CIVILITY RULES

JACQUELINE VICK

ISBN-13: 978-1-945403-39-2 (Paperback)
ISBN-13: 978-1-945403-00-2 (Ebook)

To my parents, Albert and Beverly Voirin, and to all the parents who work hard to transform little, self-centered monsters into adults who say "please" and "thank you."

Also, to my husband, Foster, for his support.

"The hardest job kids face today is learning good manners without seeing any."

Fred Astaire

CHAPTER 1

My first view of Northern Illinois farmland reminded me of something mother used to tell us when we were children. *Snowflakes come from the angels having a pillow fight.* Someone upstairs had declared war because the landscape—what I could see of it through the windshield of the rented car—consisted of a white blur. I took it slow and stuck close to the shoulder of the road.

The weather didn't improve as we got closer to our destination, Inglenook Resort, a family mansion that had been spruced up and turned into a four-star resort according to *Frequent Traveler Magazine*. Mansion. That's just a big house, but since this is the United States, you can call your home anything you like.

I heard a rustle and glanced in the rearview mirror. My older brother, Edward, was awake and taking in the view through the passenger window.

"Are you sure you have the directions right?" he asked.

"Positive."

He pulled his black wool coat tighter across his chest and told me to turn up the heater. I complied. When I glanced back again, he had shut his eyes, though I doubted if he would fall back asleep. He hated what lay in store for him at Inglenook Resort—a public appearance.

At six-feet-two, with dark hair, shoulders like a bull, a trim waist, and a square jaw, Edward presents an imposing figure, much like a defensive lineman, which is the position he played in college football—an unusual outlet for an English major. The Van Dyke beard and intelligent gray eyes add a touch of arrogance.

No matter what he looked like, he couldn't pass for a seventy-year-old grandmother type, which was everybody's first thought when they picked up one of the books he wrote under the pseudonym of Aunt Civility. Extra pre-auto-graphed copies of his latest release, *Civility Rules,* were in my suitcase, pre-autographed because his publisher's solution to the image problem was to send Edward to public appear-ances as Aunt Civility's official representative.

Edward always wanted to be a writer, though he envi-sioned a journalism career spent sitting in the press box and reporting on the latest football or basketball game. Upon graduation, he found the competition in his chosen field fierce, so when a friend suggested he apply to Classical Reads to ghost write their newest series, he sent in his resume. He had their top three qualifications: he could retain useless information (to reel off sports statistics going back to 1910 was child's play for Edward), he cleaned up well (they had requested a headshot), and he turned out copy faster than any other applicant. When the Aunt Civility series took off, he didn't have the willpower to walk away from the fat paychecks.

It's actually not that difficult to believe that Edward took to writing etiquette books. He's a romantic at heart, and he secretly sees himself in the hero role of a 1940's film. I believe his ego also played a part in his decision to stick around. People treat you differently when you say *please* and *thank you*. If you stand when a woman enters the room, you're elevated above the slobs who stay in their chairs, and when you're not intimidated by the finger bowl at a formal dinner, your fellow guests look at you with awe. As his brother, I still see the unpolished edges.

For my part, I'm thirty pounds lighter than my brother is, a few inches shorter and clean-shaven, but I do have the dark hair and gray eyes. For the record, I played halfback. My official title is secretary, which includes the usual rigmarole of office work as well as keeping the author happy by meeting his every demand. I think of myself as a babysitter.

Edward might be able to memorize facts about which fork goes where and be able and willing to advise on the proper ensemble for an evening wedding, but head knowledge and practical application are two different animals. Edward doesn't play well with others. So, I buck him up or calm him down depending on the situation and take care of all the details in between. Sometimes it gives me a pain in the side, but one of my best-kept secrets is that I'm proud of my brother.

We arrived at our destination by dusk, and the resort's private drive proved less hazardous than the open road. The tires of dozens of vehicles had already laid a trail of packed snow on a winding path lined with looming fir trees, their branches bowing forward under the weight of icicles.

It didn't look like the grounds of a four-star resort, but maybe there were bridle paths hidden in the woods, or else the tree line was hiding man-made ski hills covered with snow bunnies. I cracked my window open. Not a sound except the hiss of tires on the snow. It was cold, bleak, and dead and reminded me of the ominous backdrop of the horror movie, *The Shining,* minus the mountains.

"This can't be it." Edward's irritability increased every

time he ventured out of his familiar habitat, and the dreary weather wasn't helping.

I countered with a light chuckle. "What are you talking about? It looks like a Christmas card scene."

"Only if Santa had been slaughtered by his reindeer and buried in the woods. It's hard to believe that anyone would live here on purpose, let alone pay to come here."

I drove between two stone pillars that supported a wooden sign with the resort's name written in blood-red and caught my first view of Inglenook—an enormous shadow looming against the gray sky. By the front entrance, several small patios surrounded by snow-topped topiaries resembling wildlife met in the center at a gigantic fountain, now frozen into ice. Large planters on either side of the front door held hibernating shrubs dressed up with strings of lights in honor of the resort's grand opening.

"Not a sign of life." Edward leaned over to peer out the window on the opposite side of the car. "Not even a valet, unless he's frozen to death under that mound of white by the door."

I was distracted as the car went into a small spin, but with a little counter-steering, I got us safely into a parking spot near the end of the row. Since nobody was around to witness the arrival of the pseudo celebrity, I let Edward open his own door, while I pulled our luggage from the trunk. He took his laptop and carry-on and let his secretary handle the rest—a bag in each hand and one under my arm—and we headed for the entrance, our shoulders hunched and heads bowed against the pelting precipitation.

"I don't want to complain," he began.

"Then don't."

"We're in the middle of no-man's-land. When you said the event was in Chicago, I thought we'd be *in* the city."

"It's only eighty or so miles away," I said. "And why do you care? We're going to be indoors the entire time we're here."

"I didn't bring the right clothes for a blizzard."

I struggled to push open the front door and hang onto the luggage. "It's not a blizzard. It's snow."

A short man dressed in a red suit and black hat arrived just in time to close the door behind us. He had a face that reminded me of a bookie I knew—previously broken nose, small pale eyes, and a smile that didn't mean you were friends. It was the doorman, and his name tag read Alfred. He launched into a welcome speech, but I cut him off and told him he'd arrived too late for a tip.

Puddles of melting slush dirtied the pale marble floor of a sizable lobby where a small crowd hovered around the check-in counter and waited to be processed.

"I'm going to look for a cup of coffee," Edward said.

I told him to make mine black, thinking that if he really had manners, he would have asked me what I wanted. Once I'd found a dry spot at the end of the line and set down our luggage, I took in my surroundings. The lighting was dim on account of there not being any windows, and the dark wood paneling seemed to suck up rather than reflect the light given off by torch-shaped sconces that lined the walls. The few lamps scattered around the room on end tables next to armchairs didn't help. It looked like the Inglenooks had decorated the place with leftover furniture because nothing matched.

Behind a front counter of dark-polished wood, I could see through a glass wall into an office. Directly behind the counter, a man and woman about my age, early thirties, with matching dark auburn hair worked to process the guests, who looked like the people you'd find at a resort in the middle of nowhere. Not a group of good-looking women in the bunch.

Off to my left, a placard welcomed the Victorian Preservation Society for their annual convention, but it made no mention of their guest speaker, Edward. That would suit my brother fine because, while he enjoyed lecturing groups that shared his interests, he hated meeting the average public, whom he referred to as cretins.

"That's a nice coat." The voice came from a short, stocky woman in a checkered dress of white and gray, black stockings, and sensible shoes. She had hacked her faded strawberry-blond hair into a bob with bangs. She touched the sleeve of my leather jacket.

"My granddad brought back a jacket just like that from the war. You remind me of him. Of course, you're quite a bit younger. And his hair was blond. And he's dead."

"We almost sound like twins." I nudged the luggage forward with my foot and moved ahead with the line, and she moved along with me.

"I'm Zali." It rhymed with Sally. "Are you here for the grand opening? It's been in all the papers. So exciting. I suppose everyone wants a peek inside the old Inglenook mansion, though I can't think why. It's just a big house." Zali beamed up at me with the pleasure of a child who had discovered a new playmate.

"Then why are you here?" I said, just to make conversation.

"Me?" Her hand went to her throat, and she played with the collar of her dress. She shifted her gaze around the room and puckered her lips together. "Me?" she repeated. "I'm just taking a brief vacation." She grasped the fingers of one hand in the other, a gesture of comfort. "A little rest and relaxation."

My gaze traveled the room and landed on a geriatric group huddled in the corner, assisted by canes, walkers, and one wheelchair. "This is the place for you, then. Don't imagine anything exciting ever happens here."

Zali clasped her hands behind her back and rocked on her feet, pleased to raise my low expectations. "Oh, I would think murder's exciting enough for anyone."

Edward wandered up right then and handed me a Styrofoam cup of coffee. I pointed it at Zali and made introductions.

"She's here for rest and relaxation." I hoped to cut her off before she continued her theme of death, but she was determined to spread the good news.

"I was just telling him about the murder."

Edward choked on his coffee and pulled out a handkerchief to cover his coughing fit. "Pardon me," he said, his deep baritone smoothed out in what I called his *public voice.* "I thought you said murder."

I turned my back on her. "Don't mind her. She's cuckoo."

"I'm not crazy." Her tone held an icy edge, and I pulled a face for Edward's benefit and turned back to her with a bright smile.

"Of course you're not." I patted her shoulder and winked at Edward. He turned to stare straight ahead, like a statue trying to ignore an approaching flock of pigeons.

"There was *too* a murder. A maid went to sleep and never woke up. Something nasty put in her evening cocoa." She squinted her eyes and nodded her head. "Probably to cover the theft of the Inglenook emeralds."

It was too much for Edward. "Excuse me," he said to Zali, and to me he added, "I'll wait for you," and then he escaped like a coward to one of the armchairs.

"Inglenook emeralds, huh?" I said to Zali. "Wonderful choice. Emeralds are rarer than rubies, which would make them more valuable."

7

Zali crossed her arms over her sturdy bosom. "There's no such thing as the Inglenook rubies."

"Sure. Whatever you say."

"Next, please." The pretty clerk looked up, and I approved of the way her dark eyes and brows complemented her auburn hair. I picked up the luggage and approached the counter.

"Name please?"

"Harlow. Nicholas and Edward."

Her fingers flew over the keyboard until she paused and frowned. "The usual spelling of Nicholas?"

"That's right. N-I-C-H-O-L-A-S."

She typed again. "Let me try Nick." She stared at her computer, and then her gaze traveled from the screen to me. "I only have a reservation for Edward Harlow."

"Both rooms will be under his name."

As she continued to type, I asked, "Have the members of the Victorian Preservation Society arrived yet? They're expecting us."

"I haven't checked in anyone from that group myself. You can look in the Welcome Room. Second door on the left, past the bar." She took a deep breath. "I'm sorry, sir. There's only one room booked under Harlow."

I froze in the act of holding out the company credit card and kept my voice low. "Please tell me you're joking."

"I'm sorry, sir, but I'm not. There are two queen-sized beds in your room," she offered. "It should be comfortable."

"Comfortable my eye," I snapped with a quick glance in Edward's direction. "Have you ever witnessed a two-hundred-and-ten-pound man having a fit? I have. Just add another room to the reservation."

The clerk's coloring rose, and she ran her teeth over her lower lip. "I can't. We're fully booked this weekend. You'll have to share a room."

I leaned across the counter and attempted to reason with the clerk. Her name tag read Claudia. "Claudia, you see that man seated in the armchair directly behind me?"

She stood on tiptoe to peer over my shoulder.

"If you don't fix me up with another room, I'm going to have to explain it to him. I don't want to explain it to him. He's already jittery because he hates to leave home, and he's here on important business. He's the guest speaker for the Victorian Preservation Society. That's Aunt Civility's official representative."

She took one last look and put her focus back on me. "I'm afraid there isn't another option, sir."

I rubbed the back of my neck, a habit of mine when I'm distressed, and wondered how to break the news to Edward.

"What seems to be the problem, Claudia?"

The second clerk moved over and peered at the computer screen. "I'm Robert. How can I help you?"

"I'm taking care of it," Claudia said through clenched teeth. "No need to jump in and save the day."

"Everything is perfectly fine," I said, knowing how Edward would react to a scene. "This woman is being very helpful. Or trying to be."

Robert laughed. "You hear that, Claudia? Your job is safe."

"Don't be an idiot. It's just that there's only one room reserved in Mr. Harlow's name, so he and his brother will have to share."

"Could I speak to the manager?" I asked, darting my gaze toward my charge. Edward had his face buried in a magazine. "Quietly?"

Robert grinned. "Who's the manager today, Claudia? Shall we flip a coin?" To me he said, "My sister, Claudia, and I own the place. You can't get any higher than us. Robert and Claudia Inglenook, at your service." Robert leaned over his sister's computer screen. "Let me see what we can do."

Claudia stretched her hands over her keyboard to block Robert's access. "I'm perfectly capable of performing a search. There isn't. Another. Room. Available."

Her voice had risen in volume, so I told them to forget it and just give me two keys.

She made a few changes on the computer and hit a button. A form shot out of the printer. I signed, took the old-fashioned skeleton keys, and signaled Edward. He joined me as I headed toward a gated lift near the base of a marble staircase, and I waited until there were several people gathered there before I gave him the news because he'd keep his tantrum to himself if there were witnesses.

"There's a slight catch," I said. "We have to share a room, but there are two beds, so don't make a big deal out of it."

"I wouldn't dream of it." He then suggested we take the stairs, as if he were unaware that I was loaded down with luggage. That's how I knew he was ticked.

We found Room 220 halfway down the upstairs hallway, directly across from a nook housing a statue of a bored-looking goddess. I unlocked the door and let Edward inside.

"Good grief."

I left the luggage and nudged past him. The first thing to assault my eyes was the wallpaper. Bunches of whimsical bluebells cascaded down the walls. Deep royal-blue velvet curtains accented two queen-sized beds covered in sky-blue quilts, and an oval throw rug made of various shades of blue spiraling out of control looked like it had been inspired by a drug-induced nightmare.

"It's colorful." I went back for our bags and set them down on the floor next to a loveseat bulging with large, stuffed pillows. It resembled a blueberry about to pop.

"It looks like it was decorated by Picasso," Edward said.

"Yeah, yeah. I get it. During his Blue Period. Hilarious.

But don't think I'm going to wrangle us another room, because this place is packed."

I sized up the cherry wood armoire, offered as a humble substitute for closet space. I could see we'd have to fight to the death for hangers. Edward refused to let me wear anything convenient that I could fold and put into a drawer, like sweatpants or jeans, while I was on duty.

While he carried his precious laptop to a writing table that stood in a small enclave in the corner, I dug out our shaving kits, put them in the bathroom, and returned.

Edward pulled back the curtains and looked out a set of French doors that opened onto a balcony. A small circular table and two rattan chairs peered out from under mounds of snow.

"I imagine the place looks much better in the spring," I said, as I joined him to study the advertised view of expansive gardens and manicured lawn, now indiscernible under layers of white. He gave a long and dissatisfied sigh.

"It's bleak," I said. "I'll admit that. But it's the middle of a winter snowstorm, which has its own beauty, and once the weather clears, the sun will shine, and the ground will sparkle like diamonds." He grunted. "It's pristine, just like it must have been when Victorians walked the earth. Your group will love it."

I took off my leather jacket and folded it over the arm of the loveseat. "I'm starved. Let's find the restaurant." I headed for the front door. "I can unpack when we get back."

"My shirts will get wrinkled."

"Then I'll order an iron from housekeeping."

"They serve dinner at eight." Edward tapped the one-page brochure that housekeeping had left on the desk. "In civilized places, dining is a formal affair. It means something more than shoving a patty of meat down your throat." He dug through his carryon bag and pulled out a stack of papers held together with a large clip. It was the dreaded speech. "Let's start on page ten."

"I can't. Not again. If I hear one more time how I should never play with a room's curtains or fiddle with the doors unless the hostess is present, I'll lose it."

He harrumphed, something I swear he must practice when I'm not around. "At least you've been paying attention."

"I could probably give the speech myself. It's seared into my brain."

"Try clearing your mind. It shouldn't be that hard."

"For someone who needs my help, you're an ingrate." I tossed it off as a comment, not intending to spark anything, but since gratitude and manners liked to hang out on the same corner, Edward took it as a personal attack and felt the need to defend his honor.

"I'm paying you for your services."

"After deducting room and board."

"If you managed your finances better, you wouldn't need to live with me." He waved his speech. "Or work for me."

My jaw muscles twitched because that had been a low blow. In my very first attempt at venture capitalism, my partner had disappeared with all the money, including thirty thousand dollars that belonged to me. I'd sold everything to pay back the other investors. I'd also tracked the guy down, and after making it clear without words how disappointed in him I was, I helped send him on a long vacation, courtesy of the State of California. With no money, no home, and no immediate prospects for employment, I'd accepted Edward's offer to work for him after his secretary of fifteen years had discovered the opposite sex and decided to get a life. In other words, not my fault.

My brother didn't offer an apology. Instead, he said, "I'll take the top drawer."

I finished unpacking my suitcase first just to annoy him,

but I was quick and efficient, and soon I'd finished the job, with everything that should be on hangers in the armoire with less than an inch to spare. As I closed the top drawer on Edward's underthings, he said:

"Why don't you make sure the hotel has the right equipment for my speech?"

"That's the job of the VPS volunteers," I protested, but understanding how Edward's mind worked, I knew the outcome of any discussion would have me doing their job to help Edward score brownie points.

"They haven't arrived yet, or you would have told me. I want to make sure it's done properly. Besides, it would be a gracious gesture to help them. I'll meet you in the dining room at a quarter to eight."

That's how I wound up on my way downstairs—alone but dressed for dinner in a slate-blue suit, white dress shirt, and rose-colored tie.

The maid who serviced our floor was pulling a tray out of a dumbwaiter. She carried it to the room two doors down from ours, set the tray on the floor, knocked on the door, and stepped back. From inside the room, someone jangled a bell with the enthusiasm of a Christmas Santa collecting for charity. The door to the room next to ours opened, and a woman with purple hair marched over to the tray, picked it up, unlocked the door, and went inside, kicking the door closed behind her. The ringing stopped.

I grinned, sharing a moment of camaraderie with a fellow servant.

"I'm Nick."

I held out my hand, and we shook.

"Maggie."

I ran an appreciative gaze over her petite figure, skin the color of latte, and curly brown hair. She wore a traditional uniform—a black dress that ended right above shapely calves, a pure white apron, and a matching cap. I could have pulled it off a costume rack at any theater. She also had a crooked front tooth that gave her an adorable goofiness, and I thought beneath that professional exterior lurked a woman who wanted to snuggle—or at least wouldn't slap my face at the suggestion.

"It's like watching one of those cuckoo clocks," she said with a nod toward the door. "The ones where the soldier marches out when the clock chimes. They went through the same routine at breakfast and lunch. I'm supposed to set the tray down and knock, then Mrs. Waterford rings the bell and Ms. Mayfield takes it into the room. I suppose I could just leave after I knock, but I can't resist watching the entertainment."

"If that's entertainment, you must be hard up for laughs."

"I suggested to Ms. Mayfield that it might be more convenient to use the communicating door, but she said that Mrs. Waterford keeps it locked."

"I shudder to think what she's hiding," I said, and Maggie giggled. Edward's the only one who doesn't appreciate my wit.

"The stories I could tell you about guests of hotels I've worked at. You wouldn't believe half of them." She flushed. "I'm so sorry. I didn't mean—that is, I don't—"

"No worries," I soothed. "I'm not a guest here. I'm a prisoner, dragged here by my brother."

She giggled again, but I could tell she felt she had stuck her foot in it. "Enjoy your stay, sir," she said, and I watched her walk back to the head of the stairs, her hips swaying under her crisp black dress. She stopped before a door on the opposite side of the hallway marked Private, and she glanced back once before stepping inside.

I made my way to the staircase. A few ladies in heels waited for the elevator on the other side of the landing, but I jogged down the marble steps to reach the lobby. The crowd had cleared up, so I crossed to the front desk and asked Claudia Inglenook if the conference room was ready for the VPS gang.

Her brow wrinkled. "Ready? There's not much to do. It's in the Gold Room at the end of the north wing, but the waiters won't set out the water glasses and such until tomorrow morning."

"Is the projection screen permanently installed, or will I have to carry it over there? I'd also like to test the microphone. And I'd like to see where the outlets are so I can position the podium. I don't want the boss's laptop to run out of gas before he does."

Her cheeks flushed a light pink, which would have been attractive if I hadn't suspected the cause. I leaned my elbow on the counter. "It will be easier if you take a deep breath and let it all out at once. What do I need to come up with?"

"Well, we don't have a podium."

"He can stand and hold his speech. He won't like it, but he can do it."

She shuffled a few papers for something to do. "Or a microphone."

I saw that one coming. A place that doesn't have a podium probably isn't prepared for speakers. "He has plenty of hot air, so we'll make do."

She opened her mouth and closed it, and my shoulders tensed.

"Okay. I'm going to assume you don't have a projection screen." She nodded. "Is the wall white?"

She shook her head. "Wood paneling."

I rubbed my hand across the back of my neck. This was a problem. Edward was proud of his samples of early photography, and he had handpicked images to go with his topic. I wasn't sure where I was going to come up with a portable wall, but I slapped my palm on the counter twice and thanked Claudia. It wasn't her problem; it was mine.

I got in contact with Alfred, the doorman who was still miffed over the missed tip. Once I handed him a twenty, he helped me search a storage room for partitions, screens—or anything that might work as a screen. We found zilch. I had to give him another twenty in exchange for his oath to rig a white sheet against the wall at the front of the Gold Room by tomorrow morning.

My watch read seven-thirty, so I made my way back to the dining room to prepare the way for Edward.

CHAPTER 2

I passed through the lobby and followed the sound of raised voices and background music to the dining room, which was marked Ballroom by a gold sign above the open double doors. Inside, it was a large octagon marked at the center by a gigantic chandelier. The flooring was a dramatic pattern of white and black tiles that made me feel like a chess piece. White tablecloths and fancy dinner service covered round tables for eight. As I walked into the room, the maître d' stopped me, checked my name from a list, and pointed out my assigned spot. I ignored his protests when I took the clipboard from his hands and scanned it to make sure that Edward's name was at the same table.

I made use of the cash bar in the back of the room, and as I waited for my drink, I studied my fellow guests. Most were old enough to be my parents, or even grandparents. At two nearby tables, a dozen senior voices shouted in competition. I christened them the Happy Homesteaders. Against the wall farthest from the doors, a six-piece band played *Yellow Bird*, while a few couples from the Lawrence Welk era worked up an appetite for dinner as they twirled around a space cleared for dancing.

When my drink was ready, I paid for it, stuffed a tip into a plastic cup on the bar, and then carried my scotch and soda to the table. The set menu for the evening waited on our plates and offered a choice of beef, fish, or vegetarian main course. I was the first to arrive, but my rump had hardly hit the seat before Zali, the bizarre woman who had approached me in the lobby, plopped down in the chair to my right and said:

"How do you do? I'm Zali."

If she'd been young and beautiful, I would have taken offense at her forgetting me so easily. Instead, I said, "I'm Nick. We've already met."

"What a surprise! I love surprises." She reached for the flower arrangement in the center of the table, plucked out a rose, and stuck it behind one ear. "What are you here for? Vacation? Business meeting?" She eyed my suit. "You don't look like a businessman."

"I'm from the health department, and I'm undercover."

She brushed off my lie with a wave of her hand. "That's old news. You won't find another rat within miles of this place."

I felt my left eye twitch. After a day spent traveling with Edward, I had an excess of nervous energy that needed an outlet. A set of glass doors across from me probably stood open in the summer as an invitation to enjoy an after-dinner stroll, but right now, the view consisted of a moving blur of snow. Inglenook didn't strike me as the kind of place to have a gym. I might have to resort to doing jumping jacks back in our room.

Arguing voices brought me round. A trio of people deep in conversation paused when they reached our table. The eldest, a thickset balding man in his early sixties, had his hand on the arm of a gorgeous young thing. Her hair, the color of sunlight, was swept up into a chignon that accentuated her slender neck, which seemed an oddly demure hairstyle to wear with a sparkly pink dress and a plunging neckline.

The saxophone player played the first notes of *Blue Velvet*, and the woman reached for the hand of the third member of their party, a man in his late twenties. He had the build of a wrestler—medium height, wiry, with enough muscle to fill out his shirt, and his spiked blond hair came from a bottle. I could see his dishwater brown roots from where I sat. I took an immediate dislike to him because "roots" and male pronouns should never be in the same sentence unless the subject is trees. Some women might have found him handsome, though when he smiled at her, I thought he had too many teeth.

The woman told the balding guy, who I assumed was her father, that "they" were going to work up an appetite. His expression as he watched them take the floor told me he shared my opinion about the boyfriend. He plunked down in his chair and kept his scowl fixed on the couple.

"That's Luigi Ferrara," Zali whispered. "Felicity is his fiancée." Amused by the alliteration, Zali chanted, "Felicity the fiancée. Felicity, the flipping fiancée. The affianced Felicity."

My eyebrows shot up. "Really? Then who's the boyfriend?"

Zali nudged my ribs. "Careful. That's friendly Felicity the fiancée's cousin Jake. Jake Battencourt. Sounds like the name of a king, doesn't it?"

I watched the dancing couple with more interest until the next guest arrived wearing an intelligent and aloof expression that was in direct contrast to her hand-knit dress in a shocking combination of colors, high leather boots, and happy purple hair. It was one half of the cuckoo clock routine I'd witnessed in the hallway earlier.

I rose to my feet as the new arrival took her seat and pulled yarn and needles out of a red tote bag.

"That's Amanda Mayfield," Zali said in a loud whisper as I sat back down. I knew who she was from Maggie, but I let Zali fill me in. "I think she's Griselda Waterford's servant. That's the gasbag who hasn't left her room since she got here. She makes up for it by calling the front desk to complain every other minute. Sends Amanda scurrying around to do her bidding."

"Amanda has my sympathy."

Zali rubbed her nose. "Wish *I* had a servant. Sounds convenient."

When Felicity and Jake returned to the table—she with flushed cheeks and he looking pretty pleased for a cousin—Zali grabbed the opportunity to make new friends and called out in a loud voice, "Why don't we all share something about ourselves? Me first." She sat up, hands in her lap, and cleared her throat, as if she were about to recite her pedigree to prospective in-laws.

"My name's Zali, and I'm here for rest and relaxation. I love kittens, though I haven't got one myself, and I enjoy gardening."

She broke out in a grin and pointed at Luigi. "You're next!"

"What's there to tell? I'm here with Felicity, and if it weren't for her shadow, I'd be having a good time."

"Lou!" Felicity gasped and covered her mouth, a maidenly movement whose effect was spoiled by her cleavage. She saw me staring and narrowed her eyes in disapproval, which only made me grin. My theory is that if women really didn't want men gawking at their goods, they wouldn't put them on display.

"Not that kind of good time," Luigi grumbled.

"I wonder why anyone would build a house in the middle of nowhere. I wonder why anyone would come." Amanda's gaze roamed around the room. "There isn't a decent city for miles."

Zali raised her hand and held it there until I called on her, and then she recited facts as if she had crammed for the exam and this was her final.

"The first Inglenook came over to the States in the early nineteen-hundreds and modeled the mansion after his family estate in Devonshire. He picked Northern Illinois because he fell in love with the wooded areas, the apple orchards, and the farms. They reminded him of home."

"Until his first winter here," Luigi snorted.

She frowned. "The weather probably was a shock."

"I overheard an old woman talking." Felicity pointed a slender finger toward the Happy Homesteaders. "She said somebody was murdered here."

"Did you hear right?" Luigi glanced at the old folks, his gaze lingering on an old man in a wheelchair. "Probably somebody died in their sleep. People used to die at home, you know."

"Friendly Felicity is correct," Zali said, giving the young woman a verbal gold star. "A maid died."

"How do *you* know all this?" Amanda said.

Zali lifted her chin in defiance. "I have family in the area. I'm visiting them. They knew the Inglenooks, and I heard the story when I was a child."

"That's a harsh story to tell a kid," Jake said.

I succumbed to the urge to disagree with anything the guy with the dye job said. "Fairy tales are filled with violence. Murderous witches with poisoned apples. Woodcutters abandoning the kiddies to the wolves. It's a wonder any of us can sleep at night."

Zali sat on the edge of her seat wearing the hopeful look of a puppy in a room full of bones. She was dying to tell her story, and since murder sounded more interesting than anything else going on in the room, I egged her on.

"Well," Zali said, "Annabelle Inglenook was a sweet kid, and she didn't have a lot of experience with men. Her father, silly twerp, was overprotective, so when she met a man and fell in love, she kept it a secret."

"How romantic," Felicity said.

Zali broke into a pleased grin. "It is, isn't it?"

"When does the murder come in?" I asked to prod her along, hoping she would finish the story before Edward arrived.

"The couple eloped."

"And?" Felicity raised her delicate brows.

"They slipped something into the cocoa belonging to Annabelle's personal maid so they could make their escape, and the maid died."

"So, she was poisoned?" I nodded approval. "A good old-fashioned murder."

Zali squashed her brows together and puffed up her cheeks. She finally blew out a big huff of air and said, "I think she had been drinking, or maybe she'd already taken a dose of sleeping pills. Whatever the combination, she never woke up."

"So, it was an *accident*," Luigi said. "That's all."

Zali glared. "The family emeralds disappeared that same night. Pretty big coincidence, don't you think?"

"Did you say emeralds?" Felicity's eyes glittered.

Luigi said, "Probably one of the staff stole them."

Amanda snorted. "Do you think so?"

"I never trust anyone on minimum wage," I said with a sarcastic eye roll aimed at Luigi.

Amanda Mayfield laughed with a loud unrestricted bark.

Since Felicity was spoken for, I naturally took a closer look at Amanda. Underneath the purple hair and questionable dress, she had a cute figure, and her full lips, when at rest, curled up at the edges in a private smile. I could ask her for a drink after dinner. I'd just made up my mind to make the best of my stay here when I caught sight of a tall broad-shouldered man in full evening dress, and I lost the desire to be happy. It was Edward, and I couldn't see him giving me the evening off, especially when he found out about the conference room amenities.

Luigi spotted him and said, "Who's the guy in the monkey suit?"

Edward pulled at his bowtie, and I had the urge to go over and slap his hands. If he felt that the requirements of representing Aunt Civility included an immaculate and formal toilette, then he should suffer through it like a man. He spotted me and held up a hand in acknowledgement.

My brother likes to keep a low profile because he doesn't want to mingle with the rabble, but the rabble buy books. It was an argument we'd had even before I signed on as his secretary. He might even be right about their being cretins, but should those cretins ever need to impress the boss or a future spouse, I wanted his book to pop into their heads as the solution to all their problems. I'd already summed up my tablemates and took the approach I thought would get their interest. I leaned my forearms against the table and said:

"He has to put on his best face in public. That's one of the crosses of being the mouthpiece of a famous author." I shrugged to show that we all had problems. Then I lowered my gaze to the menu, peeking up through my lashes to watch their reaction.

"What's the author's name?" Felicity took a sip of wine, letting her gaze wander to my brother.

I studied the menu for a count of two and then jerked my

head up. "What's that? Oh, right. Aunt Civility." Three of them gasped and turned respectful gazes in my brother's direction. Without looking at any of them, my eyes back on the menu, I added, "Between you and me, he taught Auntie everything she knows about the social arts."

When he arrived, I introduced him as my brother. It wouldn't hurt for some of that respect to rub off on me. He seemed pleased at the enthusiastic reception he received and then moved to a chair two places away from me. It wasn't because I had body odor, or he thought I would embarrass him with my table manners. The purpose was to leave room for proper boy-girl seating. Just one of the many rules he carries around in his head like chapter headings to his books.

"I'm Zali." She bounced in her chair as if waiting for the games to begin and then winked at Edward.

He gave her a pained smile and took his place, pausing to move a rebellious fork to its proper position in the place setting.

"And order was restored to the universe," I muttered.

"What's that, Nicholas?"

Edward thinks he can train me not to make smart-mouthed comments by calling me out on them. He should know better by now.

My response had to wait. A new guest had arrived. He had a tall physique and a thin face that brought up images of Ichabod Crane. Around his throat, he wore a clerical collar which may have explained his ruddy complexion. Too much communion wine. He introduced himself as The Reverend Bartholomew Markham, and he spread his benevolent smile around the table.

"Did you say Ferrara?" he asked after Edward introduced Luigi.

Luigi met his puzzled gaze with a steady stare. "Luigi Ferrara."

"Oh. I thought—I thought you said Ferrari, like the car." He tittered and pulled out the chair between Edward and me, but I placed my hand over the cushion and instructed him to take the chair between Zali and Amanda. "You know. Boy, girl, boy, girl."

"Mr. Ferrara and Ms. Hartwell are engaged to be married," Edward said. I'm sure he brought it up as a topic of mutual interest to make the cleric feel included.

"So, there's going to be another wedding?" Markham scooted his chair up to the table. "How nice."

The waiter showed up with the soup, and conversation dried up while we ate. When Edward finished his main course, he turned his fork tines down to signal the waiter to take his plate. Soon, sponge cake topped with whipped cream had replaced everyone's dinner plates. Then coffee was served and, once the cups were filled and sugar and cream had made the rounds, the Reverend Markham jump-started the conversation.

"My first parish was just down the road. There weren't many members in the congregation. This area wasn't as populated back then." He beamed at the guests. "I remember every face, every service performed, as though it were yesterday." Then he told us a remarkably unfunny story that revolved around his role as shepherd to his tiny flock.

Zali leaned her hefty bosom onto the table and pointed at Edward. "It's your turn, Eddie. Tell us about yourself."

"I prefer Edward," he said, but Zali shook her finger at him.

"Don't be a stiff sock."

Rather than break that sacred rule, *Avoid Confrontations*, Edward deflected the conversation over to Luigi. "And when is the wedding?"

Luigi's face fell into a grim scowl. "Tomorrow, if I had any say. I don't know why we don't take care of things at the courthouse and get it over with."

Felicity massaged his arm and rested her head on his shoulder. "You know it takes a girl a long time to plan that special day." Then she turned her mouth up to his ear and whispered, "I want everything to be perfect."

She tilted her head, exposing her delicate neck. Remembering Zali's story about the Inglenook emeralds, I imagined how the missing jewels would look sparkling from between Felicity's breasts. She'd have to ditch the sparkly pink dress.

"Fancy weddings are overrated," Lou grumbled.

She turned up the wattage on her smile and aimed it at Edward. "Let's ask the expert. What do *you* think? I mean, if I wrote to you and asked you for advice?"

"Wrote to *me?*" Edward's brow furrowed, the corners of his mouth turned down, and a gigantic imaginary question mark hovered over his head. He covered his surprise by raising his coffee cup to his mouth.

"Why not? You're Aunt Civility's representative, aren't you?" Felicity said.

He shouldn't have gasped while swallowing. It made him choke, and he covered his mouth with his napkin until the fit subsided. "I'm just surprised you recognized me." He narrowed his eyes at me. "Quite a surprise."

I met him head on and turned my chair to face him. "How would Aunt Civility respond to Miss Hartwell if she wrote to you and asked whether she should hold out for the perfect wedding or run to the courthouse and get it over with? Let's say she is looking for an avuncular point of view."

After shooting me a look that should have made me burst into flames, he realized the rest of the table was watching, so he stroked his chin thoughtfully. I could have taken a picture and called it *Society Man in Deep Thought.*

"I wouldn't want to presume to answer for Aunt Civility,

but I think she would say that both members of the union should be happy. The wedding ceremony—religious and legal implications aside—is traditionally more for the woman. I would suggest that the gentleman give way to the young lady's wishes."

The women applauded.

"Bravo, Eddie," Zali shouted.

Only the presence of so many witnesses kept him from tweaking my ear. Fortunately, Amanda Mayfield directed the conversation elsewhere.

"No one's dragging me down the aisle," she said.

"I'm with you," I said. "I'm going to take my time and find the right person."

"I'm shocked to hear you're so discriminating," Edward said in what he considers a whisper. I'm sure the entire table heard him. "And I shudder to think what qualifications your *right woman* would need to have."

"Oh, Aunt Civility." I looked him right in the eye, so I had a good view of his orbs when they popped open wide. It was a satisfying reaction, but I put him out of his misery by adding, "What would *she* say about such an uncivil comment."

"I get it," Zali said, pointing at me. For one panicked moment, I thought she might be one of those idiot savants and that she had seen through my comments to the fact that Edward was Aunt Civility, so I was relieved when she added, "Your brother means that you're a stinker with women." She swung her attention to the happy couple and, oblivious of the thirty-something-year age difference between the future bride and groom, asked, "How many kiddies are you planning to have?"

Felicity gave Luigi's hand a squeeze, while he tugged at his collar.

"You see, well, I already have a daughter." He shook his

head with great emphasis. "It ain't easy being a parent. Not so sure I want to go through that again. Barbara has turned out to be a disappointment."

"You did your best," Felicity said.

"I would have loved to have had children," Markham said. "But God rarely takes our wants into consideration. Only our needs. My wife died without fulfilling that duty."

Amanda Mayfield took exception to this statement. She excused herself from the table, saying in a sarcastic voice that she had to go to the little girl's room and visit all the other potential breeders.

"Oh ho!" Zali nudged the cleric in his side. "I think you've lost a friend. So important to have friends, isn't it?" she said, a wistful note in her voice. "They help you out during those dark times, when the Nasties come."

That killed the conversation. Edward rose along with Amanda, as did I. It looked as if he might make a break for it, so I reached across the empty chair and took a firm hold of his arm.

"Don't leave us, Edward. We're just getting to know our fellow guests."

They urged the pseudo-celebrity to stay on, and he graciously sat back down, while I continued to play get-to-know-you. "What seems to be the problem with your daughter, Mr. Ferrara? Nothing serious, I hope."

"Barbara needs a little self-control with money," he said. "Young people don't know the meaning of frugal. They cringe at the thought of leftovers and throw out perfectly good appliances because they're bored with them. Hand-me-downs are unheard of. Clothing has to be trendy and new. And expensive."

Jake grinned. "Maybe you're just cheap."

"I don't see the point in waste. It's unnecessary."

"When's the last time you bought a new suit?" Jake prodded.

"Don't need one." Luigi pulled open his jacket to display the pristine lining. "If you pay for quality, it lasts."

"Or bought fresh pasta from the deli?" Jake raised his brows in challenge.

"Dried cooks up just fine."

"There's a point where frugality becomes self-abuse. Didn't you ever see the movie *Mother*?"

Edward, not having been to the theater since they had an anniversary screening of *Lawrence of Arabia*, was completely lost.

"Albert Brooks tells Debbie Reynolds, his mother, to stop being cheap with herself," I explained. "To buy a small wedge of nice cheese instead of a giant wheel of cheap stuff that dries out in the freezer. To treat herself right."

Luigi snorted. "Easy for him to say. It's not his money."

"Good point," Zali said, keeping score for the rest of us. "It's your volley," she told Jake. "Better make it a good one."

Felicity's cousin rose to the challenge. "You don't have to spend money to treat yourself right. When's the last time you poured a nice hot bath and just lazed around for an hour?"

Luigi looked scandalized. "I take cold Navy showers. That's all you need. And cold water gets the blood circulating."

"I bet you use the same towel all week," Jake said.

"I do. I'm clean when I use it, and it dries. What's the point in doing all that extra laundry?"

"There's something to be said for frugality," Markham piped in. "*A man's life consisteth not in the abundance of the things which he possesseth.*"

"Remember Lot's wife," Zali declared, pleased to have her own Biblical quote to offer.

Amanda Mayfield returned and announced that the gals in the powder room were ready for duty, and Zali offered her a salute. As Edward and I moved to rise, she waved us off.

"The old tartar has called for me. I just came back for my bag." She picked up her satchel of yarn and bid us goodnight.

Luigi held up his glass to signal the waiter. "The point isn't how to have a good time on a buck a day. It's that people have to pay for their mistakes. That's how they learn. You spend more than you can afford, you should have to dig yourself out. There's right and there's wrong. Gray is an area invented by those who want to get away with things they shouldn't have done in the first place. I believe in justice."

"But you'd forgive me if I made a mistake, right Sweetie?" Felicity pinched Luigi's arm.

He gave her hand a squeeze in return, but he didn't say yes. She slipped a worried look to her cousin, as if just realizing that her fantastic figure was only going to get her so far with Lou. He responded by asking her to dance, and when she stood, all the men rose along with her. Did I mention that manners are contagious, like the flu?

There was no stopping my brother this time. Hoping to get a free drink out of him in the bar, I moved to follow, but as I left the dining room, I spotted something more interesting. A woman with determinedly blond hair, dressed in a dazzling white silk suit, peered into the dining room from behind a ficus tree like a furtive squirrel judging how best to grab a nut from under the whiskers of a cat. She directed her gaze at our table, but I couldn't tell who the target was, so I strolled up to her and said, "Lost something?"

She stood straight and jammed a fist into her hip. "What's it to you?" She played it tough and wandered away slowly as if to say that if standing behind ficus trees was her favorite pastime, who was I to say different? She may have been dressed like a charm school graduate, but she walked with the sway of an angry bulldog.

"What now?" I asked Edward when I caught up to him in the lobby. I could tell from his expression that he was just about to lay into me, but his attention moved to someone over my shoulder. The scowl melted off his face, and he took on the appearance of someone about to spout poetry. I stepped sideways and turned my head, expecting to see a member of the VPS, but it was only Claudia Inglenook headed our way. Her outfit of choice was a simple black sheath with high heels and a string of pearls. She looked wholesome and good, like somebody's pure granddaughter.

When Claudia had first spoken to me at the front desk, her voice had that soft, sweet quality that tickles the air, and so my ears enjoyed it when she asked, "Are you finding everything all right?"

Edward answered for both of us. "Yes. Thank you." The way he said those few words made it sound as if we owed her our lives.

I made the introductions, and Edward complimented her on her name, as if she had had any say in the matter, and he asked if someone named her after a family member.

"My mother loved that movie *It Happened One Night.*"

"Wasn't that Claudette Colbert?" I asked. If I want to watch a movie made before 1965, I have to sneak it into the house. I'd probably seen more old movies than Samuel Goldwyn had.

"When she realized the star's name was Claudette," Claudia explained, "it was too late. I had already been baptized, but she still wanted to change it legally. My father convinced her that Claudia was much better. It was the feminization of Claude, and since she liked *Casablanca* best of all, she agreed."

"Ah," Edward said. "Claude Rains. A wonderful actor." He

paused to allow for a change of subject. "Have you heard from anyone else in my party? That's the Victorian Preservation Society."

Claudia gave her head a sad shake.

"The snow has caused delays at the airport," she offered. "I don't think anyone's allowed to land." His smile faltered, and she hurried to add, "But that shouldn't last. I mean, they *must* let them land eventually, right? There's only so much fuel."

As we imagined a tragic possibility that hadn't occurred to us, she struggled to defeat the awkward silence with, "How do you like your room?" She addressed this question to both of us.

Edward jumped at the opportunity to offer a compliment. "Truly creative."

I couldn't stop the guffaw in time, so I turned it into a combination cough/throat clearing, but she wasn't listening, anyway. She looked up at Edward with a pleased smile.

"All the rooms have themes. I just picked up on what my grandmother had done. Your room was the Blue Room. Now it's the Blue-Bell Room. But you already know that. Griselda Waterford is in Red Rose, Amanda Mayfield has the Darling Daisy Room, and Luigi Ferrara is in Birds of Paradise." She stopped with a self-conscious laugh. "I'm boring you."

"Not at all," Edward said.

Between their polite banter and all the underlying attraction, I felt the danger of an Oscar Wilde play breaking out. "It's fascinating," I added in a formal tone. "Just fascinating, but I need to take care of some duties. If you'll excuse me." I clicked my heels and bowed.

Claudia murmured something about neglecting her other guests and turned her attention on a middle-aged couple, which gave Edward time to grab me by the collar before I got away.

"Have you been talking, Nicholas?"

I tugged my jacket straight. "I don't know what you mean."

"We have this conversation at least once a week. I don't want to play Aunt Civility to every Tom, Dick, and Harry who has a question about whether he can wear a baseball cap to a wedding."

"That's sexist. It could be Tom, Dick, and Harriett. Women wear baseball caps, too."

"You know what I mean." Two old women passed by at a crawl, pointing and whispering, and the one with lipstick on her teeth gave him a huge smile. He returned the favor at a lower wattage and then lowered his voice. "Everyone seems to know who I am, or at least who I'm supposed to be. How did they catch on so quickly if you haven't spread the word? It's not as if members of the Victorian Preservation Society were here to mention it."

"Maybe your fans recognize you from the dust cover of your books."

"My picture isn't on my books."

"Or they read the advertisement for the convention."

"There's no mention of my name on the placard."

So, he'd noticed.

"I haven't told anyone about your not-so-dirty little secret." I put my hand on my heart and held up three fingers. "Scouts honor."

"You were never a scout." And with that, he turned on his heels and strolled into the bar. I followed him in, and he informed me he preferred to be alone. After he left with a cognac, I started a tab. While I drowned my boredom, I half-listened in on conversations about what a good time Cousin Emily had visiting the girls, and how great Matt looks since surgery.

When I started on my third scotch, no soda, I picked up my drink and moved around to clear my head. I wandered into the next room, the Welcome Room. Reaching for cultural heights, the Inglenooks had laid out a board game. Something catastrophic must have occurred because there were whoops and moans coming from the spectators.

Most of the guests had planted their rumps on the couch and chairs that faced the large-screen television, and they watched a sitcom play out a scene that the majority used to consider unsuitable viewing before ten at night. It felt too much like a public orgy for my taste, so I moved back to the game table. On my way across the room, I overheard a piece of information that made my blood run cold. I set my glass on an end table and headed for the room I thought most likely to attract Edward.

As I entered the library, my brother stood over an old man in a wheelchair, looking as if he had no idea what to do or say. He relaxed when he saw me and stepped to the side of the chair, inviting me into the conversation.

"You're very kind," the man said. "It shouldn't take me long to pack, and then I'm sure someone at the front desk can arrange for a ride. I'll leave right away."

"I don't think so." I crossed the room to a set of thick gold curtains that ran the height of the wall. I grabbed hold of one panel and yanked it open. At this time of night, there wasn't much of a view, but they couldn't miss the pile of snow pressing against the window.

"We are officially snowed in."

CHAPTER 3

On the way back to our room, Edward explained the intense scene that had taken place before my arrival.

When he had first reached the library, he'd found it empty; the ambiance was perfect. A warm glow crackled in the generous stone fireplace, and shadows from the flames reflected off books that encircled the room on three sides. Against the far wall stood an enormous mahogany desk, where the first Inglenook probably wrote important letters to other rich people and politicians. The smell of good leather hung in the air, and Edward had just settled into one such chair directly in front of the fire when the sound of squeaking wheels interrupted his peace.

"And so, you hid," I said.

"I settled down in my chair, which just happened to have a high back, and didn't make myself known."

I let out a snort. "Same thing."

Thumping footsteps followed close behind the squeaking wheels, and a voice called out:

"You've got a lot of nerve!"

"Excuse me?" an old man's voice asked with surprise.

"Coming here after everything you've done to my family."

"I'm afraid you must have me confused with someone else," the old man insisted.

Edward peered around the chair back and watched as Robert Inglenook verbally accosted a frail old man in a wheelchair. His first instinct was to jump to the victim's aid, but curiosity took hold, and anyway, he reasoned, it seemed too late to explain his presence. He might cause the men an *Uncomfortable Moment*.

"How many Henry McShanes am I likely to find at Inglenook?" Robert swept out an arm to encompass his surroundings. "Well? What do you think? Does it make you happy to see that our low finances have forced us to take paying guests?"

Henry McShane wheeled around the young man to make his escape.

"I really am sorry if someone has hurt you or your family, but you must believe me when I say it wasn't me."

Robert rested his hands on the wheelchair arms and loomed over Henry. "Where are they? What did you do with them?"

"I don't know what you're talking about. I really don't."

Robert stared down at the man with obvious disbelief. "I want you out of here."

"You bet," Henry answered. "First thing tomorrow."

"Now."

"I'll have to call a handicapped taxi, but as soon as it arrives, I'll leave."

Apparently satisfied, Robert left the room without another word.

Henry studied the floor and murmured, "Oh dear. I had no idea. No idea at all."

Compassion overcame Edward's desire to steer clear of

other people's complications, and he cleared his throat and stood. He met Henry's embarrassed gaze and said, "I couldn't help overhearing. Do you need any help?"

And that's when I walked in. Edward tends to romanticize events. I didn't take his version as gospel because if Robert had actually manhandled the old man in the wheelchair, Edward would not have sat on his fanny and watched. However, I accepted that he had given me the gist because I heard the last part of the conversation myself.

"What did Robert Inglenook mean by *where are they?*" I wondered aloud.

"I didn't ask."

"Of course you didn't. Curiosity is not one of your virtues."

"You have enough for both of us. And curiosity isn't a virtue." Edward stopped walking. "What on earth?"

A ficus plant, tall as a small tree, tipped to the left as if it were losing a fight against gale force winds. Clumps of dirt surrounded the base of the pot, dirt whose rightful place was in the pot holding up the plant.

"I haven't noticed a dog running loose," I said. "Have you?"

Edward ignored my suggestion that we let the resort staff deal with it and instead insisted that two perfectly healthy men were capable of clearing up the mess. Since I was the mere secretary, he held the trunk in place and made me replace the soil and pat it into a firm base.

"If you heard the conversation in the library correctly—" I said with a grunt as I bent to scoop up another pile of dirt.

"My hearing is perfect."

"Then the old man—Henry McShane? —pulled something over on the Inglenooks. Something *not nice.*"

"That would be a reasonable conclusion."

I dumped the last clump in place, held my hands away

from my suit, and rubbed them together to dust off the remaining dirt.

"What do you think it was?"

"I'm not about to speculate on something that is none of my business."

As we passed through the lobby, I noticed the reception desk was unattended. "Maybe the Inglenooks are off murdering Henry McShane right now." Edward didn't appreciate the joke and walked ahead of me, pretending I didn't exist all the way to the room. Once there, I grabbed my pajamas and headed into the bathroom but found Edward blocking the door.

I took a step back and dropped my shoulders with an audible sigh. "What now?"

"On my way to the library tonight," he said, "a strange woman asked me if her marriage could be saved. She told me about her husband's affairs in chilling detail." He stared at me, waiting for an explanation.

I kept my poker face in place. "Shocking," I said. "Just shocking."

"You've probably told every person in this resort I'm Aunt Civility's representative and my fondest wish is to speak with them."

I thumped his chest with my index finger. "If you'd get off your high horse and schedule *public* book signings like a regular author, I wouldn't have to work so hard to make sure your books didn't fall into the cemetery," which was my name for the remainder pile, where unpopular books went to die.

I should have known better than to tempt my brother with physical contact. He grabbed my finger and twisted it back, and I had to retreat a few steps.

"My sales have done fine without your help. Why can't you respect my wishes?" He let go of me and made a scrunched-up face of distaste. "I'm not some performer sent to entertain the masses. I have a specialized field and prefer to speak to groups who can at least spell etiquette." He narrowed his eyes. "You didn't tell them that I *was* Aunt Civility, did you?"

"Perish the thought." I pushed past him with more force than necessary and closed the bathroom door. When it was Edward's turn to wash up before bed, I turned off his alarm clock, which had been set for six a.m., and set my quieter watch alarm for the same time. A miracle might occur before morning. If the VPS gang made it to the resort, I wanted plenty of time to get everything in place without Edward harping at me. Besides, the extra sleep might put him in a better mood.

Normally, I'm out like a light until sunlight peeps through my bedroom curtains, but dreams peppered my sleep this first night at Inglenook. Friendly Felicity was there, and the two of us were about to hook up when Luigi started shouting insults that called into question my dear mother's morals. His voice drifted away, and I was suddenly in full panic mode, convinced that I would be late for Mrs. White's third-grade English class. It was the school bell. It rang and rang and rang. As my eyes cracked open to stare into the dark, I identified the incessant jangle as Griselda Waterford's bell.

Edward was awake. I could hear the low growl of displeasure in the back of his throat, but I considered myself off-duty. I remained still and pretended to be asleep. My brother hauled himself out of bed and stuffed his large feet into waiting slippers. He threw on his robe, marched to the door, and cracked it open wide enough to peer out. I made a show of rousing myself.

"What's going on?" I asked with a yawn, and I sat up just in case Edward actually needed me.

"That deranged-looking girl is standing in the hallway,"

he whispered, loud enough that the entire floor of guests probably heard. "She's unlocking the door. She's going inside."

The ringing stopped.

Edward muttered all the way back to bed and made a huge ruckus trying to get comfortable, but eventually we both made it back to sleep.

CHAPTER 4

My teenage years had given me a lot of experience at sneaking out of the house, or in this case, the room. I'd set out my clothes last night, and I carried them into the bathroom on tiptoe. I could hear water running from the pipes next door, so I knew taking a shower would make too much noise. Instead, I turned on the sink tap, splashed my face with water and just avoided letting out a yell. The temperature was freezing cold. I brushed my teeth first to let the water heat up, but it wasn't cooperating.

For some reason, I thought cold water on a washcloth wouldn't be as bad as straight from the faucet. I was wrong. I got everything washed with maximum speed, and then it was time to man up. I have enough natural curl in my hair to give me a case of bed head, and I'm vain enough to do something about it before I appear in front of strangers, so I accepted the inevitable, took a deep breath, and stuck my head under the flow long enough to let me get a comb through it. By the time I finished, I had to mop up the countertop and floor with all the available towels.

Once dressed and in the hallway, I leaned against the wall to slip on my loafers. I had on beige slacks, a matching turtleneck, and a navy-blue sports jacket. Edward would expect me to wear a suit to the conference, but right now, I wasn't sure there was going to be one.

The hallways were deserted except for the cleaning crew, but I found Claudia Inglenook behind the front desk in the lobby. Since she was on the phone, I decided to sooth my stomach and peeked through the open doors of the dining room. Several employees had it in high gear as they laid out the breakfast buffet. I grabbed a scone and held it between my teeth while I removed the coffee pot and maneuvered a Styrofoam cup under the flow without spilling. I cooled off my coffee with some milk and finished off the scone on my way back to the lobby.

I like moving about before the rest of the natives, when it's just me and the people who set the day in motion—cleaning crews, newspaper delivery trucks, and patrol cars carrying cops at the start of their shift. It feels like a peek behind the scenes of an elaborate play.

It surprised me to find Claudia Inglenook still on the phone. I looked at my wristwatch. A quarter to seven. I set my cup on the counter and waited.

"Good morning," she said into the receiver for the second time. "Hello?"

I glanced down at the caller ID and read 222, the room next to ours. She hung up with a disgusted huff. We had just made eye contact when the phone rang again. She motioned for me to wait while she took the call, so I rested my laurels on one of the armchairs and picked up a *Chicago Tribune* from the end table. It had yesterday's date on it. I tried not to let that worry me too much. There was a chance the day crew hadn't gotten around to putting out fresh copies.

I made it all the way to page three before Claudia finished

her current call, but before I got on my feet, she had to answer another. I finished my coffee and waited through two more phone calls before I crossed the room and leaned against the counter. She hung up the phone. It rang again, and when she reached for it, I gently took hold of her wrist to get her attention back on me. She raised her brows and looked at my hand as if it had no business being there, so I released my grip and begged her pardon.

"What are the chances of any new arrivals today, such as the Victorian Preservation Society members?"

Her gaze darted to the ringing phone and back at me. "There is talk that O'Hare may open up this afternoon. I haven't heard about Midway, but even if the planes land, no one's getting through until the plows have made it out to us."

"Any guesses on when that will be?"

"I sympathize with you, Mr. Harlow, but I'm afraid I don't have a crystal ball handy. Your guess is as good as mine."

The phone was still ringing, but Claudia ignored it in favor of the maid, Maggie, who had just entered the lobby at a trot and was tying the strings on her white apron.

"Sorry, Ms. Inglenook. I'm running late."

"Could you see what Room 222 wants? Mr. Ferrara called, but he hung up before he said anything." She rubbed her forehead and muttered, "I hope we're not going to have a problem with the phones." A second line joined the first one in ringing, and her expression dared me to stop her from picking up, but since I had the answer I wanted—or the answer I didn't want—I smiled my thanks and left her to it.

If the people in Room 222 were up and moving, chances were that Edward was awake. There isn't a good time to break bad news, but it's usually received better on a full stomach. I returned to the dining room and grabbed a blueberry muffin, Edward's favorite, wrapped it in a paper napkin, and poured out a cup of coffee. More people were up and at 'em now, so I had to wait my turn, but it still couldn't have taken me more than fifteen minutes before I jogged up the stairs and found Maggie pulling a covered tray out of the dumbwaiter in the wall. It was a heavy one-piece tray with the handles built in.

The sight of her reminded me that I needed to put our bathroom back in order, so I waited for her to deposit the meal on the floor in front of Griselda Waterford's door and knock before I said, "I have a towel emergency."

She motioned me to follow her through the door marked Private—the last door before the landing—and I stepped inside after her, tucking the muffin into my jacket pocket. It was a small room crammed with stacks of sheeting, a rainbow of towels, cleaning supplies and the like.

"Nice office," I said.

She smiled. "And it's all mine. You're in Blue Bell, right?" I admitted it, and she crouched down next to a loaded cart and rustled through the contents. Then she stood, her hands on her hips. "I must be losing it." There were white towels lining the middle shelf in the wall, so she pulled out a few and stuck them in my free arm.

"How's Mr. Ferrara?" I said this with a grin because I wanted her to remember me as the guy who cared if I needed her help again.

"I wouldn't know. He was in the shower when I got there. That's kind of rude, don't you think?"

"Must not have been important."

A door slammed in the hallway. She leaned her head out, and the expression she wore when she turned back to the room told me her day wasn't getting any better.

"Maybe I should go back to bed and start over."

With Edward on my mind, I finished the chitchat and got moving. Zali was patrolling the halls, and she stopped to introduce herself to me. I told her it thrilled me to make her acquaintance, which seemed to please her. When I reached our door, I tucked the towels under my arm, dug my key out of my pocket and, once unlocked, gently inched the door to our room open. It closed behind me with a soft click, and I tiptoed into the bathroom to put the towels on the rack above the toilet. I needn't have bothered. I'd no sooner stepped out of the bathroom when Edward, still dressed in his pajamas and dressing gown, shoved his alarm clock under my nose and demanded an explanation.

"*Nicholas?*"

I turned over my wrist to get a look at my watch. "It's a minute fast. My watch says twenty-two to eight."

"That's not the problem."

I took it from him and puzzled over it. "Didn't it go off?"

"No. It did not."

I handed it back with a shrug. "Must be defective. I can check the gift shop for a replacement when it opens, or I could set up a wakeup call with the front desk."

He took the coffee cup from me, stepped into the bathroom, and flipped the lid up on the clothes hamper. I leaned over and saw all the used towels.

"Well?" he demanded. I stood there and waited for him to follow my gaze to the towel rack, which he eventually did. He set his coffee cup on the counter and turned on the faucets in the tub. "I tried asking the maid for more towels," he grabbed a bath-sized towel from the rack, "but she ignored me."

I remembered the muffin in my pocket and set it on the bathroom counter. "That must have been the night shift, going off duty."

"Still, that's an incredibly rude way to treat a guest."

"You're right," I said, and I promised to take it up with the management.

He stuck his hand under the tap and wiggled his fingers in the flow. "Typical."

"What now?"

"You used up all the hot water."

That tore it. "So now I'm responsible for outdated plumbing? Maybe I'm responsible for the weather, too. I might as well break it to you, since you're in a fine mood. The airports are closed for business. There will not be a conference because there aren't any attendees."

He stared, speechless. My brother could not believe he'd endured removal from the comfort of his home office in San Diego, California, the indignity of airport security, and hours of hard work spent polishing his presentation for nothing. He sputtered a few times, working up to a response, but a shriek interrupted him.

Edward turned off the faucet. We waited for a follow-up yell, but the next sound we heard was someone pounding on our door. I turned the knob, and Maggie fell into the room and collapsed in my arms. I patted her back while she tried to catch her breath in between sobs.

"Take it easy," I said.

Edward gently pried her away from me and shook her shoulders. When that had no effect, he slapped her. She hiccupped and put her hand to her cheek.

"I'm so sorry, but it had to be done. Now what is all this fuss about?"

She straightened her shoulders, stuck out her chin, and said, "Mr. Ferrara is dead, sir."

CHAPTER 5

Luigi Ferrara had the good manners to die fully dressed except for his bare feet. Since he had met his end in the bathroom, other less appealing options could have presented themselves. His corpse lay face down in a puddle of water, and he had been shaving when death caught up with him. His razor, in the sink's bottom, was still wet, and there were fluffs of shaving cream left on his face. One patch, next to his temple, was stained pink from a deep gash above his left ear.

"Are you sure he's dead?" I asked, leaning on the bathroom doorframe. Maggie held onto my arm and peered out from behind my shoulder.

Edward crouched down and felt for Luigi's pulse, then looked up at me and nodded. When Maggie gave a slight gasp, we both followed her line of sight, but all I could see was a set of blue towels on the rack above the toilet.

"Is there a doctor on staff?" Edward asked.

"No," she answered. "One guest is a doctor."

"Then you must notify him."

"I'll take care of it, sir."

"The Inglenooks will have to know. If you could get the doctor first and then let Mr. and Miss Inglenook know, they can break it to his party."

"Should I tell Alfred as well?"

I could tell from his puzzled look that Edward had no idea who Alfred was. "The doorman," I said.

"He's security, too," Maggie offered.

"Er, if you think you should."

Without glancing back, Maggie hightailed it out of the room.

As Edward moved to stand, his foot slid out from under him. I shot out a hand to steady him.

"It's slick," he said.

"No kidding. That's probably why there's a dead body on the floor."

Edward ran the toe of his slipper through the puddle of water. "How on earth did the man make this much mess with a shower?"

Thinking back to my own ablutions this morning, I said, "It happens."

Edward pulled back the sopping-wet shower curtain. "So, the man allegedly got out of the shower, dressed, and then came back into the bathroom in his bare feet, slipped and fell."

I looked at the body. "No allegedly about it."

Edward grunted in dissatisfaction and let his gaze wander the room. He stopped on the mirror where one patch looked less foggy than the rest. He wiped his finger across the edge of the glass where the film remained. "He cleared a spot."

"You're a genius," I said. "Of course he did. The man wouldn't be able to shave in front of a foggy mirror, so he wiped it down with a towel."

Edward tipped open the clothes hamper and pulled out a single damp, orange towel. "Do *you* shave after you bathe?"

"I'm not a complete moron."

"So you keep telling me."

He inspected my face. "You didn't shave this morning."

He was right, as usual. "That's because I want a beard, just like yours."

Edward stepped into the bedroom and winced.

I peered around his shoulder and got a good look at the decor for the first time. "My eyeballs are burning."

Luigi Ferrara's room was the Bird of Paradise Room, though darker places came to mind. Not even Claudia Inglenook could have thought flaming orange an appropriate color to sleep by, yet dazzling shades of pumpkin, persimmon, orange-peel and tangerine leapt out and singed our vision.

On the bed, a suitcase lay open, partially packed. The remaining clothes were neatly folded and stacked in small piles on the comforter. I picked up Luigi's wallet from the bedside table and flipped it open. It contained a nice-sized wad of bills sorted by denomination and all facing the same direction. I put the wallet back down next to his watch.

Against the wall, by the French doors, this room had a long credenza. A large manila envelope rested on an otherwise empty surface. Edward moved to the patio, and using his robe to cover his hand, unlocked and opened the doors. We both leaned out. The thick snow cover on the balcony remained undisturbed.

The door to the room flew open and Felicity Hartwell rushed in, her delicate silk nightgown catching her in all the right places. Cousin Jake entered hot on her heels, so close that when she jerked to a stop, he careened into her.

"What's happened? Why are you in here? I heard screaming—"

"That was ten minutes ago," I pointed out.

Edward stepped forward to head her off, but Felicity had

already spotted Luigi's body. She sagged against Jake in a faint. I took hold of her ankles, trying to ignore how slender and soft they were, and we carried her to the bed.

Jake patted her cheeks and made a face in the bathroom's direction. "Is he dead?"

"I'm afraid so," Edward said.

"How?"

Edward hesitated. "He appears to have fallen."

"Fallen?" Felicity said, rousing herself. "Then it was an accident?"

"What else?" I noticed the quick look she shot Jake.

Maggie returned at that moment with a middle-aged man. She introduced him as Dr. Reeves. His shirttail hung out from his pants as if he had dressed in a rush. Edward and I followed him into the bathroom. He pulled a pair of spectacles from his shirt pocket, put them on, and then leaned over the remains of Luigi Ferrara.

"He's dead all right."

He lifted the corpse's head and studied the mark above the left ear. Then he made a dissatisfied sound and made eye contact with Edward.

"Has anybody moved this man?"

Edward shook his head. "It appears he slipped."

The doctor nodded. Then he lifted the dead man's feet and studied the soles as if measuring him for a new pair of shoes. "Have you telephoned the police?"

Felicity gasped. "The police?"

Dr. Reeves straightened up, took off his glasses, and decided. "I think someone should."

Edward stroked his chin. There was a gleam in his eye, as if his little brain was working overtime. We returned to the bedroom, and he announced, "Don't touch anything, please."

Felicity, reaching for the manila envelope, said, "Oh. But why?"

Before Edward could explain, the Reverend Markham leaned his head into the room.

"Can I be of assistance?" He saw past Dr. Reeves to the bathroom floor. "Oh, dear." He moved swiftly to the body, crouched next to the late Luigi Ferrara, and mumbled some prayers.

"This place is starting to resemble that Marx Brothers film where they try to see how many people they can cram into their stateroom," I said.

Even as Felicity, confused by the reference, wrinkled her lovely brow, yet another person joined the party. The Woman in White stayed true to form in a frilly white nightgown. She burst through the doorway with Claudia close behind, and when her gaze fell on Felicity, it transformed into one of such loathing that I took a protective step forward.

Her eye caught movement from the bathroom, and she turned and gaped at the minister kneeling over Luigi's lifeless form. She sucked in a sharp breath. "Daddy?" There was a moment of silence while she put her fingers to her lips and took in two lung-fulls of air. Giggles bubbled out, getting louder until they were shrieks of laughter.

This time, Claudia delivered the slap. The Woman in White switched from laughing lunatic to vicious viper, and she aimed her venom at Felicity Hartwell. She flew at the younger woman, screeching, "This is your fault!"

I intercepted her, wrapped my arms around her in a bear hug, and held on while she wriggled and kicked. When her frantic motions subsided, I said, "Feel better?"

"Get your hands off me."

It was a rational statement said in an angry but controlled voice, so I let go. She was wrong on one point. If Luigi had been showering with Felicity, he wouldn't have been fully clothed, and he would have died with a smile on his face instead of that look of surprise.

Now that the danger of an all-out catfight had passed, Edward got involved and instructed Jake to take Felicity to her room. Alfred, the doorman, arrived and announced that the police were on their way. While Claudia led the Woman in White out the door, Markham finished his prayers and wandered in to join us. There wasn't much left to say, so we all stuck together like sheep when there's been a wolf-spotting—comfort in numbers but useless.

"Luigi's daughter may need help," Edward suggested, and since Markham agreed, he scampered off to disperse God's blessings. My brother took a last look around the room. "We need someone to stand guard until the police get here."

Alfred volunteered. In his black hat and red tails, our little doorman reminded me of a circus ringmaster about to announce a death-defying trapeze act. With his arms spread wide, he herded us out of the room. Since his hat reached just under my nose, it wasn't difficult to turn back and take one last look at the Paradise Room. My gaze stopped on the credenza. The manila envelope was gone.

CHAPTER 6

Edward went back to our room to dress, and I took the opportunity to slip into Maggie's nook to make sure she was all right. I administered a hug and let her lean against my chest until she lifted her head and looked up at me, her brow wrinkled, and her warm brown eyes filled with confusion and fear.

"I don't understand." Her breathing came shallow and quick. If she didn't watch it, she would hyperventilate. "It—it doesn't make sense. I mean, I know that people are full of surprises." She burbled out a hysterical laugh. "I should know. Right? And it's not as if it means anything. It means nothing. No. I'm sure." She rubbed her forehead. "And it's not like I'm responsible. How could I know? Why would it be my fault?"

She was working her way toward a full-blown fit. I could have followed Edward's lead and slapped her. Instead, I took a firm grip on her shoulders and planted a kiss on her mouth. When I released her six seconds later, she blinked a few times in surprise and said, "Oh." It worked, because her next observation was practical. Silly, but practical.

"I can't imagine how Mr. Ferrara wound up with the blue towels," she said.

"You got me," I said. "It must have been awful, stumbling over a body like that, but don't make too much of it. Old people slip and die every day."

She crossed her arms over her middle and leaned against her cart. "I've never seen a dead body before," she said. "I mean fresh like that. Not all done up for the wake."

"The resort's only been open for a few days. Give it time. I'm sure people have heart attacks in their sleep with comforting regularity. Consider yourself broken in."

"Mrs. Beckwith has seen a body before."

"Who's that?"

"My boss."

"I'm guessing Mrs. Beckwith is an old woman. She's probably seen hordes of dead bodies. It comes with the territory."

"This was a murder victim. She's the one who discovered that maid who overdosed back when the Inglenook girl eloped. Quite a shock, she said, but it didn't scare her off. She stayed and worked for the Inglenooks for another twenty-five years. She retired, but when the current Inglenooks decided to open the place to the public, they asked her to come back. She's a wonderful cook."

"I'm sure she is."

"I wonder if she knows. I should tell her before she finds out from one of the junior staff."

I detected a note of relish, which was fine with me. It meant that Maggie had already moved on to the role of interested bystander. I got out of her way so she could spread the news.

An hour later, we were all back in the dining room and waiting for the police to arrive. In a violation of boy-girl protocol, I took the seat next to my brother. The only person missing was Felicity Hartwell, who was, one assumed, crying over her loss in the privacy of her room. Dr. Reeves felt it prudent to give her a sedative, and he insisted that Jake leave her to rest. He'd found a maid whose father was a general practitioner and, judging her medical skills adequate, he had left her to watch over the prostrate fiancée.

Staff members lined the walls and chatted away, enjoying the break. After all, who was Luigi Ferrara to them? In a far corner, gray heads leaned together, and I could almost hear the clack of dentures as the Happy Homesteaders gossiped about the most exciting thing to happen to them since the colonies won the war. Only the old man in the wheelchair, Henry McShane, looked shocked.

I was glad to see Edward had changed into a soft plaid shirt and red sweater vest that complimented his dark gray wool pants and leather loafers, even though he completed what should have been a casual outfit with a matching gray tie. He wasn't in a suit, which meant he was coming to terms with the cancellation of his lecture.

I leaned over and rested my elbow on the back of his chair. "So, who do you think did it?"

"Did what?"

I put the back of my fingers over my mouth to keep my words private. "Don't be coy. Dr. Reeves called in the police, and I don't think banging your head on a counter is an effective way to commit suicide. So, it must be murder."

"Must it?"

"I know you can't stand anything unpleasant, but this has been dumped in our laps."

"Oh no, no, no, no. Not in—" The words stuck in his throat and he had to pry them loose. "Not in Aunt Civility's lap. Aunt Civility and murder? Can you imagine the publicity? I'll be ruined."

"Any publicity is—"

"Don't give me that," he hissed. "My—her fans do *not* want to read about her representative being questioned in a murder investigation. Aunt Civility is *above* murder. The less I say, the better. Then I can fade into the background and wait for the Victorian Preservation Society to show up. I'll give my talk and then we can get out of this place."

"Get a hold of yourself, Edward."

"I'm perfectly calm."

"Really? Twenty seconds ago, you interrupted me." I tsked. "Breaking your own rules."

His eyes narrowed, and experience told me I was about to hear what else Edward would like to break, but then his gaze traveled over our fellow guests, some of whom were watching him with interest. His lips pulled into a tight smile, and he bowed his head closer to mine. His voice was hoarse when he said:

"I don't know the proper etiquette for violent death."

"It's every man for himself."

I admit I was interested in our fellow guests' reactions to the tragedy. Death usually brings up comments about the decedent's age—either he was surprisingly young and his passing was a shock, or else death was a blessing. This crowd showed a suggestive range of emotions.

Markham looked nervous. The reverend clutched a glass of beer, and when he caught me looking, he said, "Always a shock to see death up close. I never get used to it."

Jake Battencourt sat next to the minister, staring into an empty coffee cup. His brow wrinkled with worry, though that might have been strictly on his cousin's behalf.

Circumstances had forced Griselda Waterford to join the group. A large woman draped in black, she'd clumped up to us with the aid of two canes and then dropped into the seat next to her servant. She had been writing letters when the call to gather came, and she currently doodled something that resembled an angry troll on a piece of pink stationary. She didn't seem much affected by the death, but I figured that at her time of life, it was a blessing when the grim reaper stumbled into someone else before he reached you.

Amanda Mayfield represented the resilient youth, unable to grasp the finality of death. She jabbed and pulled with a crochet hook at yarn that looked like it had come from a yak, oblivious to the rest of us.

Across the table, Barbara Maggiano, the victim's daughter, continued her theme of white in a rhinestone-encrusted sweat suit. She had turned her chair to give her back to Jake Battencourt, which according to Edward's lecture, was a big etiquette violation. Her eyes moved from face to face, glaring at each of us in turn.

"There's an elephant in the room," Griselda snorted. "No use ignoring it."

"Were you speaking literally or metaphorically?" Barbara said, impressing me with her vocabulary.

"I'm saying a man has died, and it's ludicrous to pretend nothing's happened." Griselda fastened her attention on Edward. "You found the body. Was it suicide? Or an accident."

"I'm not going to hazard a guess," he said.

"That would be telling," Zali called out with a waggle of her finger.

"Er—yes. It would," he answered. "Dr. Reeves, one of the guests, agreed the police should be notified. That simply implies there are questions." He folded his arms across his chest. "And that's all I'm prepared to say about the matter. Anything further would be indecent."

"But interesting," Griselda purred.

"I don't understand why I have to be here," Barbara said. "I'm his daughter. I should be in mourning."

"You should," Jake said. "Why don't you practice now?"

She shot him an eyeful of daggers.

"They didn't need to corral us in here like a bunch of cattle," Markham said. "It's not as if they don't have our room numbers."

"They're probably searching the rooms," I said. My listeners let loose howls of protest, which I dismissed as a natural reaction.

"I planned to check out today," Barbara said. "I hope they don't think they can charge me if we have to stay."

Jake laughed. "You're not going anywhere. None of us are. Not in this snow."

"Then how are the police going to get here?" the grieving daughter asked.

"Maybe they'll parachute in." Zali's hopeful expression pleaded with us to agree.

"Or snowmobile," I offered.

She gave me a dirty look. "Parachuting would be more fun."

"There's a field on the other side of the grounds that meets up with a two-lane highway," Griselda Waterford said. "I think snowmobile sounds more likely."

I leaned into Edward. "If I'd known murder would put an end to this weekend, I would have killed you right after we arrived."

"No one's going anywhere," said a voice from behind me.

A stocky, broad-shouldered man wearing a blank expression to match his bland brown suit tapped Edward on the shoulder and identified himself as Sergeant David Michelson.

"I understand you two found the body." He glanced at the sheet of paper in his hands. "The Harlow brothers, Edward and Nicholas. Detective Timms would like to start with you."

Edward's shoulders stiffened. I couldn't blame him for being protective of his image because it was his cash cow, so

I patted his knee. "Relax. Just let baby brother do all the talking. They probably don't even know who you are."

"I'm capable of doing my own talking, thank you." And he stood up, jutted out his square chin, and tugged his vest down, preparing to meet the enemy head on.

The sergeant led us through the lobby and behind the check-in counter, down a short hallway that passed the main office, and into a small storage room filled with boxes and odd bits of furniture. These included a desk, and behind that desk sat a man who looked as if he came with the room. He wore a crumpled gray suit that looked as if he had slept in it. Ginger hair had retreated into a thick ring that skirted the edges of his round head. Plump cheeks and a bulbous nose held together a face that belonged on a barstool, but the hooded light-gray eyes were sharp and intelligent.

I'm not heartless by nature, but as the man stood and came around the desk while Michelson read off our names, I couldn't help scanning the room to see if there was a partition I could use as a backdrop in the Gold Room. There wasn't.

"You're Aunt Civility's representative," he said to my brother.

"Yes, I am," Edward answered, resigned.

The man grinned. "*Representing the author in all public appearances will be her nephew, Mr. Edward Harlow.*" He quoted Classical Reads' press release from memory. "I'm a big fan of her column. Not so much of her books, but if more folks read the paper and followed her advice, Michelson and I might be able to take a vacation."

"Thank you. I mean, I'll tell her."

"I don't suppose you could get me an autograph?"

Edward took the proffered business card and glanced at it. "I'll see what I can do, Detective Timms."

"That bit about her being a recluse. What happened? Is it really because of an accident? Or is she a crazy genius?"

Edward barely moved his lips. "I couldn't say."

"Couldn't? Or shouldn't?" Timms said with a wink.

I'd become bored right after *I'm a big fan.* A cop shouldn't slobber over a celebrity's representative like some star-struck teenager.

"And you're the secretary, Mr. Nicholas Harlow?" Timms said. He looked at us in turn. "Mr. Harlow and Mr. Harlow. Could get confusing."

"Make it simple," I said. "I'm Nick," and, unable to resist, I added, "and he's Eddie."

"Gee, thanks," Timms said, pleased to be on a first name basis with a pseudo-celebrity.

"Perhaps we should focus on the death," Edward said.

Timms sobered immediately. He jerked his jacket straight, took his seat, and motioned us to the two folding chairs that faced him.

As we took our places, Edward sat, shoulders squared and straight, his back barely touching the chair. He crossed one leg over the other at the knees and waited patiently, but I could tell by the tiny twitch in his right eye that the idea of Aunt Civility becoming embroiled in a murder investigation had him ready to snap. I settled in to perform the role of secretary-to-the-rescue and shield my employer from stress.

"You found him?" Timms asked.

I jumped in. "*Technically*, no. The maid found him and came to us for help. We followed her into his room and saw that he was dead. Then Dr. Reeves looked at him and suggested we call you."

"Very wise," Timms nodded. "At first glance, it looks like a simple case of slip-and-fall. The old guy, kind of a slob, gets water on the floor while he's shaving. Slips and bang, down he goes. What do you think?" He watched us for our reaction.

"That's very probable," I said, not believing it for a second. I'd seen how neatly he kept his wallet. Still, it was the answer that would get us out of here the quickest.

"Except Luigi Ferrara wasn't what I'd call a slob." The only thing Edward values more than his privacy is complete truth and accuracy. He can't control it any more than a lemming can help jumping off the cliff after all the other lemmings, and it was going to be a problem.

"You knew his personal habits?" Timms said.

"Well, no," Edward admitted. "But the man was neatly turned out."

Timms and Michelson shared a look that barely hid their amusement, and Timms leaned forward. "Thing is, we on the force find that the way people present themselves to the public is not always who they are in private."

Edward has keen observation skills, almost as good as mine, so the condescending smirks and comment irritated me. However, the goal was to make this interview as short as possible, so I kept the urge to defend my brother to myself.

To my relief, Edward left it at, "I'm sure you know best," and eager to escape, he made a move to leave.

The detective held up a hand. "Was there anything you might call suspicious-looking in the room? Anything you noticed as being out of place or odd?"

"Isn't that your job, gentlemen?" I added a chuckle to make it clear I wasn't criticizing. "You would know better than we would what to look for, and we'd never been in his room."

"You two were the first on the scene."

"Second," I said. "Maggie was first."

Timms conceded the point. "The second, then."

"What could be suspicious about an accident?" As I said this, Edward blurted out:

"It seems silly…" He hesitated when he saw Timms reach for his pen. "And I'm not saying it means anything…"

"Let me be the judge, please."

"There was an inordinate amount of water on the bathroom floor."

This Timms wasn't expecting. "Fair enough," he said.

"But the man's feet were dry."

We all stared at Edward, and then Timms shared a look with Michelson.

"You're very observant, Eddie. Dr. Reeves mentioned the same thing. Anything else?"

Normally, my brother would like nothing better than to scuttle off to some private place and practice sitting without breaking his trouser crease, or whatever he does when he's alone, but there was a gleam in his eyes and a lift to his eyebrows I'd seen on his face when he was lecturing a particularly rapt audience. After receiving one minor compliment, Edward's ego had taken control.

"The mirror was completely fogged up."

"Except for the spot he cleared for shaving," I pointed out, "which makes perfect sense."

"So?" Timms said.

I crossed my legs and deliberately kicked Edward's shin, and when he frowned at me, I raised my brows and shrugged my shoulders. As in *what are you doing?* He answered them anyway.

"You get little condensation from a cold shower," Edward said.

Timms narrowed his eyes and asked, "Now how would you know his shower was cold?"

"His morning routine was common knowledge. He announced it at dinner."

Timms smirked at Michelson. "I've been hanging around with the wrong crowd."

"Luigi Ferrara was a frugal man," Edward continued. "He made a point of telling us about his various economies, including his cold Navy showers, at dinner last night."

"Which everybody heard," I said to impress upon Timms that Edward wasn't worthy of his time.

Timms looked again to Michelson, this time for an explanation.

"Water on. Water off. Soap up. Rinse."

Timms sighed as if wondering why the Luigi Ferrara's of the world couldn't take a decent shower like a regular fellow. "I was Army myself." He turned his attention back to Edward. "You're sure? And how did this come up in conversation?"

I thought this would be a good time to put the spotlight on Luigi's disappointment in his daughter, her shaky finances, and the coincidence of her being on the spot, which made her a perfect suspect.

"His daughter—"

"I can't remember," Edward interrupted. He gave me his profile so he could ignore my pointed stare.

Timms allowed a moment of silence for us to get our stories straight, and since Edward had elected himself spokesman for the team, and I had no idea what message we were selling, I kept silent.

"We only met him at dinner last night," Edward said. "Other than that, we didn't have any direct contact with him. He was engaged to be married to a young woman, Miss Felicity Hartwell. He was looking forward to the wedding. He used the wrong fork on his salad and consumed dessert with his soupspoon. That is the extent of my knowledge of Luigi Ferrara."

Things had gotten out of hand. It was time to extricate

my brother from the interview, especially as he couldn't seem to control his tongue. I stood and said, "I think that's enough boys, don't you? With all that information, you've probably got the murder solved. Come on, Edward." I moved toward the door.

"Hold on."

With my back turned on Timms, he didn't see me squish up my face in a cringe. I had said too much.

"What made you say murder?"

I turned back and spread my arms, my palms up. "Dry feet. Cold water. Foggy mirror. I thought it had been decided."

Edward blurted out, "Luigi Ferrara had my towels."

I gave up and sat back down.

"You're what?"

"My towels," Edward said, slowly and clearly. "We're in the Blue-Bell Room. Naturally, the towels match the theme. I had to request additional towels this morning," he cleared his throat, "through no fault of my own, and the replacements were white. Spares, I would think. The blue ones I should have received were in Luigi Ferrara's bathroom."

"How do you know his towels weren't blue, too?" Timms asked.

"Because he was in the Birds of Paradise Room. The theme is orange."

"That explains it," Michelson mumbled.

"Enough to turn your stomach," Timms agreed. "So, the dead man had your towels. I assume you didn't murder him for them."

I gritted my teeth. I just knew we were going to hear about the hamper.

"But there was only one orange towel in the hamper." Edward raised a finger. "And Mr. Ferrara made a point of mentioning that he used the same towel all week, so why throw this one in the hamper? And where did the rest of the orange towels go?"

Timms mulled this over, and then he tapped his pen on the desk. "That's quite a list. Anything you want to add?"

Edward hesitated. "That's it."

"Eddie," Timms said with a reproving glance. "You have a public duty to disclose everything you know. It might even give your boss some good publicity if your tip helps us catch the killer."

That comment recalled Edward to our present situation. "If Aunt Civility and murder wind up in the same sentence in any of your statements, I'll sue."

This was the wrong thing to say. Timms didn't look so friendly anymore. "Since none of us believe it was an accident, I'm going to have to ask you where you were between six-thirty and eight this morning. Just as a formality," he added with a malicious grin.

As Edward went through his encounter with the broken alarm clock in painful detail, I tried to remember hearing a cry or a thump or anything else that might go along with an assault. I have good ears and an even better memory.

When I first went into the bathroom, I had heard water running and assumed it came from next door, but in a house this old, assuming the pipes were just as old, the source could have been any room on our floor. Then I'd washed up, and when I'd stepped into the hallway, there wasn't another soul walking the floors. In fact, the first person I'd seen had been Claudia Inglenook behind the front desk.

After I gave Timms a thorough account of my movements, he perked up and asked if I had seen anyone else running loose other than the cleaning crew, Claudia, and Maggie.

"By the time I came back upstairs, there were several other guests in the dining room, but I couldn't tell you their names. That woman, Zali, passed me on our floor. She was headed for the stairs, but don't get the idea she's a killer. If she did murder, I doubt she would remember who the intended victim was long enough to carry it out."

"A little loopy, huh?" Timms then cautioned us to remain at Inglenook, adding a slight smile to acknowledge that escape for any of the guests was unlikely in our current snowbound state.

Before we left, Edward grudgingly said, "The night maid may have seen something. The other maid. I saw her shortly after I got up at half past seven."

There was a light rap on the door, and the old woman, Lipstick Teeth, poked her head in. "I heard you wanted to talk to everyone." Behind her stood a line of guests who, too antsy to stay in the dining room and wait their turns like good boys and girls, had taken matters into their own hands. The line wrapped around the front counter.

Timms invited her to take a chair, and we stepped aside to let her pass, but when we started out the door, she said, "Aren't you staying? I hoped that Mr. Harlow, as Aunt Civility's representative, would remain to make sure the police stayed within the boundaries of good conduct."

Edward's shoulders scrunched clear up to his ears, but he had it under control by the time he turned to face her. "I couldn't possibly intrude."

"Oh." She looked with doubt at Timms and Michelson. The latter straightened his shoulders and stuck out his chin, perhaps hoping to make the impression that the local force was made up of decent men with good posture. Timms remained slumped in his chair, one elbow on the desk, but his eyes were on Edward. He motioned with his head toward the free chair.

"By all means. You're officially invited to remain."

I'll give Edward credit. He didn't fight it, moan, or throw

a fit, though his legs seemed a little stiff as he made his way to the chair. I took up my position against the wall behind his chair, directly opposite Michelson, and when Lipstick Teeth asked if I was going to take notes, I pulled out a pocket-sized spiral notebook that I carried with me to record details and reminders. I clicked my pen and sent a grin to Michelson. I hoped he didn't plan to compare notes, because I didn't intend to waste the ink.

Satisfied that she had our attention, the old woman announced that Luigi Ferrara was just asking to be killed. Not that anyone deserved to leave this earth before the good God was ready to take him, but Mr. Ferrara had certainly worked at moving his expiration date forward. He'd called that nice young man, I assumed she meant Jake, a dirty name, and it wasn't the only time she had heard him use foul language, but her main complaint seemed to be that he cheated.

A few of them had started a friendly game of Mexican Train in the Welcome Room. They had pulled the allotted number of dominos each and the remaining dominos were left face down on the table. One of the extra dominos had been face up, but she hadn't liked to say anything since she assumed she was playing with people of integrity. However, right before he won, she had seen Luigi switch out one of his pieces for the extra domino—a blatant violation of the rules.

"Did anyone else see this?" Timms asked. He bit his upper lip to keep his face straight.

"I can't be sure. I might have mentioned it to the other players as we left the lounge." Her lips were pressed together in judgment, which made me sure everyone in the resort knew about the incident by now.

She creaked her gaze in Edward's direction, expecting him to weigh in, and he delivered the verdict. Mr. Ferrara had behaved improperly, unethically, and like a cad. Satisfied, she allowed Michelson to escort her to the door.

Word had gotten around that Edward was assisting the police in their interviews, and we were forced to remain for the next two hours while guest after guest took the chair in front of Timms and gave their opinion of the murder. They didn't have any facts to share.

Even Zali made an appearance. She introduced herself and wrote down all our names.

"Oh, Eddie." She clapped her hands together, her eyes as bright as a child on a sugar high. "I've always wanted to play murder hunt. Or should it be murder*er* hunt? I didn't know games had been included in the package."

"I'm afraid this isn't a game," Edward said. "The murder is real."

Her smile faltered, but then it grew larger, and she leaned over and punched his arm in a show of team spirit. "You've got to say that, haven't you? I can see you're going to be loads of fun!"

To Timms, she offered her one observation: That a maid she didn't recognize had been playing around with Maggie's cart on the second floor. Then she asked if the police were going to share all the clues with the players so they'd all be on equal footing. Timms had to disappoint her, but he added that they were using the information provided to rank the players, and Zali was in the top ten. She skittered away, eager to improve her standing.

"How reliable is she with faces?" Timms asked us.

I shrugged. "Considering that's the fourth time she's introduced herself to me, not very."

Our chance to escape came when a sharply dressed couple entered the room, he in a dark blue suit and she in a sapphire-blue twinset and black skirt with real pearls around her neck and a pair of matching earrings that an oyster had

68

put out a lot of effort to produce. The man, an attorney, questioned our presence, and Edward was quick to agree with him and bow out. Before I followed him, I noted that, other than Zali, no one from our own table had dropped in to offer their insights.

"I didn't expect them to," Timms said. "The people who volunteer are usually the crazies, the attention-getters, the looky-loos." The man blustered, so Timms added, "Present company excluded."

I hurried to catch up with Edward, who was halfway across the lobby, because I had a point I wanted to discuss with him.

"Holding out on Timms?" I called out.

He came to a halt. "Stop babbling and say what you mean."

"Why didn't you mention anything about the daughter? Luigi said she had trouble with her finances. What if she inherits?"

"You mean slander her so she could sue me? That would look good in the papers. I can see the headline now. *Aunt Civility's Representative Tries to Frame Grieving Daughter.* You need to think before you speak."

"Me? I didn't get a chance to say much of anything because your jaw was working overtime. I could have told Timms almost everything you did except the bit about the feet because your big head was in my way, but I held my tongue because you didn't want to get involved. What's the deal? You were supposed to let me do the talking so Aunt Civility could remain unsullied by murder."

He put on a pose of righteous indignation—square jaw jutting, nose in the air, and arms crossed over his chest.

"If I hadn't given him the information I had, it might have impeded their investigation. As it is, maybe they can wrap it up quickly."

"An accident would have the same result. Why didn't you go with it? Instead, you're a material witness."

He only kept his voice low with effort. It quavered with frustration. "Because I would have looked like a moron. Did you notice the wound?"

"A gash above his left ear."

"Luigi was lying on the right side of his face. It would have taken an acrobatic feat for him to have landed in the position we found him in. And the gash wasn't the right shape for the rounded edge of the countertop. It was more of a dent. You could almost see—"

"All right," I said, feeling queasy. "Point taken. So, it was murder. But I don't remember anything lying around that could have made a wound like that."

"Another very good point." Edward's features softened, and for a fleeting moment, he wore the same vulnerable look he'd had on when, at eight-years-old, he'd found Freddie the Fish floating belly up in the tank.

"I—I don't understand what happened back there. It was as if some strange force compelled me to answer their questions with complete honesty and clarity."

I snorted.

"Yes, Nicholas. A strange force. I was almost…detached. Interested even, which I'm not. That would be morbid."

I cuffed his shoulder. "Don't worry, big brother. That was your ego talking."

"You think so?" He sounded relieved.

Claudia Inglenook was behind the counter soothing an elderly couple who demanded that extra security patrol the halls, but when she looked our way, she replaced her professional expression with a grim frown and held up her hand with the authority of a crossing guard.

"Don't move," she ordered. She hissed something at

Robert. He looked at us with interest and stepped in to take over for her.

"She was pointing at you," I said. "See you back in the room." He clamped onto my wrist and held on until she swooped in on us, hooked her arm through his, and dragged him into the corner behind a large potted plant, for privacy I assume. Like a good secretary, I followed to take notes.

"What are you trying to do to my staff?" she demanded, the sweet disposition of last night replaced by Shakespeare's shrew.

He looked down his nose at her. "You're under a good deal of stress."

"Even more now, thanks to you."

"You're hysterical. You're not making sense."

Claudia squeezed her eyes shut, exhaled, and began again.

"The police are questioning all the maids again at *your* suggestion."

I remembered Edward's ominous words to Timms and expected him to sputter an apology.

"Detective Timms must have a reason for wanting to see them. He doesn't seem the type to badger helpless women. In fact, he was quite professional."

Call me cynical, but I could only see one reason Edward would defend Timms. "He's a big fan of Aunt Civility," I said.

She paused, and when she spoke again, it was on a friendlier note. "I'm so sorry I snapped at you just now." She giggled like a naughty girl. "Biting the heads off the guests is inexcusable." She laid a hand on Edward's bicep. "The thing is, Edward—May I call you Edward?"

"You can call me Nick," I offered, and she shot me a brief smile. In hindsight, I like to think she focused on Edward as part of a plan to go after the weaker member of the herd.

With her attention fixed back on my brother, she said, "People are ghouls and will be happy to continue to book rooms, but qualified staff was difficult to come by, and now they might quit. That would leave me in a terrible position."

"I can understand your difficulty," Edward murmured. His eyes narrowed, and I could see the wheels of his brain turning, probably flipping through a mental index of social situations, desperate to come up with the right thing to say.

"I talked to Mr. Ferrara this morning," Claudia said, brushing her bangs away from her eyes. "Or at least he called. There was no one on the end of the line when I picked up. I sent Maggie to see him. You heard," she said, acknowledging me.

"I heard your side of the conversation," I said, to be clear.

"What did he want?" Edward asked, then immediately held a hand up to stop her from answering. "My apologies. That would be prying."

"Don't fight the strange force, Edward," I murmured.

Claudia pulled us even farther into the corner, searching the vicinity to make sure no one would overhear. "She never saw him. She said he was in the shower. So, I might have been the last person to have had contact with him."

"Surely, no one could suspect you," he said.

"You're so sweet." She giggled, and then she switched back to a businesslike attitude with alarming ease. "They also wanted to know about the room keys. I have a master set."

Since Edward considered prying questions an offense right up there with wearing white to a wedding—the bride excepted—I figured it came under my job description.

"Do you carry your keys with you at all times?"

"I do now. But it's like closing the barn door after the horse is gone." She held up a gargantuan key ring. "The grandmaster key is gone. I couldn't find my keys last night, and I thought I'd left them in the apartment. Turns out, they were on the floor underneath their hook in the office, but I could swear they hadn't been there the first time I searched.

Then there is the missing key. Maybe I just misplaced it, but that doesn't seem likely."

"Are all the doors the same type of locks?"

"No. The maids all have master keys that can open any guest room or linen closet. But my skeleton key is the grandmaster and opens any door in the resort, including the outside buildings."

"Do you have more than one grandmaster key?"

She hesitated. "Robert has one."

"Of course," Edward said, "Luigi Ferrara could have let his murderer into the room himself."

I nodded at her. "That's a very good point."

"Then you definitely think it was murder?" She put her hand to her mouth to cover a sob. "This will ruin us." Tears welled up and threatened to spill down her cheeks. "I wish there was someone who could help." She looked up at him from under her lashes.

"That would be ideal," he agreed.

"Someone who could talk to the police on our behalf," she said slowly, with apparent thought. "Someone who's already in their good graces."

"Hmmm."

Her voice took on an impatient edge. "Someone who the lead detective admires."

He wasn't getting it. "She's talking about us, you ass."

Edward frowned and surprised me by cutting to the core of her request.

"I can't steer Detective Timms' course. That wouldn't be ethical."

Claudia lifted her chin. "I wouldn't dream of asking you to do anything that would make you uncomfortable."

A loud whoop made me jump. Zali stood over a wastebasket and clutched a balled-up paper in her hand. She ripped it open, studied it, and then dropped it back into the bin. "Never mind," she called to us across the room. "Thought I found a clue."

Edward nodded at her, and I gave her two thumbs up.

"Thank you both for humoring Zali," Claudia said, watching as the older woman left the lobby. "She's such a dear, but she's not all there, and she really enjoys the idea of a murder hunt."

Edward pursed his lips. "I still think we should make her aware of the danger. There could be a killer stalking these halls."

I raised one eyebrow at him. Maybe he should make the switch from non-fiction to fiction.

Claudia waved off that idea. "No. I don't want her told. Zali is coming to us after a, well, a vacation of sorts. A rest."

The Victorians had been famous for their rests. Rests could mean anything from illegitimate births to mental breakdowns, and as Zali appeared to be far past motherhood...

"I see," said Edward. "How, er, fragile is she? Was it a simple case of melancholy? Perhaps I shouldn't ask. That's personal information, and it couldn't possibly have any bearing on the murder. Although I am concerned—"

"The incident involved gardening implements," Claudia said. "I really don't feel I should say more."

He gave a start. "Good grief! Is she a danger?"

"Definitely not. At least, I don't think so. It was one incident, and...well..." Claudia offered a strained smile. "The doctors are optimistic Norbert will make a full recovery."

With nothing left to discuss, she made her way back to the front desk.

"I have work to do," Edward said. He pulled his gaze away from her and issued an order. "Make sure that conference room is ready. The weather could break at any moment."

I wasn't as optimistic as Edward was, but since it was my

job to comply with orders, I convinced the staff to set out the water glasses and pitchers to prepare for the attendees. I found a box of supplies in the front desk office, shipped there early by the organizers for convenience, along with a box of books the publishers had sent, so I made sure each place at the table had a writing pad bearing the Victorian Preservation Society logo and a ballpoint pen. I set the box of books in the corner. I was chastising Alfred for not earning his twenty bucks—he refused to rig the sheet until the guests had arrived at the resort—when Timms and Michelson peered through the door and decided the Gold Room was the perfect spot to move their temporary headquarters.

This was bad. Death had interrupted Edward's steady routine, and a frustrated Edward with time on his hands was trouble. I added *Find out who killed Luigi Ferrara* to my list of duties, and I was only half-joking.

CHAPTER 7

When I returned to our room, the bolt was in place. After a loud knock, I put my ear to the door. Edward likes to handwrite responses to fan letters, and he doesn't let me see them until he's come up with a brilliant solution to each problem. The sound of slamming drawers told me that Edward was hiding his precious work like some frantic squirrel trying to bury the last surviving walnut. When he finally answered, his hearty greeting surprised me. Something was wrong.

He seemed to sense he was acting out of character because he reverted to form. "Is the conference room ready?"

I pushed past him and washed my hands in the bathroom sink. I had fixed up two more tipping plants on my way up to the room, just like the one we had found on our way back from the library last night. Then I dropped onto the loveseat.

"The police have taken possession of the Gold Room." I waved off his sputtering protest because I was cheesed-off myself. "Alfred's new duty has gone to his head. Do you know he actually told me I wasn't a *person of importance* and couldn't cross the threshold of the Paradise Room? I would have explained my connection to Aunt Civility, but I didn't want to brag."

"Why would you want to go in there?"

"You have to admit we have an interest. Someone murdered a man right next door, probably while you were still sleeping. Kind of rude when you think about it. Almost a direct affront against us."

"I'm not getting involved." He gave a derisive snort. "I know what you'd like, but I'm not snooping around and prying into people's personal affairs like some common gumshoe."

"They're not all common. Hercule Poirot was well-mannered and intelligent. Lord Peter Wimsey had class and a title, and just think of Roderick Alleyn, the gentleman detective." Edward's library was as dated as his movie selection. "And if Aunt Civility's rep solved the murder, book sales would go through the roof."

"Not a chance."

"Until the VPS gang shows up," I reasoned, "there isn't much else for me to do."

"If you're bored, you can start typing my responses to that pile of letters on the desk. When you finish those, read a book." Edward moved to leave, but he couldn't resist one last lecture. "One of a man's greatest attributes is his ability to amuse himself." Then he strode out the door with that arrogant swagger that annoys me so much. I resisted the urge to kick him. Instead, I followed to make sure he'd really gone, and then I closed the door and slipped the bolt.

Edward's books had blossomed into a column carried in over one hundred newspapers—a kind of *Dear Abby* for social situations. He received dozens of letters each week. I would date stamp them the day they arrived and then put them in order in his folder, with the oldest on top, to await his pearls of wisdom.

He wrote out his first impressions by hand, making notes directly on the letters in a kind of shorthand of his own invention. His initial responses came from the gut and would not have made him a popular guy, so he let them sit for a few days. Then, once he had refined his answers, I deciphered the hieroglyphics and typed the official responses on his letterhead.

The letters on the desk were ready to go, but they weren't what I was after. He had locked his notes in the drawer, and it only took a minute to jimmy it open with a nail file. I took out a bulging file, suffered a brief annoyance when I found the dates out of order, and then settled in to follow Edward's advice and amuse myself. The first query made me chuckle.

Dear Aunt Civility,

My grandma gave me a handmade scarf for my birthday. (Totally lame!) I called her the next day and thanked her on the phone (even though she bored me half to death.) Mom insists I write a thank you note!!! But I already said thank you!!! Do I have to thank her again in writing? On paper??? Couldn't I just email her?

Brittany Bowers, 12
   P.S. My mom is forcing me to write this.

Edward's response was curt.

Frml exp grat expted/reqred. Right thing. Email? Don't even think about it.

By the time I typed it up, it would read:

Dear Miss Brittany,

Thank you for your query. A formal expression of gratitude is not only expected but also required. It is the right thing to do. As for email? That is not an acceptable option for a young lady.

Sincerely,

Aunt Civility

In Edward's simple world, I respected his request to keep his work-in-progress private, even from me. But really, he was asking too much.

It surprised me that the books and columns did so well. Nobody cared about offending the neighbors. People felt it was their right to be rude. They carried on conversations in the theater. Why not? They had paid for their ticket. Rude to a shop clerk? The customer was always right.

Being polite in a letter was easy. Being polite to the guy who'd just stolen thirty thousand bucks from your company bank account? Not so easy. I had another reason for perusing his most recent responses. They helped me to gauge his mental state. So far, so good.

The smile left my face as I read the next letter. A sophomore in high school was planning to give her virginity to her boyfriend. She had made plans to tell her parents she would spend the night at a friend's house. She had a fake ID with which to make hotel reservations in another city. All that remained was the proper way to invite the lucky boy. Should she tell him her plans or surprise him? She signed off as Virgin Girl.

I leaned back in the chair and whistled.

If girls my age had been handing out their womanhood like a particularly popular CD, I could see how some guys would have been happy lads. As for me? However much I might enjoy some passionate snuggling, I thought a woman should keep something in reserve for the guy who respected her enough to marry her. At least that was my expectation.

It was worse for Edward. He still clung to the notion that most of the female population was worthy of the title of *ladies*. The Mister Manners act had become second nature to my brother. He'd probably convinced himself that he'd nursed at our mother's bosom with a pinkie in the air, and a letter like this could plunge him into what I called *the abyss*. I'd seen it before.

First, he would foresee the end of his book sales, since the world was obviously overrun with cretins incapable of reading his advice, let alone following it. Second, with no future for Aunt Civility's official representative, he'd revert to the pre-bestseller Edward. The football-playing ruffian who gave me the small scar next to my left eye.

I tried to be positive. Maybe he'd averted the crisis by walking away from his work. I looked up. Walk away to where?

I shot to my feet. It was too early for a drink in the library, and the VPS gang wasn't here. If Virgin Girl's dilemma with a side of murder affected him the way I thought it would, I couldn't allow Edward to mingle with the public unsupervised. After locking up his papers, I hurried out of the room to do damage control.

Downstairs, I caught sight of his back as he pushed through the resort's front doors, and I jogged to catch up. He wasn't wearing a jacket, but if he could stand it, so could I.

Someone had taken advantage of the break in the weather to shovel the cement landing and shake the coverage from the shrubs on either side of the door. Edward was moving fast on a walkway next to the building, which had been partially cleared by an employee without much enthusiasm for the job. I slipped and went down on one knee, and by the time I picked myself up and made sure I hadn't done too much damage, Edward had moved out of sight.

I caught up to him around the second corner where the two wings of the building sheltered a patio area large enough for a gala event in better weather. The blowing and drifting had exposed patches of cobblestone in between small snowdrifts.

I expected to find him kicking snowmen or breaking icicles in his teeth, but something had distracted him. Edward stood all the way back to where the lawn started, about a hundred feet, and stared up at Inglenook. I joined him in his reverie while I caught my breath. This was my first good look at the resort from the outside, now that we had clear weather. What an eye-opener.

"It doesn't do justice to the travel brochure pictures," I said.

"Mmm."

He couldn't find the words for it either.

The architect had had more imagination than talent. The brochures had shown a flat-bottomed "U," with both wings joining the main body in the lobby. A gigantic dome topped the roof, making it look like a government building, and the only purpose it served that I could see was to keep the startled eye from taking in the rest of the structure. I don't know enough terms to describe it accurately, but there were decorative touches slapped on here and there that might have looked good if they'd been consistent.

Long balconies ran the length of the second floor. These were divided with bamboo slats for privacy, probably after the Inglenooks decided to take in guests. Dead ivy clung to weathered stone that couldn't decide whether to be gray or white and, in each corner of the building, gargoyles snarled down at the guests in protest at having to watch over such an architectural mess.

"It's an attempt at..." Edward said. He tilted his head. "I just can't put my finger on it."

Steam puffed out as I breathed. "I'd put the style as Old World Tart."

Edward broke out of his daze and let loose a loud hardy laugh. The crises had passed.

"Sorry about your conference."

He let out a rumbling martyred sigh. "It's not your fault."

"You know, this murder business is too bad for the Inglenook woman," I said, hoping to make him see that others were suffering, too. "She seems nice. Or she did last night."

"Mmm." A non-committal noise if ever I heard one. "It's a problem."

"It certainly is. She's a damsel in distress. Not that I'm suggesting that you're a knight in shining armor." He wasn't interested, so I dropped it. Besides, my mind was on more immediate concerns. "Aren't you cold?" I stamped my feet and flapped my arms.

"No," he said, sounding surprised, but then he noticed I was shivering. "You need to get your circulation moving."

We kept walking, and just as Edward maneuvered around a large drift, something struck him on the back of his head. He reached up and dusted off the remains of a snowball.

"Who in all that is holy—"

I spun around and found the attacker—a plump boy trailed by a solemn little girl. I'm not good with kids' ages, but I put the girl at tricycle age and the boy at *old enough to know better*.

"You're a good target," the girl said.

"You're huge," the boy added in admiration.

"What are your names?" Edward demanded.

"Don't talk to it," the boy advised her in a voice husky with excitement. "It's our prey."

"I'm Neecie." She pointed at the boy. "He's Lucien."

Lucien pulled back a mitten stuffed with snow.

"Come here, you little rug rat." I grabbed his wrist and shook his hand clean.

"Hey! You're not supposed to touch me. It's illegal."

"If I kick your backside, then only my shoe will touch you."

The child took a step back.

"Where are your parents?" Edward demanded. "Shouldn't someone be watching you?"

Neecie jutted out her lower lip. "I don't need a babysitter. I'm not little anymore."

"That's relative," Edward said, and he ignored her puzzled frown. He spread his hands in an imploring gesture. "What's left to destroy the tranquility of this resort? A hard rock band?"

Edward and children don't mix. Not even violent death could shake him as much as these two chubby faces.

"It's not really that tranquil, Edward. There has been a—" I stopped myself in time, not knowing how much I could say about murder in front of the wee ones.

Edward was already walking away. I followed, and so did the miniature imps. He turned his bulk on them, and they took a step back. Neecie toppled and disappeared into a pile of snow, so I pulled her out by the collar and dusted her off.

"I only allow good little boys and girls to accompany me on my walks," Edward said, "and good little boys and girls don't throw things at people."

"Are priests good?" Neecie asked.

Edward, suspecting a trick question, narrowed his eyes. "Why?"

She planted a fist on her tiny hip in defiance and turned one foot inward. "Because we saw him throwing snowballs."

Lucien picked up her point with glee. "Yeah. So, you're saying the priest is bad. We're gonna tell."

Edward and I looked at each other.

"Do you mean The Reverend Mr. Markham?" I asked.

"I don't know his name, do I?" It was a saucy reply, but then Lucien seemed to feel he had pushed things too far. "The guy with the white thing around his neck."

"Where was he at when he was, er, being bad?" Edward asked.

"Under that room that has the yellow tape on it." Lucien hesitated, a solemn expression wiping away his childish excitement. "I think someone died there."

Neecie reached out and clutched Edward's hand. "Does that mean there's gonna be ghosts?"

Edward shook his hand free. "And when did this happen?" He directed his question at the boy, but the girl answered.

"Right after pancakes," she mumbled over the thumb in her mouth. "We came out to build a snowman. I don't like ghosts."

"Come on!" Lucian cried. "We'll show you!" They ran toward Luigi Ferrara's room.

We looked at each other, uncertain if we should follow, until I said, "They may be about to destroy evidence."

And we took off in pursuit.

CHAPTER 8

"I was taking my morning constitutional."

We were in the Gold Room with Timms and Michelson and the Reverend Markham, who bestowed his interrogators with a serene smile and an attitude of benediction. Edward's face couldn't decide between sadness and irritation. He was still mourning the conference that might have been.

"You called me down here to ask me that?" Markham continued. "I'm happy to assist you in any way I can, but please. Exercise some discretion."

Timms scratched the back of his head as if trying to work out a difficult problem.

"You took your constitutional in three feet of snow? They only shoveled the walkway *after* our arrival."

"I'm very particular about my exercise," the minister explained. "*So run, that ye may obtain.*"

"An admirable sentiment," Edward said, and Markham, looking on my brother with favor, launched into a detailed account of the many times he'd chosen his feet over his automobile while making parish calls.

"That's all good," Timms interrupted, "but you're telling me you walked along the side of the building and then, when you realized the snow was deep, turned back. You could have got that much exercise from walking the floors of the resort."

"A difficult lesson learned," the man conceded.

"What I don't get," Timms continued, "is why you were throwing snowballs at a dead man's window."

The minister blinked. "Pardon me?"

"Throwing snowballs," Timms repeated. "Trying to get Luigi Ferrara's attention, I assume." He paused, and then added, "You were seen."

Markham looked to Edward, and my brother gave a sympathetic nod and said, "There are two reliable witnesses, I'm afraid."

Edward refused to meet my eyes after that whopper, though all he would have seen was my deep respect.

"I see. Well, all I did was walk," Markham insisted in reasonable tones. He directed his response to Edward. "I might have tried to get the attention of Luigi Ferrara when I reached his window, but that's all."

"What did you need to discuss that you couldn't talk about in the cozy hallway?" Timms asked. "Seems like you went through a lot of trouble to avoid being seen."

"My conversation with Luigi Ferrara was private." The minister's lowered voice and solemn expression indicated that it might have been confessional in nature—something no officer of the law could force him to reveal. Or was that only a Catholic priest? "Nothing to do with his death. And I couldn't get his attention, so it's a moot point."

"And what time was this?"

"Around seven. I rise early."

"What was your connection with Luigi Ferrara?" Timms asked.

The reverend hesitated and then gave Edward a brief smile. "We knew each other a long time ago."

Timms was unable to get further details, so he let the man go with a mild warning that he may need to talk with him again. Once Markham left, Timms let loose.

"That's the type of religious guy I can't stand. All that holier than thou attitude. *My conversation was of a private nature.*"

Michelson explained. "Their pastor sided with Myra on the trial separation."

"That's got nothing to do with it," Timms snapped. "The reverend is hiding something."

"Maybe Luigi Ferrara was a former parishioner," Edward said. "The reverend mentioned at dinner that his first parish was around here. Was Mr. Ferrara from this area?"

Now that my agenda had changed from protecting Edward from the murder fallout to getting this thing solved and out of the way as soon as possible, my brother's inability to keep his thoughts to himself helped me, especially when Timms eyed him like a dog deciding how to approach a hefty bone. He parked his rump on the edge of the table.

"He seemed to trust you."

When Edward protested, Timms raised his hand. "Don't worry. I'm not offended, but I noticed he was more comfortable giving answers to you. You seem to have a way with people." He called to his sergeant. "Doesn't he?"

Michelson grunted. "Seems to."

"I assure you, I don't."

I raised my hand. "He means it. That's why I'm here."

"It's those manners of yours. People are comfortable giving you information. Look at the way they lined up to spill their guts once they knew you were in the room. You coaxed those kids to spill the beans. And you've got a good memory, doesn't he, Michelson?"

"Sharp as my mother-in-law's tongue."

Timms raised his voice to drown out Edward's protests. "You remembered that Luigi said he took Navy showers, and you remembered what Markham said about starting out in the area." Timms adjusted his bottom and became positively friendly. "I don't mind telling you we're short handed. Half the department is out with the flu, so it's just Michelson and me. We could use another man on the inside, someone who could help us with our inquiries." He looked at me. "Maybe you and your brother could work together. You know, team up. People talk more freely when we cops aren't around. I'd even let you sit in on a few of the interviews of people you're familiar with so you could give me the nod if, to your knowledge, someone is lying."

"Out of the question." Edward folded his arms across his chest to make sure we all knew his answer was final, but it wasn't final as far as I was concerned. I couldn't have him standing around with nothing to do, tempting fate to send another reason for him to leap headfirst into *the abyss*.

"I don't think you realize our position, Edward." I looked at the detective. "I imagine you're not going to let any new guests in until this murder is cleared up, once they can make it past the snow, I mean." I bowed my head and raised my brows, meeting the detective's gaze. He was quick to catch on that I had a point.

"Yeah. You're right. No one in or out. *No one*."

"So, the VPS gang will never get here unless we help move things along. They might even hold the conference somewhere else with a different keynote speaker if it looks like you're going to be tied up for a while."

Edward shifted in his chair. "That would be a disappointment."

"Especially after all the work you put into preparing your

speech. Of course, if they reschedule, we can always fly to the next conference. Maybe it will be in Alaska."

Edward began with, "I suppose–" but a knock on the door interrupted him. Off Timms' signal, Michelson opened the door and Henry McShane and his wheelchair rolled in.

"How can I help you, Mr. McShane?" Timms asked.

Henry's voice cracked when he answered.

"Actually, I'm Luigi Ferrara."

CHAPTER 9

I n the silence that followed Henry/Luigi's announcement, I picked up Michelson's pen from the floor and returned it to him. At a nod from his boss, the worthy sidekick closed the door to the hallway and settled into a chair in the corner with a look that bordered on interest.

"You'll forgive my ignorance," Timms began, "but we seem to have a corpse by the same name laid out in the cellar, right next to the produce."

I made a note to pass on the vegetables at dinner.

"Actually, *he's* Henry McShane."

Timms absorbed this and then asked if Barbara Maggiano, the daughter, was aware of her status as a Scott.

"I can't say," Henry said, scratching his chin. "If I had to guess, I'd say no." He patted his wheelchair. "It all started with this. I was twenty-eight-years-old and working for the county as a lineman when I had a little accident. It was while I was in the hospital that Henry first visited."

Timms rubbed his eyes with both hands. "Let's call him Luigi, just to keep things clear."

"I knew Henry—Lou—back in high school. We weren't all that close, so it surprised me when he stopped by to visit me. He said he had a proposition. He had some in-laws he wasn't fond of and he wanted to disappear."

"May I ask you a personal question?" Edward waited for Henry's confused consent. "Did this sound legitimate to you?"

Henry shrugged. "I've never been married. I think I should explain that I'd just been told that I'd never walk again. That's not great news to a man heading for thirty. I was depressed. Lou offered me an adventure. I had no family; my parents were dead. I grabbed it."

"May I ask another personal question?"

"Let's assume he's given you blanket permission," I said, impatient to hear the entire story.

Edward decided that was reasonable. "How old are you now?"

"Sixty-eight last July."

Timms arranged a few items on the table before asking, "You've played this charade for forty years?"

"Gosh. Has it been that long? I kind of lost track." Off Timms' look, he added, "It never affected me. Henry—Lou— deposited my disability pay into an account he opened in my name and added a little extra for the inconvenience."

"But now Luigi Ferrara is dead, as far as the government is concerned."

"That's what's got me worried," Henry said. "I don't want to defraud anybody, but I do want the money that belongs to me. But now—"

"What about taxes on the income that Luigi made under your name?" Timms asked.

"He told me he only worked for cash," Henry said. His eyes popped open. "Don't tell me I've got to worry about the IRS!"

"It certainly is a mess." Timms flipped his hands in the air. "Thank God it's not my mess."

"Did Luigi Ferrara invite you this weekend?" I asked.

"I came with my friends from the senior center. It was a complete shock to see him here."

Edward leaned back in his chair and studied Henry. "Had you ever heard of Inglenook Manor or Inglenook Resort before this weekend?"

"Well, I'd heard of it, having grown up a few towns over," Henry said. "Lou and I both came from Winnebago. But I didn't know them personally."

After giving his whereabouts this morning—alone in bed —Henry McShane wheeled out of the room.

While Edward sat there frowning, I said, "It's starting to feel like some kind of creepy reunion."

"It does." My brother stroked his chin. "Henry McShane comes to the injured Luigi Ferrara and tells him he wants to hide from his in-laws. So, when Robert Inglenook was talking to our Henry McShane in the library, did he know he was talking to Luigi Ferrara?"

Too late, Edward realized he had set the hounds on Robert Inglenook's trail.

Timms' nose twitched. "What's that? Robert Inglenook was talking to the victim in the library?"

"No, no, no, no. Not the victim. The man in the wheel-chair. Nothing to do with the murder."

"What were they talking about?"

"I can't remember," he lied.

I had to do it for Edward's own good.

"I can."

I repeated back the conversation as Edward had related it, verbatim. Edward bared his teeth at me in the semblance of a smile, but Timms appreciated my efforts.

"That's interesting, don't you think?" He directed his

question at Michelson, who gave a brief nod. "Sounds like Robert Inglenook had a grudge against the man he thought was Henry McShane."

"And since that man wasn't murdered, it doesn't really matter." Edward gave it his best shot, but Timms' mind was already playing with the possibilities.

"He might have had something against the real Henry McShane, known to him as Luigi Ferrara, but had never met the man in person. Then, when he figured out his mistake—"

"I saw no indication that he thought Henry McShane was anyone other than who he said he was," Edward said, and I gave him a broad grin.

"I thought you couldn't remember."

"Here's what we have so far." Timms rapped his knuckles on the table to call us to order. "We've got a man murdered sometime between a quarter to seven when he called down to the lobby and about a quarter to eight, when the maid discovered his body. Now Markham says no one responded to him when he tried to get the victim's attention around seven o'clock, but Luigi could have been in the bathroom getting ready to shower, or maybe Markham has poor aim. Maggie says she heard the shower a little after seven. She went into her nook right after that to prepare for her day, and then she found him about a half an hour later. Anyone could have walked the hallways during the time she was in her room and she wouldn't have noticed. So far, everyone seems to have been tucked in bed. They didn't see or hear a thing. Nicky here was out taking a walk." Timms motioned to me. "Markham was outside lobbing snow at the deceased's window. And you say you saw a maid?" he asked Edward.

"Yes. She was heading down the back staircase. One of the night shift going off duty."

Michelson stopped writing in his notebook and looked up. "The maids don't have a night shift."

"Interesting." Timms said it as if he meant it.

"Why did Maggie go into Mr. Ferrara's room?" Edward suddenly asked.

Timms nodded his approval as if Edward had just aced the detective's exam. "We asked her that. She said the shower was off when she knocked on the door again, so she should have gotten some kind of response from Mr. Ferrara, even if he told her to get lost. She got a creepy feeling, and she thought she'd just peek in the door to see if everything was all right. The maid called inside and then got concerned when she saw the empty bed and a light coming from the bathroom which meant the door was open and he should have heard her calling."

"Very conscientious," Edward said.

"Her first job was with a retirement home, and she says that makes her extra jumpy about accidents in the bathroom."

Timms stood. "When we questioned the staff, no one admitted to being on the second floor at that time, but maybe one of the maids was lollygagging around and doesn't want to admit it. I'm more interested in Robert Inglenook. It would be a favor if you'd come along and clear up any points on that meeting between Mr. Inglenook and the man known as Henry McShane."

"You mean you want to catch him if he lies," I said.

Edward jumped up and led the way out, and I stifled a grin.

CHAPTER 10

From behind his desk, Robert Inglenook looked up with mild interest as we entered the office with Edward in the lead. My brother had a game plan. That was apparent from the way he took up a position in the middle of the room, facing Robert, and waited as if he had thought everything through and just needed the right moment to act. I stood close by him so I could follow his lead.

"I need to ask you about your relationship with Luigi Ferrara," Timms said.

Robert set down his pen and leaned back in his chair. "We didn't have a relationship. He was a guest."

"What's going on?" Claudia Inglenook abandoned her post at the front desk and stepped into the room. She crossed to her brother and rested a hand on his shoulder, meeting Edward's gaze.

"As long as you're here, Ms. Inglenook," Timms said, "I can question you both at the same time. Let me rephrase my question. Did either of you harbor ill feelings toward Henry McShane?"

Robert's brows shot up. "What's he got to do with anything?"

"Just answer the question, please."

"All right. No."

"That's not technically true." Edward's abrupt tone told me this was what he'd been waiting for—to attack. Not the approach I would have taken, and Claudia Inglenook agreed with me. She came out from behind the desk with a fury that made me step back. Edward held his spot.

"Are you calling my brother a liar?"

She stood, head thrown back and eyes narrowed, as if she were considering how high she'd have to jump to sock him in the eye. Edward bent his head to meet her glare.

"You misunderstand me." He used that level, cool tone that made it impossible to argue with him. It was about time he used it on someone other than me. "I think we should clarify who's who. Detective Timms?"

So that was it. He wanted to keep Timms from ambushing them with the victim's actual identity. Timms shook his head and blew out a stream of air. He hadn't wanted to show that card yet, but Edward had forced his hand.

"The deceased Luigi Ferrara was, in fact, Henry McShane," Timms said, trying to keep an eye on both siblings. The color drained out of Claudia's face and she blinked a few times.

I found Robert's reaction more interesting. He didn't have one, and I wasn't the only one who noticed. Edward had an unobstructed view over Claudia's head, and he was giving Robert his best unflinching stare. The one that has me confessing sins I've only thought about committing.

"You didn't, say, confront either man about their real identities?" Timms asked.

Robert shrugged his shoulders. "This is the first I've heard about it."

"Is this about last night?" Claudia asked, resuming her place beside her brother. "That's all been straightened out."

Timms nodded. "Let's talk about last night. I understand you and the man calling himself Henry McShane had words. What about?"

"It was a personal matter."

"Personal nothing. A man's been murdered."

Robert turned his palms up. "But not the man I spoke with."

Timms rested his bottom on the edge of the desk and twisted to keep both sibling suspects in view. "I've got a little idea. You asked the man what he'd *done with them*. I think you knew Henry McShane was the name of the man your Aunt Annabelle ran off with, and I think you were asking him about the Inglenook emeralds, which disappeared the same night."

Claudia tightened her hold on her brother again, something Edward didn't miss. I sensed him stiffen at my side. I was too busy trying to figure out if Timms' information was certain knowledge or a guess based on our conversation about how far a man would go to hide from his in-laws. If it was the latter, his move paid off.

"Okay. I recognized the name. And now you're telling me that the dead Luigi Ferrara was Henry McShane." Robert looked up at his sister. "I think the detective is wondering if I killed the real Henry in revenge for his stealing the emeralds. Or maybe he thinks I was avenging Grandfather, who was against the marriage."

"That's ridiculous," she sputtered. "That happened years ago. What does that have to do with us?"

"The two of you are very understanding," Timms said,

"considering you've recently been forced to open your home to the public to make ends meet."

"And you think it would be different if Henry McShane hadn't run off with Aunt Annabelle and taken the jewels with him?" Claudia made a short, harsh sound intended to be a laugh.

Robert sighed. "My father drank himself to death. He wasn't good at managing money, and if he had gotten hold of the Inglenook emeralds, he would have cashed them in and lost that money, too. We would have wound up right where we are with or without Henry McShane." He shifted in his chair. "It's embarrassing now, but I asked the man I thought was Henry McShane to leave. I thought he had come back to Inglenook to gloat. I was wrong to let my emotions get the better of me, and I planned to apologize this morning, but I got caught up with paperwork. Then, with the murder, it slipped my mind."

"And you didn't have any suspicions that Luigi Ferrara was actually the man who made a mess of your family?"

"As far as I knew, the man I talked to last night was Henry McShane. That's the name he registered under, and I don't perform background checks on my guests. Besides, the incident happened a long time ago. Before my time."

I raised a hand. "How long ago did the elopement-slash-theft take place?"

"About forty years ago."

Zali had said she had been a mere child at the time, and she was in her sixties, but I didn't make a big deal out of it. She wouldn't be the first woman to lie about her age.

"And where were you both this morning, say, between six-thirty and eight?" Timms asked.

"Here. At one point, I went to check the boiler," Claudia said. "I'd received several phone calls complaining that there wasn't any hot water."

"That's true," Edward said in support, but Claudia kept her eyes fastened on Timms and pretended my brother didn't exist.

"Where exactly is the boiler located?"

"In the cellar," Claudia said. "The access used to be from outside the house, but Grandfather added an entrance right off the original kitchen."

"Could anyone have seen you?"

"I can't remember. My mind was on the boiler."

"And was anything wrong with it?"

"No."

"I see." Timms allowed us to appreciate the significance of her statement before moving to Robert.

"And while your sister was in the basement, you were…"

"I was balancing yesterday's receipts right here at this desk."

"Did anyone come to the front desk during that time?"

"No."

"Any phone calls come in?"

"No. Correction. Claudia was handling the front desk, so I didn't pay attention to the phone."

"And when she went to check the boiler?"

Claudia answered for her brother. "I sent the calls to voicemail when I left the desk."

Timms surveyed them with a pleasant smile. "So, neither of you has an alibi."

As we left, Claudia Inglenook grabbed Edward's arm with both hands and pulled him back into the room. "Robert, please leave us."

Robert Inglenook closed his ledger and slid it into the desk drawer. "Someone's in trouble," he sang. I had to admit that Claudia's brother was either a fool, or he wasn't particularly worried. To clown around right after you've been told your alibi isn't worth a cent takes a brave man or a simpleton. As he passed Edward on his way out, he whispered, "Look sorry and beg forgiveness. Works for me."

"Robert!"

With the soft click of the door, Edward was alone with Claudia Inglenook, but by leaning on the wall next to the doorframe, I could hear their conversation perfectly. So could Robert Inglenook, who took up the same position on the other side of the door. After trying to be casual about our eavesdropping, we gave in and grinned at each other.

"What are you trying to do to my brother?" Claudia said. "I thought you were above getting involved?"

"You strike me as an intelligent woman," Edward said. "Surely you can't believe lying to the police will bring you anything but problems. Robert's omission would have appeared suspicious. As it is, I think he's cleared himself nicely." He added in a low growl, "Thanks to me."

"How do you mean?" Claudia's tone was what I would call *snippy*.

"Obviously, when your brother confronted Henry McShane in the Welcome Room, he believed that to be the man's true identity. Why would he bother killing Luigi Ferrara? He didn't know that Luigi was an imposter."

"You're right," Claudia said, but her voice sounded far away. She repeated, "You're right. Although it's strange they knew so much about Robert's conversation with Henry McShane."

"Of course they knew, and if he had lied about it, they would have been highly suspicious."

"What do you mean, *of course they knew*? How are you so certain? Did you hear Mr. McShane tell the police about it?"

He'd dug himself into a hole, and I was curious to hear how he'd climb out of it.

"Well, no."

And he should have left it there, but his crippling honesty got in the way.

"I may have told them."

Robert's eyebrows shot up. I shrugged.

"You what?!"

"With no malicious intent. It…slipped."

A moment of silence followed. "You're fired. We don't want your help."

"Fired? I never agreed to help you in the first place."

"Good. Let's leave it that way."

"Fine. I'll see myself out."

Edward yanked open the door so hard it slammed against the wall. As he stalked off, Robert slipped past him back into the office dripping with curiosity. Before the door closed, I heard him say:

"So, am I cleared?"

She responded, "I can't be sure."

CHAPTER 11

T hat last snippet of conversation between Claudia and Robert Inglenook left an uncomfortable sensation in my stomach. There could be several interpretations. Robert could have been more disturbed than he let on about Timms' accusation because he was innocent, or he could be guilty, and his sister knew it.

Either way, Edward was back on his high horse where he was easier to handle. I decided to let my brother cool off and do a bit of digging on my own, and I had a hunch my best source of information on the guests was Maggie.

I found her on our floor, and it was like déjà vu. The dumbwaiter door hung open. She stood before Griselda Waterford's door with a tray at her feet, and she knocked. The bell rang. Amanda popped out of her door like a live Jack-in-the-box and made the delivery.

When Maggie looked my way, I grinned at her, but she wasn't in the mood to return it.

"I have a couple of questions for you."

She turned her back on me. "I'm fresh out of answers." Her cart was a few doors down and she moved toward it, but

I took her arm and steered her back to her nook, talking on the way.

"Don't be like that," I said. "You'll wind up with frown lines between those beautiful eyes."

"I don't like being called a liar."

Once I got her safely inside, flipped on the light switch, and closed the door behind us, I mustered up some indignation, dropped her arm, and stepped back. "Who called you a liar? Did I?"

"No," she reluctantly admitted.

"Did Edward?"

She kept her hands busy straightening sheets that didn't need straightening. "He must have because he's the reason the police called me back and questioned me for half an hour. That's what Miss Inglenook said."

I put one hand on my heart and held up the other, taking an oath. "All he said was he saw a maid in the hallway, and she ignored his request for additional towels."

"I never—!"

"That's what I told them."

Her tone softened. "You did?"

"Yeah. But the fact remains someone dressed as a maid was walking these halls before you came on your shift. They figured if anyone could help them, it would be you." I brushed at the air in a dismissive gesture. "The police treat everyone like suspicious characters. They've got to. What if you were a master criminal putting one over on them, and they had offered you tea and crumpets? They'd look silly, and the cops don't enjoy looking silly any more than the rest of us do. That's all."

"I guess they weren't that bad," she said. "Still, it was annoying."

I grinned. "Just like the guests here." Once I had her laughing, I hooked a leg over one stack of sheeting and set down my rump. "So, who do you think was dishonoring the uniform?"

"Isn't what I told the police confidential?"

"Only for those not helping the police. Say Mrs. Waterford clumped out and started asking you questions. You could tell her to go back to her cave."

That got me a full chuckle. She stopped playing with the sheets. "I can't even guess."

"Sure you can."

"Really. I can't. I didn't see or hear anything."

"I find if I replay a scene, it helps jog my memory. Let's go back to this morning. I followed you in here after making my request." I pulled down some white towels. "You efficiently met my needs. I asked you about Mr. Ferrara. You said he was taking a shower. A door slammed. You peeked out. By the way, who was in the hallway? Was it Zali?"

She gave a little jump, and I homed in on it. "What do you remember?" I tried to look her in the eye, but she wasn't having it. She bowed her head to avoid me.

"I said I didn't see or hear anything, didn't I? I don't want to talk about it."

Her tone made it clear she'd given her final answer on the subject, so I moved on to a friendly conversation about her job, what she did with her free time, and then I led the topic around to vacations and back to the guests. In her present state of mind, she was happy to slam them. By the time we were through, I had plenty of starting places should Edward agree to focus on the murder, and on impulse, I leaned in and gave her a peck on the cheek. I went straight to big brother to share the news.

When I opened the door, I checked my step and held my breath. Edward was at his desk, but he slumped forward in his chair with his chin on his chest and his arms hanging limp at his sides. My first thought was the killer had struck again, but then his chest expanded with a low snore. I closed the door with more force than necessary and took my time turning back to the room to allow him a minute to muster his dignity.

"Where've you been?" He cleared his throat to get rid of the frog and said it again. He leaned back in the chair with a pen in one hand and a page in the other, pretending to proof it. I explained I had been picking up tidbits about the guests.

"That's gossip," he said without looking up from the page.

"It's information that may help you clear up the mess you made with Robert Inglenook," I said, hoping to stir up some guilt.

"That woman fired me."

Edward dropped his pen and paper on the desk and repeated himself with additional emphasis.

"That woman *fired* me. How can you fire someone who isn't even working for you?" He looked at me, his brow creased with puzzlement and indignation. "Everything I said to the police was true. It's not my fault if her brother behaved like an ass." He shook his finger at me. "Henry McShane was in a wheelchair. A *wheelchair*! What kind of man accosts a man in a wheelchair? Robert Inglenook must be unstable."

He reached for his paper. To keep the conversation going, I'd have to get him away from distractions, so I looked at my watch. "What do you say we get something to eat and forget about this business?"

He stood without argument, tugged his vest down, and straightened his tie. "Good idea." He led the way, and as I locked the door behind us, I heard him mutter, "They're all mad."

CHAPTER 12

They served lunch in the Atrium, a glass room filled with enough greenery to give it a tropical feel. Snowdrifts pressed against the windows, reminding me we were stranded. If I dwelled on that thought, I could have worked up a panic attack, but then I saw the food. At least we wouldn't starve.

Buffet tables lined one wall and overflowed with a variety of thick sandwiches, several salad choices, teacakes, and beverages. We filled our plates and sat at a small, wrought-iron table near the entrance. I waited until Edward had unfolded his napkin and spread it across his lap before I tried to lead the conversation back to the murder, taking the roundabout way.

"It's interesting the different types of people you find at a resort, don't you think?" I aimed my fork at an elderly couple across the room.

"Don't point."

"For instance," I said, making it up as I went along, "that couple has been married sixty-five years. They met on her father's dairy farm, where she used to wake at three every

106

morning to help milk the cows. He stumbled across their house and knocked on their front door about ready to collapse from walking the ten miles from his car, which had broken down on a dirt lane. He was only on that road because he'd gotten lost on the way to sell a tractor to a guy with a field of corn to plow. Doesn't that make you believe in true love?"

"It's called harvesting, and they use combines, not tractors."

"Listen to you, full of information. Well, I have a tidbit for you that you *don't* already know. You remember those little gremlins we met outside?"

He made a noise of acknowledgement because his mouth was full.

"They belong to Claudia Inglenook."

Edward stopped chewing and swallowed. "You mean she's married?"

He covered his interest by playing with his silverware.

"She's watching them for a cousin."

He kept his eyes fastened on his fork as he polished it with his napkin, so anyone who didn't know him like I did would have thought his next question a casual inquiry. "Are you certain? I mean, how do you know?"

"I had an interesting talk with Maggie about the guests."

"Who is Maggie?" he demanded. "Our *maid's* name is Maggie. Are you seducing the staff?"

"It's not a crime to say hello to a beautiful woman regardless of what her job is. And it's a good thing I started a conversation with her because I learned a lot of tidbits that could be useful for Timms. He asked us to keep our eyes and ears open."

"Like what?" His tone put the stress on reluctance, but I could see an interested gleam in his eyes.

The first person to catch my eye was Griselda Waterford.

I wondered how much food she put away in one day, since Maggie had delivered a tray to her room less than an hour ago.

"Just as an example, Griselda Waterford seems to know a lot about proper service techniques for an independently wealthy widow."

Edward took a slow drink of iced tea and peered over the rim of his glass at our subject as she loomed over an enormous pile of desserts. Next to her lay an empty plate filled with crust corpses. Across the table, Amanda Mayfield chewed slowly, her bored gaze wandering the room. She made eye contact with Edward and winked. He gave her a stony stare. When she winked again, he looked away.

"Maybe the Mayfield woman is her personal maid," he said, "and Mrs. Waterford has picked up tips."

"Amanda Mayfield's not a maid, believe it or not. She's a companion. An odd job for a young American woman, don't you think? Anyway, her boss demonstrated to our dear Maggie the proper way to make the bed because she wasn't satisfied with the way the corners were tucked. According to Maggie, the old woman was good at it."

"Who cares?" Edward slid a glance toward Griselda and shuddered. Her attention no longer diverted by dessert, she eyed a nearby ficus plant as if she were sizing up the enemy.

I tossed a crouton at him to get his attention.

"You should care," I said. "Especially if you want the police to catch the killer so the VPS gang can settle in and have their conference. Now, back to Amanda Mayfield. She's been with Griselda for two years, ever since Mr. Waterford gratefully checked out. Her only vice is she thinks she can crochet."

I leaned back and popped a cookie into my mouth, enjoying myself. Edward says he doesn't like gossip, but I could tell he was interested, and it's not often that I have anything to say that holds his attention. "Then there's the dearly departed's daughter."

"Stop talking with your mouth full."

I swallowed and took a long drink of iced tea to make him wait. "Barbara Maggiano," I finally said, nodding to where she sat.

Barbara had changed into a blinding white cashmere sweater and slacks. A woman I dated told me a simple black dress should be a part of any well-dressed lady's wardrobe. Still, I hesitated to judge. I think the Japanese, or maybe it's the Koreans, wear white for mourning. Who knew what the Scots did?

"According to Maggie, when they swiped the woman's credit card, it left a trail of smoke. She said she had handed over the wrong card by accident, but I don't believe it. Anyway, that just confirms what we already know. Barbara Maggiano's finances are shaky. An inheritance would be welcome."

"And how would the maid know about Mrs. Maggiano's finances?" Edward asked.

I smirked, something Edward says I do too often. "Maggie doesn't miss much." To make my point, I adjusted my chair to give me a view of my next subject. "The Reverend Markham understated his desire to speak with the victim. Maggie noticed him hovering around Luigi's room several times last night. Whatever it is he needed to discuss, he's not saying. Yet. He seemed to get along with you. Maybe you can get him to spill."

"A man of the cloth must use his discretion about what's confidential. I wouldn't dream of prying it out of him." Edward continued to watch the reverend, his gaze thoughtful and his hand stroking his chin.

I passed over Zali, who was plunging headfirst into a bowl of mixed greens, sending bits of tomato and lettuce flying. Edward moved his gaze away from the cleric when I pronounced her name.

"Maggie didn't have much to say about Zali."

His gaze lingered on her; his mouth drooped in a frown.

"You know, Edward, if you're really worried that she's a danger, we can ask Claudia to take away her steak knife."

"As much as I enjoy listening to you drag our fellow guests through the mud," which meant he didn't, "we know nothing about the victim."

I grinned. "Luigi Ferrara was a retired accountant and as interesting as stagnant water. He must have been loaded. There's no other explanation for the delicious Felicity Hartwell. And her cousin is a shady character, or at least he doesn't have any self-respect."

Edward's brows lowered. "You don't mean—"

I nodded. "Luigi Ferrara paid for all three of them. I'm not sure about the technicalities. Does that make Jake a gigolo?"

Edward plucked his napkin from his lap and lobbed it onto the table. "All that tells us is that Mr. Ferrara was a generous man. In fact, there is a simple explanation for everything you've told me. Maybe Griselda Waterford was in the army. Or was a nurse. Either profession would teach her how to make a bed properly. Amanda Mayfield works as a companion. An unusual field, but hardly sinister. The Reverend Mr. Markham is trustworthy, and Barbara Maggiano is broke, which isn't a crime."

"So, you're going to pretend there aren't motives hiding under that pile of facts I just gave you? There's a murderer stalking the halls," I said, using his dramatic statement against him. "You can't be squeamish. We may find out things about our fellow guests we'd rather not know." I leaned forward, elbows on the table just to annoy him. "Seriously. What do you think?"

Edward pushed his chair back, stood, and looked down at me. "I'm going to work on my column."

I gaped. "There's been a murder, the police have invited us to help them solve the crime, and you're going to write letters?"

"Those letters are paying for this trip."

As it turned out, Edward didn't get to the letters that afternoon.

CHAPTER 13

"**C**an you believe I'm Scottish?"

It seemed that Barbara Maggiano's Italian in-laws would accept a murdered father without a blink, but a tartan-sporting ancestor would elicit boos and hisses. We were in our room, with Barbara seated on the blueberry loveseat. Edward had moved up his desk chair, and I was standing on the other side of the coffee table, facing her. My brother had informed me it would be unseemly if I sat on the edge of my bed with a lady present, and after the Woman in White's hostile entrance, I didn't want to share the loveseat with her.

She had pounded on the door so hard that when I opened it, she tumbled in. When I caught her by the arms to keep her from falling, she had bared her teeth at me. From what I understand about dogs, that means *trespassers beware.*

Though Edward and I had said nothing about the suspicious circumstances of Luigi Ferrara's death, the way the police kept questioning people made it clear they weren't satisfied with the accident theory. The word *murder* was being whispered among the staff and the guests, and Barbara Maggiano had come to us for advice.

"You say you had a fight with your father, and now the police are trying to blame you for his death?" Edward asked.

Her tense smile pleaded for understanding. "You know how we Italians are. Vocal. But then it's all kisses and hugs."

"Except you're not Italian," I pointed out.

She turned her head toward me. "I was until ten minutes ago. Look. We had an argument, and it was a lulu. Afterwards, I felt bad. He was getting up there in years, you know? I couldn't stand the thought of him dropping dead from a heart attack with bad feelings between us. I followed him down here to make it up with him. I had nothing to do with his death, but I can't say the same about his tart."

Edward's left eye twitched. "You mean his fiancée."

She pulled open her purse and took out a packet of cigarettes. "Do you mind?"

I grinned and looked at Edward. She had asked nicely, and she was definitely under high stress, yet there were the resort rules. How was Edward going to handle it?

"Of course," he said. He stood and motioned toward the balcony. "The ashtray is this way."

I lost the grin. It was cold outside, but I wasn't going to stay inside and miss out on any insights we might gain from our first interview. She raised her brows and stared at him. If she thought he'd change his mind on account of her being in mourning, she was mistaken. All she got was his back as he led the way.

The hotel staff had swept the snow away, but the chairs were still damp and definitely too cold for comfort. We all three stood as she lit her cigarette.

"Your father was engaged to Miss Felicity Hartwell." Edward made it sound like a question.

She blew out a mixture of smoke and the condensation

that comes from breathing in a freezing environment. "He was infatuated with her. He would have come around." Barbara leaned one arm across the balcony but pulled it back as soon as she touched the cold metal. "My father had a rigid sense of right and wrong, and that girl is a wrong 'un. She would have slipped up eventually, and that would have been the end of her and Jake. You were at her table last night." She pointed her cigarette at me. "You saw what she was like."

"I pass." It seemed the safest answer.

"Most guys don't see through her, but I'm a woman." She tossed her head to show us how much she loved being a woman. "I know how much work it takes to be that effortlessly perfect." She threw a challenging look at us, and neither of us had the nerve to disagree with her expertise. "No woman puts out that much effort unless she expects a big payoff. My dad was that payoff."

I raised one eyebrow. "He's worth that much?"

"He was good with the market and he never spent a dime he wasn't forced to." Her mouth twisted into a smile. "The police checked with Papa's lawyer. His will leaves everything to me. As it should. Bet little Felicity is in for a surprise."

"Ah," Edward said. "Then you think Miss Hartwell murdered him for the money she thought she would receive upon his death?"

I interjected to keep the focus on Barbara and her obvious motive. "The money from your father should come in handy."

"There's a recession on," she said. "How are your own bank accounts doing?" She caught my frown as I remembered my current balance, and she laughed. It wasn't a happy, kind sound. "And yet you haven't killed anyone, I assume."

"So, did you?" Edward asked. For a moment, Barbara looked startled, until he added, "Make up?" When she hesitated, he asked if she had seen her father anytime last night.

"N-n-n-o."

I looked straight into her eyes. Though she didn't bat a lash, I recognized that no—the drawn-out *n* and the drop in pitch at the end meant to convince the listener. I used it all the time. It meant yes. She stubbed out her smoke in the ashtray on the table and led the way back inside.

Edward said, "I still don't understand why you're here."

She sighed with impatience. "I just told you."

"Yes, I got that. You had a fight with your father; you followed him to Inglenook. But what are you doing *here?*" He motioned around our room.

"Oh. I saw you in with the police. You were with them for quite a while, long enough to get an idea what they're thinking."

"I can't read minds. You'll have to ask them directly."

"They wouldn't answer. As ridiculous as it sounds, I'm a suspect."

"Most likely, yes."

There wasn't much to say after that, but Barbara Maggiano submitted one last request. "Maybe you could put in a good word for me. Explain that it was just a simple argument. I may be a lot of things, but I'm no murderer."

Edward spread his hands, palms up. "And why would I do that? I've never met you before today. Even if I wanted to, as you said, put in a good word for you, why would the police listen to me?"

"Because you represent a famous author. That has pull. Even if you are the biggest crook in the world, and I'm not saying you are, your association with Aunt Civility has rubbed off on you. It makes people trust you."

That seemed to square it with the Woman in White. Since Edward was speechless, I told her we'd discuss the situation and showed her out.

He jabbed his finger at the closed door. "Did that woman just suggest I'm a crook?"

"You weren't listening. She specifically said she *wasn't* saying it. But I know what she means. Look at the way celebrities sell everything from liquor to cars. And it works. Maybe you should consider lending Aunt Civility's name for advertising. Tea manufacturers and stationery companies. You might start people writing letters again."

"I know what you're really after. You made it obvious with the way you were so eager to tell Detective Timms about Robert Inglenook."

So now it was my fault.

"And your hints about the nefarious backgrounds of the guests. I'm not traipsing around this resort hunting for clues and harassing people."

"You don't need to traipse. I'll bring them here to you, like the Woman in White."

"Absolutely not."

Edward went into a sulk that lasted until the next knock on our door. Timms and Michelson were headed for Griselda Waterford's room. They didn't like being in a guest's private room without impartial witnesses, so they asked us to tag along. That made perfect sense to Edward, so he agreed.

Amanda Mayfield answered the door and invited us in. Once inside the Red Rose Room, my first thought was: *It will have blood.* Red velvet rose wallpaper; that said it all.

Griselda had a suite, so the first room was decked out with a small table with chairs, a couch, and a bookcase filled with a selection of old books. The servant allowed us to enter the bedroom only after Griselda Waterford had time to arrange herself. She sat up in bed surrounded by piles of pillows and covered by an enormous crocheted blanket that would have given Joseph's multicolored coat stiff competition. Amanda must have plenty of down time.

A magazine lay open on her lap while she worked a crossword puzzle. She beckoned us to her with a wiggle of her pudgy fingers. Before Timms could utter a word, she cut him off. "I don't see why you have to badger me. I know nothing."

He placated her with the usual general statement. "We're checking up on everyone's whereabouts this morning."

She waved her hand around the room. "My whereabouts," she said. "I was in here the entire morning by myself until Amanda brought me an unsatisfactory, lukewarm breakfast."

He looked to Amanda Mayfield for confirmation.

"Considering that she doesn't do a thing without my help, I'd say she's telling the truth. I didn't arrive here until she summoned me. I'm not sure of the time."

"The tray arrived around a quarter after seven," I offered.

"That sounds about right," she said.

Timms gave me a dark look.

"It's not as if it could be a secret." I pointed at the large bell on Griselda's nightstand. "The entire floor could give you the same information."

He moved his glare to the bell. "And we understand from Maggie that you were in the middle of, um, personal stuff when she knocked." He clarified. "The water was running."

The old lady snapped her lips into a pucker. "I hardly think that's any of your business. I was probably brushing my teeth."

"Before breakfast?" Timms asked.

Her haughty stare would have made most grown men quake, but Timms stared back, perfectly pleasant.

"Do I need to spell out what I was doing?" she threatened. "And afterwards I went to the telephone to make a complaint about the lack of hot water."

Timms included Amanda Mayfield in his next question. "How well did either of you know Luigi Ferrara?"

Griselda plucked her blanket up around her armpits, giving the impression that his question wasn't worth her attention. "Not at all."

Timms seemed to debate something in his head, and then he brought out the zinger. "Did you know that Luigi Ferrara was actually Henry McShane?"

Her face remained a blank. "How odd," she said. "But that would mean—"

"That Henry McShane is Luigi Ferrara," Timms said, nodding.

"Sounds like a childish game." Griselda raised a large penciled eyebrow. "Did it involve sex?"

"Oh, good grief," Edward muttered in exasperation. I elbowed his ribs twice, once to shut him up and once for the pleasure of it.

"We're checking out all possibilities," Timms answered. I gave him points for not flinching.

"Well. It sounds as if I knew even less about the man than I thought I did. Inglenook sounded like a charming place to visit, but I won't be returning." Griselda clasped her hands together on her bosom. "Is there anything else?"

"Hmmm." Edward stroked his chin.

Timms gave Griselda Waterford another look and then asked, "What is it, Eddie?"

My brother waved him off. "I'm sure it's nothing."

"Enlighten me."

"May I ask a personal question?" Edward said. When Griselda didn't say no, he proceeded. "Have you been to Inglenook Resort before?"

She narrowed her eyes in a predatory fashion. "Why do you ask?"

"You knew there was a farmer's field on the other side of

the grounds and that it leads to a two-lane highway. That suggests you're familiar with the area."

Griselda stated this was common knowledge.

"Then you aren't acquainted with the family?"

She said she wasn't.

"How about you, Ms. Mayfield?" Timms asked. "Have you ever heard the name Luigi Ferrara or Henry McShane before?"

"You're barking up the wrong tree," Amanda said. "I'm at this resort in the middle of nowhere because I have to be."

"You and me both, sister," I said under my breath, and the corners of her mouth turned up a notch.

"Did either of you hear or see anything this morning? Anything unusual?"

When they insisted they had not, Timms gave both women the speech about making themselves available for additional questions. He motioned for us to leave. As I passed Griselda's bedside, I looked down. In a blank corner of her magazine, her doodle had captured Michelson's stoic expression perfectly.

CHAPTER 14

My new friend, Charlie, was in rare form. He and his traveling companions who included a guy who had a permanent lean—one leg was shorter than the other—were on an annual ice-fishing trip. They'd decided to try Inglenook to take advantage of the grand opening specials, but current weather had defeated them, so they picked their second favorite sport. Hanging out in the bar. They hailed from Chicago, and I put down their occupation as dockworkers. They all had squints that might have come from daily exposure to sunlight reflected off Lake Michigan, and they all looked strong and tough.

I was still recovering from a joke about a politician nobody liked when Charlie leaned in and muttered over his shoulder.

"I heard you were helping the police." He added a conspiratorial wink. "Thought you'd like to know about the argument, that's all." He leaned back and stared at his empty glass.

Argument sounded promising. I motioned to the

bartender, and while Charlie got his refill, I asked, "Who argued?"

He took a long pull on his fresh beer and wiped the foam from his upper lip with the back of his hand. "The dead man and that little filly he hoped to marry."

"Hoped?"

"You got it. To set the scene, I'd been celebrating hard, and I didn't get to bed until after one in the morning. Me and Joe were talking about playing a round of poker, but I thought I might nod off in the middle of the game. It's happened before." He grimaced. "One of the joys of getting older. Did I mention this was the night before Luigi died?"

"And all through the house, not a creature was stirring, yadda, yadda, yadda," I said. "Get to the good part."

"Gee. Try and do a guy a favor."

He really looked hurt, so I apologized. "I'm just anxious. I can't claim experience at this kind of thing, but it seems to me an investigation should have some life to it. This one isn't going anywhere."

He took pity on me and continued, though with less relish. "Seems the old geezer was having a blowout with Miss Prissy-pants in the hallway. Couldn't help overhearing."

"What was the cause?"

He took a drink, plopped his glass down for effect, and said, "Her cousin." He allowed me some time to absorb this information.

"I know I wouldn't have wanted a tagalong if I had such a beautiful fiancée. Really, though, I just think they're close, like Siamese twins."

"He caught them," Charlie said.

"Caught them?" I asked. Then I scrunched up my face. "You don't mean—"

"I do."

I stood up and sat back down because the thought gave

me a major case of the creeps. "That's just sick."

"Seems Mr. Ferrara agreed with you. The engagement was off. And the last thing I heard the young stud say to his *cousin* is that he would *take care of everything.*"

I whistled.

"And did you tell the police?"

"I will when they get around to me."

"Why don't you offer the information like a good citizen?"

Charlie scrunched up his face. "I don't want to get involved if I don't have to. This isn't the city; it's the boonies. A murder *means* something out here, and the press will have a field day. Would you want the papers reporting that you were a snoop? Besides, if I figured it out, the police should be able to. And now that I've told you…" He shrugged.

There wasn't anything else to do but to buy another round. I enjoyed Charlie's company, but the reason I had entered the bar twenty minutes ago was I'd followed Barbara Maggiano inside. She hadn't met up with anyone but had taken a table in the middle of the room. I gave a quick glance in her direction. She was still there, and she was still alone.

Charlie didn't miss my interest. "I wouldn't waste my time on the dragon lady. First night we were here, Joe tries to start a conversation with her. He's still looking for his *cojones.*"

"Maybe she likes her men younger and better-looking." That got me a chuckle, and I took my drink and wandered over to her.

"Is this seat taken?"

Her upper lip curled. "Does it look like anyone's sitting there?"

I accepted that as an invitation, sat down, and did us both a favor and was direct. "So, what did you say to your father when you saw him the night before he died?"

"You heard what I told your brother."

"I know what you *said*."

She didn't appear to hear me, so I repeated myself.

"I heard you the first time." She stirred her drink with a swizzle stick laced with olives. "First, it's none of your business. Second, what makes you think I saw him?"

"Because I would have." I grinned at her look of surprise. "I sympathize with you. If some piece of goods was working her way into Edward's good graces and he was contemplating changing his will..." I trailed off because I didn't even know if Edward had a will, or if it mentioned me. I'd have to look into that. "Well, I wouldn't just sit on my thumbs."

That garnered me a respectful glance. She seemed to decide I was worthy of her confidences.

"You strike me as a shallow man." When I protested, she snapped her fingers to get my attention. "I mean that as a compliment. All these idiots pretending to care. My father wasn't an easy man to like. His standards were high, and he rubbed my face in every mistake I ever made."

I started to sympathize with her.

"I went to talk to him about my problem." She whispered the word *problem* as if she were sharing feminine hygiene secrets.

"We are talking about money," I said, just to clarify.

"What else?" She threw back the rest of her drink and wiggled her painted nails toward the bar.

"I'll get it," I said, motioning to the bartender. She scooted her chair closer with an admiring smile.

"Finally. A gentleman."

I made a note to report the compliment to Edward. "So, you asked him to change his mind about helping you out. Seems reasonable."

"Entirely," she agreed. "That floozy thought she was going to snatch up my inheritance. I'm sorry my father's dead, but if he had to kick off, I'm glad it was before he changed his will."

I must have registered surprise because she clutched my hand. Her nails dug into my skin.

"*You* know what I mean. And Daddy would have regretted it. I'm sure of it. A few months with Felicity and her cousin and he would have been—Hey! You don't think they planned to murder him after he changed his will, do you?"

I didn't know how many drinks she'd had so far, but it must have been a few, and the alcohol had loosened her train of thought along with her tongue.

"You mean you think they killed him? If that's the case, they jumped the gun."

She snorted with laughter. "A premature eja—"

"Point taken." I cut her off because I don't like to hear crude language from women. "Just to be clear, you talked to him the night before he died, and it was to suggest he reconsider changing his will."

"Got it in one," she said, changing out her empty glass for the fresh drink handed to her by the cocktail waitress. I put some bills on the tray.

"And did he agree to think about it?"

"No." She shrugged it off as if it hadn't really mattered. "But I didn't expect him to. Not at first. But he would have come around."

Perhaps she had expedited matters.

With that in mind, I went to find Edward, but when I turned the corner into the main hallway, I spotted danger ahead. Zali sifted through the dirt of a large plant with her fingers. According to Claudia Inglenook, Zali's gardening exercises had painful consequences, and her puzzled expression made me wonder if the "Nasties" had taken hold of the woman again.

However, I could solve the mystery of the tipping plants

with a direct question, so I set my shoulders, approached her with a confidence I didn't feel, and said, "Can I help you find something?" I caught the extra cheerful note in my voice and hoped I didn't remind her of a condescending mental health professional.

She whirled on me, and it took everything I had not to make a run for it. Then she tucked her hands behind her back and stared at me. I waited her out. Zali blinked first. After blowing her bangs out of her eyes, she dusted her hands together, dropping large clumps of dirt on the floor.

"Caught me in the act. Looking for clues. Makes a mess when you do it with your hands, but Claudia's certain she doesn't have a spade handy."

"That's pretty clever." I nodded at the plant. "What made you think of it?"

"Well, I have to admit it wasn't my idea. I saw—" She stopped with a sly smile.

"Saw what?" I asked, and then I mentally kicked myself for fumbling it.

"You just want to get the jump on me."

I held my palms up. "I'm banned from the competition."

"I don't think I should tell you. I've seen you with the coppers. You're probably a judge. Can you tell me if I'm warm? Or have they forbidden you from helping us? Probably." She started down the hallway and paused to ask, "What's the prize? They haven't said."

"It's still under consideration."

Since Zali had gardening on her mind, my feet took me in the opposite direction. Who knew if those thoughts would remind her of Norbert and lead to a second attack? I hit the top of the back staircase just as Michelson, Edward, and Timms came out of Felicity Hartwell's door. Jake escorted Felicity across the hall and Timms unlocked Luigi Ferrara's door and motioned them inside.

I jogged up and leaned against the doorframe, right behind Edward, and glanced over the proceedings. Luigi's room was just as I remembered it, though a dead body no longer stretched across the bathroom floor.

"Your fiancé was very neat," Timms said to Felicity. He caught my eye as he spoke and acknowledged me with a nod. Edward turned his head.

"There you are."

"Here I am."

"Lou's motto was everything in its place." Felicity wrinkled her forehead. "He had a lot of mottos."

"Just like you." I nudged Edward, who had his arms crossed over his chest. I could have sworn I heard a crinkling noise, but when I raised an eyebrow at him, Edward met my gaze without a hint that anything was up.

Felicity wandered to the bedside table, picked up Luigi's watch, and played with the clasp while she searched the rest of the room. "I don't see anything missing."

"There was a manila envelope on that desk by the window," I offered.

The way Felicity studied me sent chills down my spine. She only looked away when Timms asked her, "Do you know what was in it?"

"Envelope?" she said, dropping the watch on the bed. "I suppose there might have been one. I didn't pay attention."

She was lying. I'd seen her make a grab for it while the corpse was still fresh.

The lady led the way out of the room, and Timms, lagging behind, whispered to Michelson, "There's something familiar about her face."

The sergeant nodded. He kept his face neutral, as always, but there was a distinct gleam in his eyes.

Out in the hallway, Felicity took a wrong step and stumbled, and she grabbed onto my upper arm with both hands and leaned her head into mine. She whispered something and then apologized in a normal voice. With one glance back at me, she allowed Cousin Jake to lead her to her room.

"I see you traipse halls after all." I said this to Edward's back because he went straight to our room and unlocked the door. "Not that I mind being left out of things. I've got so much to occupy me at this fabulous four-star resort."

As soon as I closed the door behind us, he said, "Lock it." His tone was so serious I did as he said and followed him to the desk. He pulled his shirt loose from his waistband, reached inside, and pulled out a manila envelope.

"You little devil," I exclaimed as Edward carefully opened it and pulled out a single sheet of paper. "Was it in Luigi's room all this time?"

"I found it in Felicity Hartwell's room," Edward said, distracted as he studied the page. It was a colored pencil sketch of Inglenook Manor from the outside. A man sat on horseback, his trusty hunting dog at his side. He gazed up at a woman who waved to him from a window on the second floor. The flame-red of her dress matched her hair, and around her neck, she wore a green necklace.

"Luigi Ferrara had a romantic side," I said. "That must be a rendition of his first love wearing the Inglenook emeralds. It seems callous to carry that around on a vacation with the woman who was primed to become the next Mrs. Ferrara."

Edward grunted. "Why would Miss Hartwell take this from her dead fiancé's room?"

"Maybe it has sentimental value."

Edward raised his eyebrows. "She coveted a picture of his first wife?"

"Good point. What else did you find out about Felicity Hartwell, or Jake?"

"Nothing important. They claim they didn't know Luigi

was Henry McShane, but they would say that, wouldn't they?"

"Huh. Sounds like you're interested in the murder."

He met my gaze with no sign of embarrassment. "I'm interested in anything that will get the VPS—the Victorian Preservation Society members here as soon as possible."

"Okay then." I reported what Charlie had told me and my conversation with Barbara Maggiano. He didn't seem surprised, or if he was, he kept it from his face.

"Maybe Luigi wasn't avoiding the reverend like I thought," I said. "Maybe he was in Barbara Maggiano's room discussing finances, which she didn't mention to the police."

"If either Barbara Maggiano or Felicity Hartwell is hiding something, she's not alone. That field Griselda Waterford mentioned. The one on the other side of the resort? I can't see why anyone would have casual knowledge of it. We didn't pass it on the main road."

Edward pulled a blank sheet of stationary from the middle desk drawer and set it alongside the drawing.

"I want to study this before I hand it over to Detective Timms."

I leaned over to get another look. He uncapped his pen and looked up at me, waiting.

"Well?"

"Well what?"

"Is there anything else?"

What he meant was he wanted me to leave him alone to play with his little clue. I'd been about to share what Felicity had whispered to me after her stumble, but he ticked me off. I didn't need to look at our SAT scores to know that Edward was smarter than I was, but to dismiss me like an errand boy? That tore it.

"I'll leave you to play detective," I said with a pretty good sneer, and I left to keep my date.

CHAPTER 15

Felicity Hartwell had invited me to meet with her in the bar. The offer surprised me, not because I had any illusions about the depth of her mourning, but because I thought she might hold a grudge. It was clear she was interested in that envelope, the one I told the police about, so the timing of her move made me wary.

While I waited for her to show up, Amanda Mayfield waved at me from a barstool.

"Join me?" she said. "Not really anything else to do in this place."

I told her I'd take a rain check. When Felicity Hartwell slid up behind me and rested her fingertips on my arm, Amanda turned her head with a sniff, as if I suddenly smelled funny.

We took a booth at the back of the room, and I sat on the side facing the door. Felicity ordered a margarita, and I asked for a Manhattan. I excused myself, caught up with the waitress at the bar, and changed mine to an iced tea in a cocktail glass—no ice. She raised a brow at me, but like a pro, she said, "Whatever you want."

Not that I had any reason not to trust Felicity Hartwell, other than she was a flirt and a liar, but I chose to be on the safe side.

Once we had our drinks, Felicity waited for me to go first. I took a sip and made a face to show my beverage was strong, and she merely touched her own liquid to her lips and put her glass down. She unfolded a compact mirror that she got out of her purse and played with her bangs.

"I look a mess."

I considered it in poor taste to dig for compliments so soon after the death of her fiancé. "The love of your life has been murdered. You're a step away from hag, but that's to be expected."

She snapped her compact shut. "Maybe I need something stronger to buck me up." She reached across the table for my glass, but I held it out of her reach.

"You might have cooties."

Her mouth didn't drop open. That would have spoiled the effect she was going for. Instead, her full lips merely parted.

"You look just fine and you know it."

That appeased her. She looked up at me through full lashes. "Everyone assumes there's nothing more to me than what's on the outside."

"Sure." I nodded. "You're a decoration."

She stood and did a good impression of being offended. "I thought you might be different."

When she moved to pass me, I put my arm out to stop her. It didn't take much effort because she wasn't ready to leave. "I'll admit there's something behind those big blue eyes of yours if you'll drop the injured act and get down to whatever it is you wanted to discuss." I grinned. "I don't suppose you asked me here to admire my manly profile."

She gave a small laugh and tried to slip into the booth next to me, but I firmed up my thighs and refused to budge.

There wasn't much dignity in having half her fanny hanging off the seat, so she returned to her side of the table, folded her hands in front of her like a junior executive, and lifted her cute, pointed chin. I tried to match her serious expression and waited for her to begin.

"You seem smart."

"Shallow *and* smart. I'm getting a reputation among the ladies at Inglenook." She frowned, and I told her to forget it. "Let's say I am."

She folded her arms in her lap and leaned forward, emphasizing the cleavage overflowing from the V-neck of her black sweater. "I want you to find whoever killed my fiancé. I know you're working with the police, but I think they'd like to call it an accident and let it go."

"You miss him already?"

"I know it was a strange match, and I will not pretend that I was in love with Lou, but he offered me security. I was grateful for that. He didn't deserve to die."

I pretended to think it over. "Okay. If we're being frank, what were you arguing about with Luigi the night before he died?"

"Arguing about?" She wrinkled her brow.

"You were overheard, and it sounds like it was a lulu."

"Oh. That." She laughed, but just barely. "Lou could be possessive. I had already stopped seeing most of my friends —male and female—and then he started in on Jake. But Jake is the only family I have. When he saw I was serious about keeping my cousin in my life, he got mad. But it wasn't a big deal."

She didn't seem embarrassed, so I figured that Charlie had gotten it wrong. Maybe Lou had caught her but with someone else.

"There wasn't, say, another man in your life?"

She gave me a genuine laugh. "I had enough on my hands

with Lou being jealous of my cousin. I didn't have the energy for more complications."

"Okay. You knew him best. Who do you think did it?"

Her brow crinkled again, and I put her age at closer to thirty than twenty. "Lou wasn't exciting enough to have enemies. I know everyone thinks Barbara probably did it for the money, but I don't believe it." A soft sigh escaped her lips. "Poor thing has lost her father. It's terrible."

Either she was sincere, or she wanted to reiterate Barbara's position as a suspect.

Suddenly, she decided she'd had enough talk about murder, and she asked me about myself. That's one of my favorite topics and, since the company was pleasing to the eye, I let myself loosen up enough to enjoy the conversation keeping in mind that she might like to bludgeon people to death while they shaved. She told me she was a slow drinker and encouraged me to order another, so I asked the waitress for one more of the same.

After I'd been served, Felicity brought the topic around to my job. I let loose a few frustrations without giving up any secrets, and I was just about to decide that Felicity Hartwell was in the clear when, without warning, she slid out of the booth and said:

"I'm tired of everybody staring at the bereaved fiancée. Let's go for a walk."

The only gazes I'd seen land on her were the appreciative kind, but I agreed out of curiosity. Maybe she planned to lure me into the shower and then crack my skull with a bath brush. We didn't go far, just across the hall. My eyebrows shot up when she peeked into the dining room, took my hand, and led me inside. The room was empty as far as I could tell from a quick survey, but the possibility of Felicity and Jake teaming up for murder crossed my mind, and I stopped all forward movement.

"I'm not hungry."

She made a pouty mouth, which was adorable on her. "You know I'm not broken-hearted over Luigi. Just sad, and when I'm feeling down like this, there's one thing that can cheer me up."

She dropped my hand and sashayed toward a large folding curtain against the wall that acted as a partition, not waiting for me to follow. As she slipped behind it, she said, "Coming?"

I figured, what the heck. As soon as we were out of sight from all those imaginary prying eyes, she pressed against me and slipped her arms around my neck. There was only one polite way to respond, so I did, though I kept my eyes open so I could see it coming if this were a setup.

Ten minutes later, a tiny hand ripped back the curtain. Felicity pushed away from me and screamed. Two children stared up at us with wide eyes, and behind them loomed Edward. To be fair, he looked as surprised as I was.

"Nicholas," he growled.

"I'm busy," I said. "Comforting the near-widow."

Felicity brushed her fingers through her hair and rubbed her hands down her sides, making sure everything was in place.

"You were sucking her face." The girl giggled.

I looked down at our young audience. "Miss Hartwell had something in her eye. I was removing it for her."

"What are your names?" Lucien asked.

"None of your business."

Felicity seemed to think bending down to the child's level and playing along would make Lucien our friend, and she gave him an answer.

"Nich'las and F'licity, sitting in a tree!" he bellowed.

I grabbed his arm. "Don't do that."

"You're not supposed to touch me!"

"It's illegal, you know," Edward finished with a smirk. He appeared to be warming to the child.

Felicity sobbed something about being distraught and abandoned me, and I watched her nicely shaped backside with regret. She just avoided running into Claudia Inglenook as the latter leaned her head into the room and called out, "There you are!"

Auntie Claudia profusely thanked both of us for watching over her charges, and when she reached out her hand for Neecie, the little girl motioned Edward toward her. He bent down, and she wrapped her arms around his big head and whispered something into his ear. His lips twitched into a smile.

"I solemnly promise." He actually crossed his heart. Then she kissed his cheek. To my amazement, he didn't wipe it off after they'd left the room.

"You haven't adopted them, I trust," I said, shoving my hands into my pants pockets. "You're playing hide and seek with two kids while we're surrounded by murderers and lunatics who talk about the Nasties—"

"I don't think Zali's technically crazy. And don't change the subject." He waved a hand at the curtain. "What were you playing at?"

"For your information, I was following a lead." We faced off, each one standing with his arms folded and chin out.

"You were being led all right."

"I'm not a moron. I knew she was playing a game."

"Murder's not a game."

I dropped my hands. "Are you saying that Felicity and Jake—"

"I'm not sure, and until we know who murdered Luigi Ferrara, I don't trust anyone."

"I guess you'll find out before I do. What's the idea of

going on an interview without me? I thought Timms wanted us as a team."

"I told you. I couldn't find you."

"Did you even look?"

"I'm not your nanny." He tilted his head and then shook it slowly. "Nicholas, Nicholas, Nicholas. You always needed constant amusement, even as a child."

"I'm as introspective as the next man."

He grinned at me. This always disarms me because it happens so rarely. "Okay, man of action. An important task needs our attention right now. Are you up to it?"

I twisted my head sideways to crack my neck. "Just lead the way."

CHAPTER 16

Edward had given his word to the child, Neecie, and he was forcing me to aid and abet in the commission of a crime—namely, larceny. We stood in front of the open door of the cellar and stared down into the darkness.

Edward jerked his chin and said, "Body or no body, we have to go down there."

"Couldn't you just ask Mrs. Beckwith for a carrot?"

"As you can see, she's not here to ask, and according to the child, she already tried that route. Mrs. Beckwith's selection fell short. Apparently, there is a proper length for a snowman's nose. I have strict orders for nothing shorter than *this big*." He held his hands apart to demonstrate the desired length.

"Turn on the light and let's get this over with."

Edward felt along the wall. "There isn't a switch."

Waving his arms above his head, Edward descended the stairs with me close behind until he found a cord hanging in the middle of the room and pulled. We took a moment to allow our vision to adjust to the dim lighting.

This first room was an empty twenty-by-ten-foot rectangle, with walls made of stone, and a low ceiling covered in some craggy-looking crud. The dirt floor under our feet sloped down in the center into a drain that smelled of damp earth, mold, and sewer. I shivered at the cold and eyed several doorways that led to other rooms.

"If I were a carrot, where would I be?" Edward asked aloud.

I peered through the closest doorway and saw the shadow of a large furnace, so I crossed to another doorway and said, "I choose this way." The temperature dropped as we entered. I found a light switch on the wall—one of those numbers with a button you depress. It hardly made a difference. The walls were lined with wooden nooks that had warped with age. The nooks overflowed with produce. In the middle of the room, distinctly out of place, some unlucky person had set up a cot and laid out the body of Luigi Ferrara. Thank the heavens they had enough sensitivity to cover him with a sheet.

"Go right ahead," Edward said. "I'll keep a lookout."

I gave him a dirty look and then scooted around the makeshift morgue. Fruit occupied the first shelves I reached, and I worked my way back until I found the vegetables.

"Parsnips, potatoes…or are these sweet potatoes? Aha!" I grabbed hold of a green leafy top and yanked out a gigantic carrot. The children's snowman had better be huge, or the face would be all nose. I lowered the carrot and leaned over. "What have we here?"

Edward shimmied past the corpse and looked over my shoulder at something bright orange that had been crammed into the bottommost shelf. I stuffed the carrot into my pocket and reached around a box of turnips. It took both hands to loosen and remove the stiff bundle of material, and

I carried it with me to the top of the stairs to look at it in better light.

"Towels?" I said.

Edward set his mouth in a grim line. "Bright orange towels."

"They're stained."

Edward ran his finger over the largest rust-colored blotch. "It's stiff. I think it's blood." He reached for our find and said, "We need to take these to the police."

As I handed them over, something black fell to the floor.

"What are you doing here?"

Our heads snapped up in unison. Mrs. Beckwith loomed in the doorway, and her sturdy figure blocked our escape. In her hand, she wielded the largest rolling pin I'd ever seen. I picked up the fabric, but Mrs. Beckwith swooped in and plucked it from my hands. She shook it out and stared.

"It's one of the maid's uniforms," she said. "Now what would that be doing here?" She raised the rolling pin. "And what business do you have, poking around in private rooms?"

"Madame," Edward said, "I believe the police will want to see what we found."

"Let's make sure they do." She snatched away the towels. "I'm going with you."

At least she didn't take the carrot.

Timms accepted his prize with mumbled thanks, and Mrs. Beckwith, considering her duty done, left us in the Gold Room.

"If we had the proper amount of men available, we would have searched that room and come up with this evidence ourselves."

"I'm sure that's the case," Edward soothed. "We were only there by chance in response to a little girl's request." He explained how Neecie had recruited him to help the children with their snowman—an excellent specimen except for his lack of a nose.

"Pure chance," Timms said, much cheered.

"Yoo-hoo!"

Zali stuck her head in the room, her hand raised in schoolroom fashion.

"I have a question about the rules," she sang, and she tottered in and plopped into a chair.

Timms, apprised of Zali's *special circumstances,* welcomed her with exaggerated heartiness and asked how he could assist.

"I've never played a murder game before," she said, struggling to remain in her seat like a good girl, "and it's loads of fun, but I expect there's rules." She looked at us with bright eyes, apparently hoping they were Marquis of Queensberry Rules as applied in the movie *The Quiet Man.* A free-for-all.

"Rules. Yes. Let's see." Timms was out of his depth.

"Why don't you tell us your specific concern?" Edward suggested.

Her smile turned coy. "I wouldn't want to give away my strategy."

After the two detectives, Edward, and I had, at her suggestion, sworn secrecy, crossed our hearts, and shown her our opposite hands to prove we weren't crossing our fingers to negate the deal, she told us her dilemma.

"You already saw me looking through the plants." She gave me a reproachful glance. "So I've had to give that up. You've done a bang-up job of hiding the clues, but they've got to be somewhere. I was wondering how much destruction was allowed?"

"Destruction?" Timms repeated.

"The plants will survive a little digging. Probably it's good for them. But would we be off track if we, say, looked in the statues?" She peered at Timms sideways.

"In the statues?" Timms seemed unable to hold up his end of the conversation.

Zali opened her purse, a large tapestry satchel that carpetbaggers might have carried while ravaging the USA's South after the Civil War. She placed various resin body parts on the desk in no particular order.

"I admit I've already had a go at one, and then I thought I'd better ask, though it's not as if there's much of value left in the old place. And Claudia's so understanding." She leaned in. "I've had my eye on that portrait of Old Inglenook that hangs over the lobby. Might be a paper clue attached to the backside, and I wouldn't mind taking a pair of scissors to him. He looks mean."

Doing his best to be pleasant, Edward said, "I assure you the clues are in the open. In places everyone has access to."

"Like the dining room?" She watched his face when she asked, ready to pounce on any subtle reaction as proof she was on track.

"A definite possibility," he said.

She sprang up from her chair and dropped to her knees in front of the box in the corner. "Or in here?"

Before I reached her, she had already yanked open the cardboard box and pulled out a copy of *Civility Rules*. After frowning at the book as if it were a personal insult, she tipped it, pages down, and shook the living daylights out of it.

"You're supposed to read it." I took away her new toy, got a firm hold of her elbow, and helped her to her feet. She shook everything back into place like a wet dog.

"Back to the plants," Edward said, controlling his voice to keep out his anger over the assault on his latest child. "You said you got the idea by watching someone else." I tried to warn him off with a gesture, but Edward didn't catch it. "Who was that?"

She lifted her chin and strode back to her chair, where she picked up her purse and clutched it to her bosom. The look she gave us said that we had bottomed out in her estimation. "I think I can say I've never been a snitch. That's the kind of vicious thing the Nasties might suggest."

At the mention of the Nasties, I felt my leg muscles twitch and resisted the urge to run from the room, but I must have made a movement because she looked at me when she said, "And everyone can agree I don't have a vicious bone in my body."

"Yes, ma'am," I replied.

Timms proved that he was made of braver stuff. "What about Norbert?"

Zali blew out a breath. "Even I can be pushed past my limits."

She cast one more searching glance over the room and then scuttled away, but Felicity Hartwell replaced her. Judging from the way she brushed past me without a second glance, she wasn't in the mood to flirt.

"I want my drawing."

Timms leaned back in his chair. "Drawing?"

"It's missing, and it was there when you came to my room. No one else has been there. I want it back."

The manila envelope rested on the table a few inches from Timms' hand. He reached for it. "You mean this envelope? The one that was taken from the victim's room as he lay dead on the floor?" He slid the drawing out and studied it. "It's an interesting theme."

"It was a gift, and I want it back."

He pointed at the woman in the window. "I never met Annabelle Inglenook, but I'm guessing this is her with the red hair."

"Since I never met her either, I wouldn't know. It's a romantic picture my fiancé gave me on our arrival here.

141

Maybe he secretly preferred redheads, and it was a hint. You have no right to keep it."

"I think the young woman has a point," Edward said. "It seems cruel to keep this treasured remembrance of her loved one, especially when it probably has no bearing on the case."

Timms opened his mouth to argue, but then he narrowed his eyes at Edward and changed his mind. He slipped the drawing into the envelope, folded down the clasp to seal it, and handed it to Felicity.

"I'll want to see it again if it becomes relevant."

She took the envelope and, with a last glare at me, left the room with head held high and dignity intact.

"One moment, Mrs.—"

Felicity froze.

"Pardon me. *Miss* Hartwell. All that talk about weddings…" Edward gave a fake jolly laugh as he pulled one of his books from the carton and handed it to her. "I'd like to make a gift of this. As you can see, it's autographed by the author." He shrugged. "For all the trouble we've caused you."

"*Civility Rules?*" She looked at him as if she were waiting for the punch line, and when it didn't come, she said, "Um, thank you."

Edward's distraction had ruined her exit.

"I assume you have a good reason for letting her take that drawing back," Timms said.

Edward reached into his shirt pocket and pulled out a folded sheet of paper. "I took the precaution of copying it." He unfolded the paper on the table, and we all rose and leaned over his shoulder while he looked down on his masterpiece with pride.

I resisted the urge to laugh aloud. "I take it the large box is Inglenook, and that single piece of wood falling out of the upper-story window is the woman wearing the necklace." I tapped at the bottom of the page. "That man has six legs."

"He's on horseback," Edward growled.

"And the deformed child next to him?"

Edward snatched his drawing back. "It's the hound. I admit I'm not an artist, but I've captured all the relevant information from the original drawing. If there is a clue in this scene, it's still here. All we have to do is figure it out."

"As long as that's all," I said, and from Timms' low mumble, I could tell he agreed with me.

CHAPTER 17

Edward made me carry his books back to the safety of our room, and then we dressed for dinner. Apparently, the slaughter of a guest alters the tone of a place, because Edward left his tux in the closet and put on a gray pinstripe suit. An hour later, we were seated for dinner, which started out with a near crisis when Edward noticed one of the place settings was missing a steak knife. After the chastised waiter had corrected this disastrous error, we placed our drink orders and settled into an uncomfortable silence.

Timms had reiterated his request that we observe everyone and report back with any unusual reactions or comments, and this time Edward had given a slight nod, which meant he had committed to the program.

Griselda and Amanda were there, as was Markham. Felicity Hartwell was taking her meal in her room. Understandable. Jake, banished to dine with the rest of the suspects, kept glowering at me. To Jake's right, Barbara Maggiano tore at the communal loaf of bread as if she were wringing a chicken's neck. In Lou's place, Henry McShane sat, looking miserable. When his regular table had discovered his nefarious connection with the murder victim, they suggested he might like to park his wheelchair elsewhere.

Edward gave Griselda Waterford an over-enthusiastic smile, his attempt to bring normalcy to the strained atmosphere. "I wonder what's on for tonight."

She glanced down. "I imagine it's on the menu. The one on your plate."

"How stupid of me," he muttered, and he pretended to study the selections, now limited to chicken and vegetable courses. He should stay away from improvisation.

I thought it called for a more direct approach, and I clanked my soupspoon on my water glass until I had their attention.

"One of us is a murderer." If they weren't listening before, they were now. "The cops are doing their best to catch the right person, but we all know they'll settle for anyone they can put the blame on."

Edward closed his eyes and rubbed his forehead. I forged ahead anyway.

"So, what do you suggest?" Jake asked.

"I think we should get our alibis straight. Where was everyone between, say, six and eight this morning?"

"Where were you?" Griselda asked.

"Taking a walk," I said.

"That's convenient," Jake said. "You could have been anywhere, including in Luigi's room murdering him."

Zali wrote every word down on Inglenook stationary.

I grinned at Jake to show there were no hard feelings. "How about you? Were you tucked in your own bed like a good little boy?" I must have hit a nerve because he suddenly seemed more interested in the menu than in keeping up his attack on me.

"I was in my room," Barbara said, sounding bored with

the exercise. "I woke up just after seven. By the time Claudia Inglenook came for me, I was still trying to get hot water for my shower."

"You had that problem, too?" Griselda asked. "Very inconvenient."

Zali piped in with, "I love cold showers."

"Let me guess," Jake said. "It chases away the Nasties."

Her eyebrows shot up in surprise. "Maybe it does." Then she gave us all a large Zali smile. "I just think it wakes up the old body. Starts the morning off right."

Markham offered his religious services. "I suggest we say a prayer for the victim."

"Lou didn't seem like the praying type to me," Jake said.

"Sulking because your cousin isn't going to inherit?" Barbara tore a large bite from her bread and chewed with enthusiasm.

"Not all of us care about money," he said.

"Especially now that you're not getting any." She almost looked happy.

"I understand your father was an artist." Edward used his most charming voice, but the guests fell into silence at the mention of the dead man.

Barbara paused mid-chew. "Daddy?"

"He made a very nice drawing of this place and presented it as a gift to his fiancée."

Griselda sputtered her water onto the tablecloth.

"Did the drawing have special meaning for him?" Edward put the question forward as a polite inquiry, but his body was still and his gaze steady, and I knew he thought the answer mattered. I put my attention on her and waited.

The bereaved daughter tossed her mangled bread onto her plate. "I'm sure you all know by now who my father was." The cowards responded by looking at everything in the room but her. "Obviously, he was obsessed with this place.

He met my mother here. He came back here with his fiancée. And now you tell me he captured it in crayon."

"Not crayon," Edward said. "Colored pencils."

Barbara burst out laughing. "I'm sure dear Felicity was disappointed. An amateur drawing wouldn't be as valuable as, say, diamond earrings."

"Maybe to its creator, it was. Inglenook obviously held a special place in his heart." Markham congratulated himself on his deep insight with another sip of wine.

Edward pressed the point. "Did your father enjoy art as a hobby?"

For the first time, Barbara Maggiano looked uncertain. She blinked a few times, the angry expression left her face. For a minute, I could see the pretty young woman she must have been before cynicism had burrowed that line between her eyebrows and pulled the corners of her mouth into a permanent droop.

"I never saw him draw or paint anything in my life. He didn't sculpt or build birdhouses or assemble model ships in bottles. He was an accountant, for goodness' sake. That's a left-brained job if ever there was one."

"So, this drawing was a one time urge?" Edward persisted.

"Lou said nothing to me about an interest in art," Henry offered.

Barbara studied him as if she were thinking of how best to dispose of a particularly smelly piece of garbage. "And he shared most things with you, things he didn't even tell his own daughter." Her gaze roved over him. "You don't look Italian."

"At my age, you don't look like much." He gave her a warm pat on the hand. "How do you like being Scottish?"

"I'm not going to start eating haggis. I've been Barbara Ferrara my entire single life. It's who I am."

He sighed. "I wish I had had a daughter." Not even she could think of a snippy reply to that.

"So, what do we call you?" I asked him.

"Henry's fine," he said. "I've answered to it for so long I don't even think of myself as Luigi anymore."

"How could you give up your entire identity?" Jake asked. "Walk away from who you were?"

"There wasn't a lot to walk away from when I made my decision. It felt odd at first, but I thought of it as a game. An adventure of sorts."

"Have you considered that you might have been the intended victim?" Griselda took a sip of her water as if she hadn't just dropped a bomb.

The thought had obviously never occurred to him because Henry sat up straight and his lower lip trembled. "Why would anyone want to kill me? I have nothing. I don't know anyone's secrets, except Lou's."

Griselda ran her fingertip around the rim of her glass. "I don't know. But there was Henry McShane running around using *your* name, and now he's dead."

The woman had a point, one I hoped to discuss with Edward, but once he finished dinner, he headed for the front desk where Robert Inglenook was giving instructions to Maggie's replacement—a terrified-looking maid just on twenty.

"If you have questions about your extra duties, Mrs. Beckwith will be happy to help you."

"Mrs. Beckwith?" she squeaked.

"For goodness' sake," Robert said. "She's not going to eat you. Not unless we run out of food before the snow melts," he added. He sent her on her way and gave his attention to Edward.

"I wondered how your sister was doing. She's been through an ordeal."

148

Robert gave him an appraising but not unfriendly look. "I was just about to take Claudia her dinner." He gave a nod to a covered tray on the counter. "I'll tell her you asked after her, Mr. Harlow."

Edward looked at me and then back at Robert. "Edward Harlow, not Nicholas. Make sure she knows that." He started to leave but doubled back and rested his forearm on the counter.

"Why don't you allow me to deliver the tray for you? You'll have to close the front desk if you leave, and you might miss a guest."

"Perish the thought," Robert said. "I suppose you have a point." Then he put on a perfect imitation of Edward's serious expression, a mixture of arrogance with a touch of the humility that allegedly gives birth to good manners. "But —and I say this with the greatest respect—how do I know you're not going to slip into the south wing and murder my sister?"

Edward showed him his palms. "You're right. You don't know me, and it's your duty to protect your sister."

After holding it for a count of ten, Robert burst out laughing and continued to laugh for a full minute. "Gotcha. Claudia can look after herself. And now that I know you're going to visit her, it wouldn't be smart to murder her."

Edward took the offered tray with a slight bow. "I am honored by your logic, if not your trust."

I started after him, but he said, "I don't need any help with this. There are some letters in a folder locked in my desk. I'm sure you don't need the key. Why don't you arrange them in date order?"

I suppose he thought I'd sulk, especially after his pointed comment about me breaking into the desk, and I had a mind to do just that. Instead, I headed for the swinging doors to the kitchen. I cracked them open with the back of my hand

and looked inside at a medium-sized room with white walls, brown tile, and the typical aluminum fixtures you would see in an industrial kitchen. A few remaining wait staff leaned against one side-table covered with plastic containers of perishables resting in large, gray, rectangle containers of ice, now mostly melted. There were bowls of croutons, crackers for the tables, coffee cups on trays, and buckets of extra silverware and folded napkins. I saw another door at the side of the room opposite the dining room, so I entered and crossed over as if I belonged there and told them to keep up the good work.

I found Mrs. Beckwith in the kitchen proper, which must have been part of the original house. She hovered over a large stove set into a stone chimney. Cast iron pots and various utensils hung from hooks fastened into the wall, and in the center of the room sat a gigantic wooden table that could seat twenty. She had the oven door open, and as the aroma of cloves and cinnamon escaped, I had the urge to pull up a chair and beg for cookies and milk.

She looked up on my entrance. "Guests aren't allowed in the kitchen," she said with a slight English accent. Her features wore a harsh expression as much a part of her as the large white apron that seemed permanently attached to her wide middle. Humor and flirting wouldn't get far with her.

"But I'm not just a guest. I'm helping Detective Timms and Sergeant Michelson with the murder investigation."

She grunted an acknowledgement and turned back to the stove. "I've answered all the questions I have time for."

"Dinner's over," I said, trying to sound reasonable. "There's nothing left but the clearing up."

She stood and tucked a potholder into the waistband of her apron. "Except I'm making cookies for the Welcome Room. Some people like a snack before bed. I can't say it's good for them, but anything for the paying guests."

It was clear she didn't think much of Inglenook Manor's new status as a resort.

"Maggie said you were quite the cook. She bragged so much that I didn't believe her until I experienced it for myself." I gave a nod toward the first room. "Of course, you've got assistants now that you're not just cooking for the family."

She let out a sound like t'cha, reached for a timer, and added a few minutes. "Those are warmers in the other room to keep the food hot. I do all the cooking in here. Myself."

Since I can't do much more than make a sandwich, I didn't have to fake my admiration. She must have sensed my sentiments came from the heart because she condescended to stop fidgeting, which consisted mostly of wiping imaginary crumbs from the table, and gave me her full attention.

"It's fortunate you didn't find the body," I said. "You know, after your previous experience with the Inglenook's maid."

"That was a sad, horrible affair." The way she held her hands up to wave the memory away lacked enthusiasm. I had a hunch the episode provided her with her best story. When I expressed sympathy and told her I couldn't imagine what it had been like for her, she pressed the knuckles of one hand into the table for support, stuffed the other hand in her apron pocket, and proceeded to relive the sad, horrible affair again, for my benefit.

"Doreen Gray." She leaned back her head as she remembered her younger years. I could see she still relished telling the tale, probably with additional details each time. Now she had a brand-new audience. I already knew the dead maid's name, and I'd gotten the information from a surprising source. Zali, who was apparently a history buff, had let slip a few details of the old murder while pressing me for clues about the current "game."

"That must have been a shock, to see someone so close to you dead," I prodded.

"Oh, it was." She wiped her hands on her apron and sat down, inviting me with a nod to join her. "There I was with extra guests due at the house that Sunday morning and my only helper sleeping in...or so I thought. I marched up the back stairs to give her a piece of my mind, never knowing the poor thing was dead. I knocked loudly, loud enough to wake the dead, I was that mad, and I finally unlocked the door with my master key and...well, there she was. Mr. Gray couldn't believe the state I was in when he came home from work that night. *Lucille*, he says. *What's got into you?* I was still shaking I was that taken with what I saw."

I went back for one detail that had sent a shiver of excitement down my back. "Mr. Gray. Was that a relation of Doreen's?"

I'd said something wrong, because she was back up, checking on the cookies.

"Mr. Gray was my husband."

"Is Beckwith your maiden name?"

"Heavens, no!"

She made it sound as if I'd suggested she'd been the most notorious tart in the neighborhood.

"Mr. Gray was my first husband. He died of the flu, poor thing. Went straight to his lungs. Beckwith was my second husband. Heart attack." She sounded pleased to have outlived two men.

I thanked her for her time and went off to make my announcement. I found Edward in the hallway with his head bent in conversation with Claudia Inglenook. I raised a hand to hail him as I closed the distance. Claudia excused herself, and Edward watched her walk away with a wistful expression.

"It looks like all is forgiven."

"What do you want?"

"I've made a discovery I think you will want to hear about. It could be we've overlooked a suspect."

That got his attention. I made him buy me a drink and took the booth farthest from the bar before I leaned forward and said, "Mrs. Beckwith."

"What about her?"

"She may have the winning motive. At the time Doreen Gray—that's the maid who died while Luigi and Annabelle were making their getaway—"

"I know."

"You're interrupting."

"Sorry."

"Anyway, at the time she was taking her last breath, Mrs. Beckwith's last name was Gray. I don't know what that made her to Doreen. Aunt? Sister-in-law? All these years, a feeling for revenge has been growing inside her sturdy breast, and then suddenly—"

I stopped talking. An elderly trio, two women and a man, decided the booth next to ours was the only spot in the entire bar that didn't have a draft. As the two old women rocked their way onto the bench seating, the gentleman took their orders. From the way they shouted their preferences several times, the danger we'd be overheard seemed minimal, but I leaned in, just in case.

"Luigi Ferrara shows up and gives her the opportunity she'd waited for all those years. One murder made to order."

"Made to order."

"You like it?"

"A reference to the fact that she is the cook."

"That's the idea."

"Idiot."

I felt my face get hot. "Tell me what's wrong with it."

"Grey," he said. "G-r-e-y. Mrs. Beckwith's last name was

spelled with an *e*. Doreen's was spelled with an *a*. They weren't related."

My confidence faltered, but then I came up with a simple explanation. "Surname spellings get changed all the time. When her husband's ancestors came to this country, Ellis Island got it wrong. And how would you know?"

He let out a pained sigh. "Tell me you didn't share this flash of brilliance with anyone other than me."

I'd brought it to him first because, well, he was my brother, and there was that stupid part of me that wanted his approval. It had been the same since we were kids, but I might as well have wanted to be President of the United States. The odds were about the same. "You're right. I should have brought it to Timms. He wouldn't have been so quick to dismiss the idea."

"Ms. Doreen Gray. Daughter of Luke and Mary Gray, deceased. Older brother James died in a bar fight in 1982. No sisters. Grandparents dead. Aunts dead. Uncles, none."

I cocked my head. "Are you making that up?"

He flipped his hand in a dismissive gesture. "I suggested the possibility to Detective Timms a while ago, and he made a few calls. Rather, his subordinate made them."

"Subordinate. Like me. So, it wasn't such a stupid idea after all, not when it came from the top. How long have you known about her? And why didn't you share that tidbit with me before I—"

"Made an ass of yourself? Maybe that's why Detective Timms preferred to take *me* into his confidence."

I felt his words like a kick in the gut. Once again, little Nicholas had been left behind while Edward played with the big boys. "For someone who wasn't interested in the murder, you've been busy."

"You're the one who was gung-ho on getting me involved. Spelling it out for me that the VPS—" he caught his slip, "the Victorian Preservation Society members wouldn't be allowed in until we solved the murder. Not very subtle."

He leaned forward and lowered his volume to a hiss. "You're treating this like a joke. *Murder made to order.*" It didn't sound funny the way he said it. "I don't have time to follow you around and keep you out of trouble."

"Big Eddie is looking out for little brother. Nuts. Is that what you're doing when you disappear with Claudia Inglenook?"

"My relationship with Miss Inglenook isn't any of your business." He slapped his palm on the tabletop. "Why do you have to be so impulsive? First Felicity Hartwell, then Mrs. Beckwith." He made that scoffing noise that makes me want to hit him. "You're a terrible judge of character. That mess you made with Consolidated Capital is proof of that, but this is more serious than losing a few thousand dollars.

"Is that all it was? I can't imagine why I bothered to get upset about it."

"One of these times you're going to stumble across the real killer and you're going to get hurt."

I kept my voice level, though my insides were burning up. "Don't you mean I'm going to embarrass you?"

He made a face. "That, too."

I shoved my unfinished drink to the center of the table, and the contents sloshed over the edges of the glass. "Forgive me for trying to think. Everybody knows that you're the brilliant one and I'm just a dope who shouldn't be allowed to cross the street by himself."

"Control yourself, Nicholas."

I stood. "Tell you what. I'll just toddle off back to our room and file some papers. Or maybe you need an envelope licked."

My volume had risen, but I didn't care. Several customers

had taken an interest in our conversation, and I glared back at them. "Nothing to look at here. It's only—"

"Don't even think about it."

I stopped cold and turned my head to face him. Edward had cleared his expression, but his eyelids were half-closed, and his tone had dropped to that dangerous silky level. He was looking at me as if I were the enemy. I blinked a few times, shocked to find that at the bottom of it, Edward didn't trust me.

"You actually thought I was going to give away your secret. Well, for once you were wrong. How does it feel?" I swallowed down my anger before it could get loose. "I was *going* to say it's only my brother. Lucky me."

CHAPTER 18

When I got up the next morning, Edward was seated at his writing desk in a posture of deep thought. I dressed in silence and went down to the Sunday breakfast buffet, where I took two eggs, a slice of ham, and an orange juice, but I might as well have been chewing cardboard for all the enjoyment I got out of it.

I wanted to get out of here. I wanted Timms to come walking through the door and announce he had caught the killer and we could all go home, except going home didn't sound so good either. In my head, I ran through the figures in my bank accounts and compared them to the average cost of rent in California for a cave, including utilities and food, and decided I'd have to make the best of my situation.

Edward hadn't been best friends with his former secretary. He probably didn't even know the man's middle name. I'd just remain professional and aloof, friendly without the friendship. Just to show my brother I was the bigger man, I brought an egg sandwich back to the room, which he took with a brief nod. But I wasn't ready to play nice. If he rubbed me the wrong way, I might punch him, so I took myself off to the library.

Not surprising, I had the room to myself. *The Mummy* was playing in the Welcome Room and had captured the attention of most of the guests. I flipped open my notebook and organized my thoughts about the people I considered the prime suspects.

Griselda Waterford ranked high on my list, probably because I wouldn't care one way or another if they arrested her for murder. She could probably pack a wallop with those canes of hers, and she was familiar with Inglenook and didn't want to say why.

Her companion, Amanda Mayfield, was a victim of circumstance. I knew nothing about her, but I suspected that the only thing she wreaked havoc on were unsuspecting balls of yarn.

Felicity and Jake. There was something odd about their relationship. They probably had the best opportunity, with Felicity as the lure, but I couldn't think of a motive. A dead Luigi wasn't worth much to a gold digger, especially as he had left all his money to his daughter, Barbara Maggiano.

Barbara had the motive, and since she saw her father the night before he died, she could easily have arranged the opportunity. I moved her to the top of the list.

The Reverend and Henry McShane tied for the position of dark horse. I couldn't think of anything that would drive a man of the cloth to kill a man, and Henry, if I believed what he said, didn't have problems until after Luigi died.

Claudia and Robert Inglenook rounded out the list. They had the best opportunities, and not just because their alibis stunk. This was their home. They had access to the entire resort, had keys to every door, and probably knew which floorboards creaked. But would they kill a man just for revenge with no payoff? The emeralds were long gone, and it wasn't as if Luigi had molested their aunt. She'd run away with him of her own free will. Heck, they hadn't even been born until after the scandal had taken place.

I thought about putting Mrs. Beckwith on the list, but I didn't want to give Edward the opportunity to mock me. I might not be the only brother who pried into private papers.

I shoved the notebook into my breast pocket in disgust and returned to our room. I heard voices inside and leaned my ear against the door, but that only works with raised voices, so I went inside.

Edward sat on the loveseat next to Markham, and they were drinking tea, or I assumed so from the spread on the coffee table. There was a teapot wrapped in a pink, fuzzy cozy and a little tray of cakes, mostly crumbs by now, and the cups and saucers they held were too dainty for coffee.

"I'm sure you understand," the reverend said. Since he spread his smile to include me, I sat on the end of my bed, facing them. "I had no idea what Henry was up to, so I kept quiet about his identity."

"Even after the man was murdered?" Because Edward was fond of the clergy, he kept his disapproval mild.

"I was going to tell you, only the man calling himself Henry McShane had already gone to the police. I'll admit I was relieved."

"Do you have any idea who would want to kill the real Henry?" Edward asked. "Did he have any enemies?"

"I didn't know the man at all. My relationship was with the Inglenooks. When Annabelle came to me, she was adamant the two of them were going to get married no matter what, and I felt it was my duty to at least make sure the marriage was blessed."

Edward set down his cup and saucer. "You should repeat this to Detective Timms at once."

"That policeman doesn't like me," Markham protested,

but he went with us to the Gold Room all the same. I tagged along because Edward didn't give me a choice.

"I want you where I can see you," were his exact words. I would have told him to go soak his head, but I still needed my paycheck.

Back in the Gold Room, Markham repeated his story and, as he feared, Timms didn't respond with gratitude.

"Don't you know it's an offense to obstruct an investigation?"

Markham crossed his long arms on his lap. "The small piece of information I've offered you could hardly be that important."

"I'm surprised at you. A man of the cloth lying to the police, putting the public at risk."

"You're exaggerating, which is a form of lying. I simply married the couple. The only time I met Henry McShane was at the wedding."

"I ought to put you under arrest. As it is, you better cancel your lunch plans. We're going over every interaction you ever had with the Inglenooks."

"Why pick on me?" Markham demanded. "I only married the couple. Why don't you talk to Griselda Waterford?"

"And why would we do that?" Timms asked.

"Because Griselda Waterford worked at Inglenook. She would have had much better access to any secrets the family had."

The reverend delivered his knockout news with a satisfied smile. He'd gotten in the last word with Detective Timms.

We found Griselda Waterford in the Atrium hunched over a large palm plant. Her ample rear stuck in the air and jiggled under black silk with each movement. Michelson took a step back, and Timms muttered, "Jeez."

"Who's there?" she shouted. To say she spun around

would give her an energy she didn't possess; however, eventually she faced us, though my attention was on the tiny spade in her hand. I hoped Zali didn't get wind of it. She followed my gaze, set the implement on the nearest table, and dusted off her hands.

"Gardening relaxes me."

She seemed to be the only party to benefit from her ministrations. The palm leaned to the left as if trying to peer around Griselda's colossal form and communicate distress signals.

"Have you done a lot of this?" Edward asked, motioning toward the spade.

"All my life."

"I meant since you arrived here."

She pulled a wayward strand of hair out of her eye, leaving a smear of dirt that connected her right eyebrow to her temple. "I might have found an occasional plant that needed tending. The quality of help has declined over the years."

"And you would know that how?" Timms asked.

"I assume the original owners of Inglenook Manor took better care of the place."

"I have a few more questions, Mrs. Waterford." Timms pulled out a chair for her. "It should only take a couple of minutes."

"Very well," she sighed, implying great sacrifice.

Everyone pulled up a chair except me. I remained standing, and when she sent an expectant look my way, I cured her of the notion I had anything to do with Edward and his gang. "I'm not allowed to sit at the grown-ups table."

Timms glanced over his shoulder at me, shook his head, and then he started on Griselda Waterford, slow and friendly. "You knew the Inglenooks forty years ago."

Instead of a frontal attack—letting her know he was

aware of her status as ex-employee—he was going to see if he could trip her up. I guess Timms didn't like being lied to, even if it was by omission.

Griselda admitted that she and the Inglenooks had traveled in the same circles.

He nodded. "That would be around the time a very fancy necklace disappeared."

"It was in all the papers. It wouldn't surprise me if the notoriety attracted some of the guests who showed up this weekend."

"Almost four decades ago. That's a long time. I doubt most people would remember." He leveled his gaze. "Tell me about it."

"Why should I know anything?"

"You and the Inglenooks traveled in the same circles. I imagine you were both plugged into the same gossip network."

"What's there to tell?" she said. "The necklace was here before *he* took off with Annabelle. When the happy couple disappeared, the necklace did, too."

"Do you have any proof that Henry McShane alias Luigi Ferrara stole the necklace?"

Griselda smirked. "Quite a coincidence, isn't it?"

"What did the family members have to say about it? Did they take steps to trace the couple or the necklace?"

Her smile faltered, and when her thick lips recovered their original position, it was more of a grimace. "I wouldn't know. I moved on after Annabelle left. She was my primary connection to the family."

"Did you go to school together?" Timms asked.

"I was educated in a different county."

"How did you meet?"

"A mutual friend introduced us."

"Who?"

"It was so long ago. An acquaintance. Not someone I kept in touch with."

"How long did you know Annabelle Inglenook?"

"Five years? Ten?"

Edward leaned forward. "Annabelle Inglenook was younger than you. By how many years?"

"What difference does age make?" Griselda snapped.

Timms, sensing my brother had a point, deferred. "Answer the question, please."

Griselda waived a hand. "Seven years? It's difficult to remember."

"That's quite an age difference for friendship when one of you is a teenager, as Annabelle must have been when you made her acquaintance," Edward observed. "But it sounds like a splendid arrangement for a sheltered daughter and her companion." He sat back with a satisfied smirk and all but forgot Griselda Waterford, addressing his next comments to Timms. "It's an old term, but many wealthy families still employ nannies, governesses, companions and the like to watch over and guard their precious pearls." He beamed at Griselda Waterford, oblivious to the rage mottling its way across her complexion. "We know you used to work here. I'm betting that before you became a companion, you were a maid. I've heard you demonstrated your skills to Maggie."

"Is that true?" Timms asked.

Griselda puckered her face into a scowl. "Annabelle and I *were* friends. But, yes, I looked after her."

"To keep people like Henry McShane away," Edward said with more logic than sympathy.

Griselda took offense. "I could hardly be with her twenty-four hours a day. And I tried to talk her out of it once I'd heard they had fallen in love." She said love as if it were a disease. "He wasn't good enough for her."

"But she ran off with him anyway," Timms observed. "A maid died that night. A close friend of yours?"

"Doreen was a stupid girl. It was her fault Annabelle became infatuated, with all her stories about true love and happily ever after. But even so," she conceded, "the girl had a right to live."

"And you believe Luigi was responsible for her death?" Edward asked.

"Of course."

"Did he actually administer the sleeping pills to her cocoa?"

Griselda flushed. "He might as well have, even though he denied responsibility."

Timms was quick to notice the key to her comment. "You talked to him, then? After he disappeared?"

"I ran into him in the hallway after dinner the night before he died. He was self-righteous, claiming *he* was the actual victim, forced to sneak away with the woman he loved. Ha! The woman he loved. He comes into her home, *Annabelle's* home, with his current floozy. It's disgusting. Annabelle gave up everything for him—her family, her wealth, her position." Griselda added, ominously, "Her reputation. With Doreen's death, Annabelle's elopement became a tawdry affair. I warned her…"

Timms slapped his palms on his knees. "After all the lying you've done, I don't suppose you would admit it if you followed him up to his room and killed him."

"I should have, but I'm a coward."

"There's something I don't understand," Edward said. "Doreen was the romantic who encouraged the affair, and you were dead set against the union. Why didn't they drug you instead of Doreen? Or both of you? Why Doreen at all? Surely, she wouldn't have given them away."

"Doreen was Annabelle's personal maid. She knew too

much. And the girl couldn't keep a secret if her life depended on it, which, as it turns out, it did."

Timms asked a few more questions, but Griselda's answers became short and noncommittal. He finally gave her leave to continue her assault on the plants, but only after he clarified that her lies had put her on his short list.

"That's one angry woman," he said as we made our way to the lobby.

"Angry enough to kill," Edward agreed.

"Nice work on getting her to admit to having worked for the Inglenooks," Timms said.

Edward puffed up like a peacock and, eager for more compliments, offered another suggestion. "I wonder if she requested a room on the second floor."

"To get close to the victim? Good one, Eddie. I like that idea."

They were falling all over each other. It was disgusting.

"How did an overweight woman dependent on canes sneak up on Luigi Ferrara?" I asked politely.

Timms gave me a pitying glance. "She knew him from before. Let's say she set up the meeting, for old time's sake. I bet those canes pack a pretty good wallop. And maybe she had help with the cleanup. Like Amanda Mayfield."

But Amanda didn't agree when we asked her ten minutes later.

"I do what I'm asked to do," Amanda Mayfield replied, "and no one has never asked me to commit murder or get rid of a corpse."

She sat on the couch in her room and crocheted, working three strands of improbable colors together into what promised to be a pillow.

"How long have you worked for Mrs. Waterford?" Timms asked.

"Two years and five months," was her quick response.

"Keeping track, are you?" Timms chuckled. "Not that I wouldn't do the same thing. She seems a bit of a—"

"You seem young for a companion," Edward interjected. "What I mean is that most girls your age wouldn't consider it a...calling."

Amanda let loose with a shriek. "A career? Hardly!" She took pity on us. "When my mother died, I found out she hadn't kept up on the house payments. Mom was one step ahead of the bank. The foreclosure notice came one month after her funeral. I had no training, and my savings went to the bill collectors. When I saw the ad, I thought why not? It paid well. I get room and board."

"And you liked it well enough to stay?"

"I don't have a choice. Like I said, it pays well. Once I've saved up enough, I'm out of here."

"To do what?" Edward asked.

Amanda rubbed a hand lovingly over her white sweater. I assumed it was one of her creations. Covered in bumps, it looked as if it had succumbed to the mumps.

"Open a yarn shop." She got a dreamy look. "The Nappy Barn." She smiled. "You like the name?"

"Sounds, er, promising."

"Anyway," Amanda continued, "Griselda's all right. She likes to bully people, but if you ignore her, she's harmless."

"We've got a corpse in the freezer who might disagree with you," Timms said.

We congregated in the hallway outside of Amanda's room while Timms decided the next step. Edward had stopped listening and stared over my shoulder. He took a step forward, and I turned to see Claudia Inglenook standing outside our door. Her eyes were wide open—I could see the whites—and she swayed back and forth. She cleared her throat several times and then croaked out, "Maggie."

Edward caught her right before she hit the floor.

CHAPTER 19

"She's dead all right," Dr. Reeves said, lifting his fingers from Maggie's throat and forever closing her beautiful brown eyes. The cause of death was a knife sticking out of the back of her uniform. Someone had stabbed her while she was down on her knees, cleaning the tub.

I stared because I felt I owed it to her not to look away. With my thumb and index finger, I pinched the skin on the inside of my elbow hard and waited for feeling to break through.

"Can I go now?" the doctor asked. "I'd like to spend at least part of my vacation with my wife."

"Is that a steak knife?" Edward asked abruptly, and I groaned.

"Dammit! Don't tell me there's a proper utensil for killing!"

Edward took hold of my arm. "I'm sorry, Nicholas. You've had a shock."

He tried to steer me out of the room, but I put on the brakes and insisted on sticking it out. Reeves confirmed

Edward's guess, and while my brother explained to Timms that one of the place settings at dinner last night had been missing a steak knife, the physician shot me a look of reproach that dared me to suffer a mental breakdown and delay his return to Mrs. Reeves.

"And the incomplete place setting belonged to—?" Timms asked.

"The knife didn't belong to anyone," I snarled. "No one sat there, and it was missing at the beginning of the meal, so any one of the staff or guests could have taken it before we all filed in and took our places."

We heard a low moan coming from the bedroom. Two corpses were too much for one cleric. The Reverend Markham sat on the edge of a floral loveseat, far from the bathroom. After knocking on the door, a maid entered with a tray of whiskey and glasses. Claudia Inglenook took the tray from her and then served the reverend a healthy dose. She held another out to me.

I shook my head. "I'm already numb, but you go ahead. You don't look so good."

"Drink it. You're pale as a ghost. Here. I'll join you." She only poured about a shot in hers, but she drank it like a man, without sipping, and I followed suit.

Timms came into the room and stood over Markham, looking down with an impatient expression.

"You're sure the bathroom door was locked when you got back?"

"Of course I am! I called Ms. Inglenook to open it for me. I thought maybe I hadn't released the lock all the way when I last closed it." He looked to Claudia for confirmation. Her coloring looked better, but she limited her response to a slight nod.

Timms bent down to look Markham in the eye. "Were you present when Maggie arrived to clean your room?"

"No. But I think I saw her in the hallway earlier working on—" he looked to Edward, "Was it your room? I can't be certain."

"I had the Do Not Disturb sign out," Edward said. "She skipped our room."

"Did she keep to a schedule?" Timms directed his question to Claudia Inglenook. "Take the rooms in any special order?"

"She was very punctual. A very hard worker."

"Whatsoever thy hand findeth to do, do it with thy might." The quote seemed to pop out automatically. The minister's heart wasn't in it.

"Right," Timms said, watching Markham with a wary eye.

Claudia blinked back tears and took a deep breath. "When she trained the other maids, Maggie told them to start at the far end of the hallway and work their way back to the supply closet. That way, they could stock up again before finishing the other side of the hallway. I assume she followed her own advice."

"Who are the other guests on this floor?" Timms asked. Markham's room was the last one on our side, farthest from the stairs.

Claudia explained the room assignments, which included Griselda, Amanda, us, Luigi (though that room was empty now,) Felicity, Jake, and various members from the Chicago group.

Edward wandered aimlessly as we talked. This was the Tulip Room, with softly flowered wallpaper and cream-colored furniture. My brother had no sense of timing. If I had liked Claudia Inglenook in *that way*, I would have been at her side offering my shoulder. Instead, he had his arms crossed tight across his chest, and he looked as if he were hugging himself, which if he kept ignoring Claudia Inglenook, he would be doing for a long time to come.

"Who was Maggie closest to at Inglenook?" Timms asked.

"That's easy," Claudia said. "She admired Mrs. Beckwith."

"Then I suggest we continue this discussion in the kitchen."

We followed him out, down the back stairway, and through the double doors to the kitchen.

Mrs. Beckwith clutched a handkerchief in the hand held stiffly at her side, as if daring the tears to come in front of an audience.

"Poor girl." Her voice quavered as she spoke. "Don't know who's going to take over her duties," she said, struggling to stay focused on the practical details instead of the murder. Claudia squeezed her free hand, and the older woman's lower lip trembled.

"Did anything unusual happen with Maggie lately?" Timms asked.

"Everything was right as rain. Always was with Maggie. She did her job like a professional, without whining like most young people today. And she was proud of her work."

"Was it possible she knew Luigi Ferrara before he came to the resort?" Edward asked.

"Anything's possible," Mrs. Beckwith said. "But what would she be doing with the likes of him? He wasn't her type at all. The only contact she had with him was as a guest." She heaved in a ragged breath. "She was in this room having her breakfast only this morning."

"What was her routine the morning of Luigi Ferrara's murder?"

It was clear from the concentrated look on her face that Mrs. Beckwith was trying to be exact. "I had an order to make Mrs. Waterford's breakfast early, and I sent it up the dumbwaiter so Maggie could take care of it."

"Then I saw her in the lobby and told her about Luigi

170

Ferrara's phone call," Claudia added, and I repeated how I'd asked her to get me some towels.

"How much time elapsed between the phone call and your talk with Maggie?" Timms asked Claudia.

"Ten minutes at the most. I couldn't get away because we had a lot of phone calls that morning."

"When she came into the lobby, she said she was running late," I offered, and Claudia confirmed. I had a sudden vision of her trotting along the hallway, her curls bouncing and her brown eyes bright as she tried to tie her apron strings, and I swallowed hard. Twice.

"Well, she's dead," Timms said, "and I have to assume it's because she knew something about the murder."

"Nothing other than the information she passed on to you," Mrs. Beckwith said.

"She didn't have much to say when I talked to her," Timms said.

"The second time. Or the third. When she went to you of her own accord."

"Maggie didn't come to me on her own," Timms said. "Are you telling me she had additional information? What was it?" he demanded.

Mrs. Beckwith opened and closed her mouth several times, trying to force the words out. "She didn't tell me except to say it was something so small it couldn't possibly matter."

"Did she see something? Overhear a conversation?"

"I tell you, she didn't say!" The old woman turned away from us as the tears started to fall. She marched to the oven and jabbed a wooden spoon into a pot that simmered on the burner.

Timms gave a small nod to Michelson, and the latter closed his notebook.

"Thank you, Mrs. Beckwith."

She jerked her head in response, and we left her to mourn.

We parted company with Timms and Michelson in the lobby, and I was talking to Edward with my head turned to look at him, so I didn't see it coming.

The punch caught me in the stomach. Unprepared for it, my knees buckled, and I went down. I swallowed against a wave of nausea, and when I looked up, I saw Jake Battencourt, his upper lip curled in a snarl and his fist pulled back, right before it connected with my jaw.

The blow laid me flat on my back, but the adrenaline kicked in and I rolled to my knees. When I raised my head and saw him standing there, it was as if a red veil fell over my eyes, and all my rage against whoever killed Maggie suddenly had an outlet. I leaned back on my toes for leverage, my entire body tightened like a coil, and right before I let loose, I heard Edward cry, "Nicholas! Don't!"

I sprang forward with all I had and caught Jake around the middle with my head low. The tackle carried us both to the floor. I heard a dull thump as his head connected with carpet, and a woman screamed.

He grabbed my collar and jerked me sideways, but I had one knee on his chest and that spoiled his momentum. With his shirtfront clutched in my left hand, I pulled back a fist and slammed a solid punch across his face, and it felt so good that I did it again.

When I pulled my fist back for the third time, two arms hooked under my armpits and jerked me back and to my feet. I was too far gone to think straight, and I spun around, ready to fight the next enemy, but Edward clamped his hands around both of my shoulders.

"Easy, Nicholas. Take it easy."

He held tight until my eyes started to focus again and my panting slowed to deep breaths.

"You're causing a scene," Edward said in the same tone he'd use to tell me to file his letters, but his jaw muscle pulsed and his nostrils flared. I think the old Edward smelled blood.

About twenty people stood around gawking at us including Lipstick Teeth, who had genuine fear in her eyes. That made me turn my gaze to the floor, which was a dumb thing to do with Jake Battencourt still running loose.

"Watch out!" someone cried.

Edward gave me a hard shove sideways. I stumbled but caught my balance and turned. Jake had a fist in the air, only it was attached at the wrist to my brother's hand. It did not surprise me that he'd been ready to hit me from behind, and probably would have if not for Edward's quick reflexes.

"Hitting a man when his back is turned isn't fair play." Though he spoke in a quiet voice, my brother was furious. He has an iron grip, and while Jake struggled to get free, Edward's free hand clenched into a fist. He was fighting the urge to smack him. When my brother finally released him, Jake reconsidered the odds and stalked off.

I leaned forward, hands on my knees while my guts went back to normal, and Edward clapped me on the back.

"You all right?"

"Just dandy." I looked after Jake's retreating form and coughed. "Pretty sensitive for a cousin."

Edward narrowed his eyes. "Exactly what I was thinking."

CHAPTER 20

"I really liked her," I said, my arm flung over my eyes as I rested on my bed with an icepack on my jaw. There wasn't anything I could do about my sore stomach muscles. Edward was at his desk adding notes to some letters from his file. He completed a sentence and slapped the pen down.

"Not enough to keep you away from Felicity Hartwell."

I ignored his jab and said, "Maggie made me laugh."

"When did you last see her?"

"This morning. We passed in the hall on my way down to breakfast."

"Did she seem like herself?"

I moved my arm and squinted at Edward through one eye. "She was actually in high spirits. Positively glowing." I gave a weak laugh and then decided I wouldn't do that again. "I thought it was my company."

"What did you two talk about, other than the personal lives of the guests?" Edward asked, adding, "I assume you didn't discuss me. Did you get the impression she had ambitions?"

"We might have discussed our work. And she did say she had plans. She wanted to open a bed-and-breakfast someday. Something to provide her with an income. Nothing extravagant, just three or four paying guests. Lace curtains on the windows and a long wooden table in the kitchen where guests could eat home-cooked meals. It sounded nice."

I caught Edward's amused look. "What?"

"You're a better listener than I thought. But that sounds like an expensive dream."

"She was saving up. She knew it would take a few years."

"Maybe she found a faster route. If she knew something that could implicate one of the guests in Luigi's murder, and she offered to keep quiet..."

"You mean blackmail?" I considered. "What a woman."

"A dead woman," Edward corrected. Then he asked me a highly inappropriate question. "Did Miss Hartwell seem focused on anything in particular during your, er, time together?"

"It surprised me when she asked to meet, so I went along with whatever she wanted. Apparently, she wanted me."

"You really think so?" Edward asked. He had an unreadable expression on his face, and he took his time asking the next question. "Did you play up the importance of your job?"

I turned my head to look at him. "I didn't hand her my resume."

Edward waved off my answer. "It was a silly question. Of course, you did. It would only be natural." He rubbed his chin. "Did you talk about your position in life? Perhaps your financial situation? Money."

"She did ask me about myself, but that's only natural. I might have mentioned that I was independent, but I was referring to my relationship status." An uncomfortable sensation tingled at the base of my spine. "What are you getting at?"

He gave a slight shake of his head and moved on to another suspect we hadn't yet considered.

"Henry McShane could have wanted his identity back and Luigi refused."

"It didn't sound as if he cared about the switch," I said. "And his identity problems didn't start until after Luigi's death."

"But what if he were set to inherit from a family member? He couldn't claim the money unless he was Luigi Ferrara. And I'm sure there are other possibilities I haven't considered."

The flaw in Edward's reasoning was obvious. "You're forgetting. Henry McShane doesn't have any family."

"Do you believe everything you're told?" He crossed the room to my bed and lifted the edge of the ice pack. "The swellings not too bad, but you're going to have a hell of a bruise."

"Aunt Civility's official representative shouldn't swear," I mumbled.

"There has to be something we're missing," Edward said. "No one can commit murder in the middle of a resort without somebody witnessing something. I hate to bother them and disrupt their routine, but maybe we should talk to the staff."

I flipped my legs off the bed and stood up, which was a mistake. The room spun and I had to steady myself with one hand on the nightstand. "Then we should talk to whoever's in charge of the plants first. The gardener needs to set up a twenty-four-hour security patrol. I'm getting tired of fixing them up. Of course, if we locked Zali and Griselda in their rooms, that would take care of it."

I walked on stiff legs to the desk and flipped through Edward's handiwork. "Are you ready for me to type these? Because I'm fine. Sore, but fine." My eyes stopped on the third one from the top. It was Virgin Girl. Edward had crossed off his old comments and added new ones. Once I had put his notes, written with an excess of underlines and exclamation points, into full sentences, it would be a zinger.

Dear Virgin Girl,

I can't believe with one in seven teenagers harboring a venereal disease you are willing to risk infection. I'm certain you think that this boy will be your great love, that he has never before laid a hand (or anything else) on another girl, and that having sex will bind him to you emotionally for the rest of your silly life. I have news for you. You may not be a one-night stand, but he will move on. I hope he won't leave you with any reminders, such as a baby or VD. I hope it's worth it.

Sincerely,

Aunt Civility

"You might want to reconsider this one." I held it up, and he barely glanced my way, which meant he knew exactly which letter I meant. "Look. I know you're ticked off because I lost my cool and embarrassed you, but that's no reason to take it out on your fans."

"So, I'm ticked off at you. That's what you think?"

"Sure. I'd be ticked off at me too. I'm sorry."

He narrowed his eyes and stared at me until I got uncomfortable and sat down and faced the computer.

"My answers stand as they are."

The next breakthrough came from Timms. I'd just finished the last letter and saved it to the hard drive so I could print it as soon as we returned home when there was a knock on the door. Don't ask me to explain, but it was an official-sounding knock.

"I thought you might have a vested interest in this one," he said to me. Michelson was already knocking on Felicity Hartwell's door.

I leaned into the bathroom and saw a red spot on my jaw. My scraped-up knuckles looked worse.

"Maybe you should sit this one out," Edward said.

"If you're trying to spare my feelings, I wouldn't give Jake the satisfaction."

When we entered the room, I made eye contact with the angry cousin, but he had his focus on Timms and Michelson and didn't give me a second thought. Too bad because he would have seen my grin. With a puffy, bruised eye and a cut on his cheek, Jake's face looked much worse than mine did.

Michelson took up a position against the wall, while Timms pulled up a chair a sympathetic distance from Felicity Hartwell. Her cousin, seated on the couch next to her, held her hand in both of his.

"I know this is a hard time for you, but I have a few additional questions," Timms said.

Felicity sniffed. "I'll do anything I can to catch Lou's killer."

"That's good to hear...Mrs. Kelsey."

I had my arms folded in a tough-guy stance, but on hearing *Mrs. Kelsey*, they dropped to my side. "Missus?"

Edward gave me a warning glance, and I showed him my palms to let him know I wasn't going to lose it.

Jake's arm went around Mrs. Kelsey's shoulder.

"If this is some kind of joke..." he said.

"Not at all," Timms said with an affable grin. "Mr. Kelsey."

Jake's arm dropped into his lap.

"I like the new hair color." Timms gave a nod in Felicity's direction. "Blond suits you. Both of you. And it's grown out since we last met."

"We've never met," Felicity said, her pointed chin stuck out in defiance.

"Not formally, that's true. However, I saw the picture album when I met your last fiancé, Jonathon Reier. Of course, he wasn't really your fiancé, since you're already married. I don't think you realize how close he came to pressing charges. He told us his story, how you teased him along, and when he was panting, suggested something kinky. Then you showed him the pictures of his backside along with a shakedown for cash. We were ready to move in on you, but then his daughter became engaged to the Fallows boy. The Fallows aren't the sort of family to put up with any scandal, but you were counting on that, weren't you?"

Jake dropped his head into his hands.

"I'm not following you," I said. "Are you saying she wasn't engaged to Luigi Ferrara?"

Timms waved a hand toward the unhappy couple on the couch. "I really have to thank Michelson. I recognized her face, but he's got a great memory for names. Eddie and Nicky, let me introduce you to Mr. and Mrs. Jake Kelsey."

"Huh," I said, giving in to the desire to be nasty. "Black-mailers. And here I got to enjoy her for free."

"Nicholas!"

It took both Timms and Michelson to hold Jake back while Edward dragged me out of the room, but I didn't put up much of a fight because I was too tired to duke it out again.

"Did you know?" I demanded after Edward had slammed their door closed.

"I suspected."

"How?"

"Luigi was half-packed the morning following the argument with his fiancée and her cousin in the hallway, so he was planning to leave, something Miss, er, Mrs. Kelsey didn't mention. Moreover, she overdid it. It seemed as if she were playing a role."

"And you didn't think to let me know? I never would have let a married woman kiss me."

"I would have said something if I had been certain."

I let it go because I took a good look at my brother for the first time in twenty-four hours. He had circles under his eyes, and he looked exhausted, and not just in need of sleep.

"Sorry about that," I said, nodding toward the closed door. "It was uncalled for."

He sighed like a big bear. "Humanity has once again met my low expectations."

As we returned to our room, I wondered if humanity included me.

CHAPTER 21

We were lunching in the Atrium, and it was my turn to worry about Edward. Timms had explained he couldn't arrest a wife for having an affair on her husband. Not only that, but Jake and Felicity would have wanted Luigi alive. They wouldn't admit that Luigi had discovered their duplicity, but it wasn't as if the couple had demanded anything illegal from him, like a blackmail payoff. As far as they were concerned, it was just a wasted effort. Nothing to kill over.

Edward let the cops out of our room and immediately sank into a funk. It was worse than *the abyss* because this mood arose from real and terrible events instead of Edward's imagination, so I couldn't even tell him he was overreacting. I tried to pull him into several arguments, figuring that anger would be preferable to his sad, moping demeanor, but no dice. The most I got out of him was a short speech.

"Human beings are incredible creatures, capable of great things. They are at their best when they live up to their dignity, but they appear to prefer to roll in the muck and cover themselves with slime."

It called for extreme action. I invited Claudia Inglenook to eat with us.

After a half-hearted greeting, he slumped in his chair and picked at his ham sandwich. She wasn't much help. She kept her eyes on her salad and her comments to herself.

"It's not the end of the world," I said. "You didn't really expect the killer to raise his or her hand and admit to murdering Luigi, did you? We just have to try harder."

He didn't answer.

"We've done pretty well for amateurs. You figured out what Markham was hiding."

He peeked under the bread on his sandwich and then let it drop. "I did, but since he's a minister whose church was in the area, and since he made a point of mentioning in front of Mr. Ferrara that he remembered every service performed, it wasn't a stretch to figure out he had married Annabelle Inglenook and Henry McShane and was giving Mr. Ferrara a heads up."

I held my palms up. "See? You're made for this kind of work. You're smart, and clever...and smart. I never would have thought of that angle." It wasn't working. He sat there like a big ape that'd just had his banana supply cut off. "C'mon, Edward. At least we're getting a vacation out of it."

Edward slammed his open palm on the table, and Claudia jumped in her chair. "We are surrounded by degenerates," he cried. "Griselda Waterford turns out to be Annabelle's old companion, and she despised Henry McShane, known to us as Luigi Ferrara. She blamed him for the death of the maid, the very stupid and very dead Doreen, and might have bludgeoned him to death with her canes. Felicity Hartwell and her cousin Jake are none other than Mr. and Mrs. Kelsey, ready to pounce on a lonely old man and steal him blind, which would have raised the ire of Barbara Maggiano, a woman who only cares about money. Maggie lost her young life, most likely in a black-mail attempt. They all have clear motives for killing him, their alibis smell worse than a boy's locker room, and the—"

He stopped mid-sentence, looked at our lunch guest, and leapt to his feet. "I'm so sorry," he murmured in a controlled voice, as if apologizing for not passing the salt. "I'm raving at you like a lunatic."

Her face turned red, and her shoulders started to shake. When a single tear squeezed out of her right eye and she doubled over in apparent distress, Edward growled:

"Damn me and damn this place."

"Edward!" I was on my feet. If there were one thing our mother had never allowed, it was cursing in front of women. For my brother to swear in front of the fairer sex, he had to have lost his senses or his self-control, and both options made me nervous. I stood there with my hands at my sides, not certain whether I should take him back to the room and calm him down or stay here and comfort Claudia Inglenook, but she decided it.

She let loose a shriek and covered her mouth. Claudia wasn't sobbing. The woman was in the throes of a severe fit of laughter.

"Sit back down," she instructed, still tittering. "Both of you. I needed that."

He accepted her offer, though he remained on the edge of his seat, prepared to run out the door if he lost control again.

"Wow. That's a big list of suspects," she said. "But you forgot two. Robert and I could have blamed the man for our current financial situation and killed him for revenge."

"That's true," I said, grateful she brought it up.

"No one could suspect you," Edward said, adding as an afterthought, "Or Robert."

"I wish the police agreed with you." She set down her

fork. "So, Jake and Felicity are married. That explains the argument."

"Which argument?" Edward asked, one eyebrow raised.

Claudia bit her bottom lip. "I guess I better come clean. The night before Luigi died, I, well, I went through the family album." She put her hand on Edward's. "The photographs go back to my grandfather's time. You'd really enjoy looking them over. The clothes, the cars. It's a stitch!"

She was stalling. Even worse, she was using her feminine wiles on my brother, so I said, "And?"

She removed the hand. "We found one of Aunt Annabelle and Henry McShane."

"You've known all along that Luigi was Henry?" My gaze locked with Edward's, but he wasn't giving anything away by his expression.

She toyed with her bangs, unable to risk peeking at either of us. "I was so upset. I went for a walk. I never really thought about the family history and how it had affected my life, but then it all came boiling up. I was furious. I wanted to talk to Luigi, to tell him what I thought of him. I've been telling Robert the past is the past and he should let it go, that things would have turned out the same no matter what. But would they have?"

"Impossible to guess," Edward muttered in a monotone.

"I stopped before I got to the top of the stairs. I could hear voices, and they were arguing. It was Luigi, Felicity, and Jake. I didn't want to listen in, so I left."

"Did Robert see the photographs?" I hoped the answer was no. If I had to pick a favorite to put in cuffs, Robert Inglenook wasn't it.

"I think so." She glanced up at Edward. "Of course he did."

"And that's why you wanted my help," Edward said. He clasped his hands in front of his face with his elbows on the table and sat there thinking. No man wants to hear he's been used, especially by a woman he has feelings for, and Edward liked Claudia Inglenook more than I imagined he could ever like a female. Now they both looked miserable, Edward violating the no-elbows-on-the-table rule and chewing the nail on his thumb, and Claudia slumped down so far her chin was about to connect with the table. Even I knew better than to make a joke.

Edward broke the silence. "Do you really think your brother murdered Luigi Ferrara?"

"Certainly not!"

"Then I suggest we proceed with that assumption."

As if a gigantic burden had been lifted from her back, Claudia readjusted her posture so her shoulders touched the back of her chair. I wasn't sure if the relief came because Edward didn't suspect Robert or because my brother was still talking to her, but I didn't care. The crisis had passed. Edward picked up his sandwich and tore off a hearty bite in an enthusiastic and uncivilized manner.

"I keep going over the morning in my mind, certain there must be something I've missed. I was working behind the counter by six that morning."

"Did anything unusual happen?" he asked.

"There were all those calls about the hot water, but when I checked the boiler, it was working properly. That was odd."

"Why didn't Robert check the boiler?"

"I am capable of many things," she said, the corners of her mouth lifting, but they drooped back down when she added, "but not murder."

For my brother's sake, I assumed she was telling the truth. "When Maggie went to Luigi Ferrara's room, his shower was running. But if he took cold showers, he wouldn't have noticed the lack of hot water."

A low rumble came from the back of Edward's throat. "His shower was running."

185

"That's what Maggie said." I looked at him, waiting.

"A Navy shower is water on, water off, soap up, water on, rinse, water off. At what point would he leave the shower running?"

"You're saying he lied about the Navy showers?" I said. "I don't blame him. People are practically hysterical about water conservation."

"You think Maggie was lying?" Claudia said.

As long as we were sharing confidences with a suspect, I explained that I was with Maggie in the storage room when she heard something in the hallway.

"She looked out into the hallway and then said she should go back to bed and start the day over, which I assume means she saw something out of the ordinary."

"But you saw nothing?" Edward asked.

"No. I just heard a door slam."

"Maybe it was Luigi Ferrara's door. It must have been the murderer leaving the scene of the crime." Claudia shivered. "He or she was probably wearing the maid's uniform, and Maggie thought it was odd that there was another maid on her floor."

"How did you find out about the maid's uniform?" I asked, and Edward shoveled in a large bite of sandwich, knowing I couldn't expect him to talk with his mouth full. It was obvious he had told her. "Don't choke." I held up one hand and crossed my fingers to show him I hoped he *did* choke.

"I should warn you," Claudia said. She picked up her fork and played with a piece of tomato in her salad. "I, um, thought the idea of Mrs. Beckwith being a murderer was so *funny*, and I couldn't see the harm in sharing it with Robert, and, well—I didn't know she was standing there! She might have overheard."

"You told her about Mrs. Beckwith?" Edward wouldn't meet my eye. "I can't believe you told her."

"Edward was so worried about you; it just spilled out." She jabbed at some lettuce. "Kind of like when he told the police about the conversation between Henry McShane and my brother in the library."

Touché.

"He certainly wasn't laughing when he told me. I'm afraid I'm the one who found it funny and only because I've known Mrs. Beckwith for ages. I'm sorry if I've hurt your feelings."

I wasn't sure how to respond. On one hand, Edward had betrayed me, and I could tell from the way he still hadn't looked me in the eye he knew he'd have to pay. However, I didn't want to sound like a whiny baby in front of Claudia Inglenook, so I told her not to worry about it. In fact, I let out a chuckle, Edward and Claudia joined in, but I made sure he saw the laughter didn't make it to my eyes.

CHAPTER 22

A weak Mulligatawny soup with a side of stale bread was the only item on offer for dinner that night. I had a feeling that Mrs. Beckwith was hoarding her food supplies, should she need to stretch them out for several days.

The other guests were unusually silent. One or the other would look up to say something, but as soon as a gaze landed on me, the focus went back to the soup. News had gotten out about my fight with Jake. When I couldn't stand the tension any longer, I went for a guaranteed icebreaker.

"The snow is melting. I should think we could get out of here by tomorrow afternoon if the plow gets to us." We'd all heard rumors about a neighboring farmer and his skills with a truck and attachable plow.

Amanda Mayfield jumped in. Her mood appeared to rise as her employer's dropped.

"I wonder how long it would take for us to starve to death," she said, cheerfully. Her eyes roamed the table. "Better watch it," she said to Griselda. "If we're forced to take up cannibalism, we could dine on you for ages."

Griselda sponged up the last of her soup with her bread. "Then you'd be out of a job."

"Lucky me."

Barbara Maggiano pushed her soup bowl away. "The police seem to be snatching at straws. Have they got *any* idea who's running around killing people?"

They all looked to Edward for answers.

"They have several solid leads," he said.

I was feeling mean. "There's not one person at this table who couldn't have murdered Luigi Ferrara. And let's not forget poor Maggie." I stared at them in what I hoped was an intimidating fashion. "That was a particularly cruel murder, and I'll happily attend the hanging." No one hangs in the States these days, but it added a nice touch.

"I don't think I would have recognized Maggie if I had passed right by her," Barbara said. "The staff all seem faceless to me."

Most of the table agreed, though Markham remarked she was that *pretty little Spanish girl.*

"At least they fixed the hot water problem," Griselda said. "And the drip in my faucet."

"There hasn't been a problem with the hot water since that morning," Edward said, more to himself. "And there are just as many people taking showers."

"Well, two less," I pointed out. Then I shrugged. "Maybe the boiler just suffered a hitch."

"There could be another explanation." But Edward kept it to himself, saying it was only a theory.

I had theories of my own, and I decided two could play at secrets.

"I'm off." I stood. "The guys at the bar…"

I was able to slip out of the room on my own. But I wasn't headed to the bar.

～

Actually, I wound up in the bar, but first I had to make amends.

Mrs. Beckwith and Alfred the doorman were in conversation, and she grabbed her rolling pin the minute I slipped into the kitchen. I held my hands up in surrender and backed against the wall.

"I apologize."

Fortunately, Mrs. Beckwith had that type of fair play that frowns on shooting a man who waves a white flag. She lowered her weapon. Alfred wasn't as eager to accept me at my word, and he gave me an evil look that said he meant business.

"My concern was with finding the killer, and I might have been too enthusiastic."

She asked Alfred to excuse us and tossed the pin onto the table. He reluctantly left the room, telling me, "I've got my eye on you."

"Heck of a thing," she muttered. "Accusing me of murder."

"When I talked to you, Luigi Ferrara was the only victim. It seemed possible."

"And now Maggie is dead. I loved her like a daughter."

I made a move forward to comfort her, but there was still fight in her eyes, so I stayed in my place against the wall.

"I liked her a good deal, too," I said. "She was sweet."

"Ha!" I'd finally made Mrs. Beckwith smile. "There wasn't a sweet bone in her body. That gal was smart and tough as they make 'em. It's a shame the killer didn't take one of the stupid ones instead."

I tried to imagine which of the other maids Mrs. Beckwith would have sacrificed, and confident she wasn't going to attack me, I relaxed and moved about the room. Though huge, the kitchen had a cozy feel that develops over years of hearth fires and cooking and laughter. It was the kind of room where a child would happily remain silent, listen to the grownups, and take in the smells. Once again, a craving for cookies and milk came on strong.

As if reading my mind, she said, "You're only here because of your stomach." She cackled and an image came to mind of an old crone stirring up a pot of bones. "The soup," she added with a knowing smirk. So, the disappointing dinner had been intentional. She might be susceptible to compliments, and I thought about congratulating her on successfully poisoning us all, but instinct told me she'd take offense. I avoided the subject altogether.

"Edward and I are doing everything possible to assist Detective Timms in his investigation."

"I know that," she said, and added with a sigh, "and I'm grateful. If I get my hands on the person who killed Maggie…" She clenched her hands, and her eyes wandered to the rolling pin. When she snatched it up, I backed up against the wall, but the only thing she attacked was a ball of dough.

"Have you found out anything?" she asked as she flipped the dough and sprinkled it with flour.

I adjusted my shoulders as I was leaning against a small door halfway up the wall and the knob poked into my back. "There are several viable suspects," I said, which was true.

"So." She gave the dough an extra whack with her pin, "Am I still in the running?"

The police hadn't eliminated anyone as far as I knew, but I didn't want her coming after me when I was so far from the exit. "A gross error on my part. I can't imagine what came over me."

She cracked a smile. Her second that day. "You are enthusiastic, I'll give you that." When she pointed at a pan of freshly baked tarts on the stovetop and told me to have a taste, I think she was just following a cook's instinct to share her creations, just as I held up my side of tradition by giving in to the male urge to stuff my face.

Preoccupied by the tarts, I didn't hear the dumbwaiter door creak open—for that's what I had been leaning on. When I'd moved, the release of pressure had popped it open. I *did* notice the expression on Mrs. Beckwith's face. Her eyes widened and her mouth opened, and she made tiny mewling sounds while she stared at something over my shoulder.

I looked back and saw an arm drop out of the small compartment. It swung gently, and I followed the motion with my head trying to understand exactly what I was looking at.

I'm not sure which one of us yelled. Felicity Hartwell's lovely features were grotesque, so it might have been me.

CHAPTER 23

Half an hour later, Timms, Michelson, and poor Dr. Reeves finished with the body. I risked a peek and wished I hadn't. Then I wouldn't have seen the bruises marking Felicity's delicate neck. Timms told me later she was clutching hairs in one hand, a sign she had fought for her life.

"Can't I leave you alone for five minutes?" Edward snapped.

"Her face...it was horrible," I said.

Edward grunted. "Strangulation will do that."

"Is that why her tongue was all—"

"Yes." Edward handed me a cup of cooking sherry. "Have a drink of this." Then he grabbed the back of my neck and gave it a squeeze in an uncharacteristically sympathetic move.

Timms and Michelson, after taking pictures, unloaded the body and moved it to the cellar to keep Luigi and Maggie company. Mrs. Beckwith held together admirably, since Felicity wasn't someone she knew personally. She explained how the discovery happened and, though she looked at me with suspicion, she grudgingly admitted I was as shocked by Felicity's appearance as she. It seemed Mrs. Beckwith would not welcome another visit from me.

"Has anyone told Jake?" I asked.

Edward nodded, grim.

"I bet it shook him up."

"If he didn't kill her, I agree. Two people are dead, yet he doesn't raise the alarm when his wife disappears."

In Edward's world, men looked after the ladies. Me, I would have put my money on Felicity as the winner of any confrontation, if not through strength, then with her abundant charms. Looks like I was wrong.

"Listen, Nicholas. Miss—Mrs.—Felicity managed to get herself killed, and it must have been for the same reason the killer took Maggie's life. Blackmail. Or, if I give her the benefit of the doubt, she might have mentioned a detail to the wrong person. You seem to be the connection between Felicity and Maggie. What piece of information did you share with both of them?"

"Nothing. Felicity and I didn't really talk about the murder." But had we? I had been killing time to see what she was up to, and I hadn't paid attention to the conversation details. Maybe I had let something slip.

"Did you, or didn't you?"

"I don't remember. I told the police everything I know. It's not as if I have a secret, like Maggie did. And I haven't tried to blackmail anybody yet."

"You know something that both those women knew, and they're dead."

That was something to think about, and I didn't want to stimulate the brain cells with Edward hovering over my shoulder. Besides, I wanted a real drink. I found Charlie and the gang planted in what was becoming their regular spot. He waved me over, and I bought a round.

"Good to see you," he said with a slap on my back that nearly knocked me off my stool. "The jaw doesn't look so bad, but your coloring is awful."

"Charlie, I'm sad."

"About the girl? She was a looker." There were mutters of approval from the men.

"Why is it always the young ones?" someone called out. They were talking about Maggie. Felicity's passing hadn't made it to the gossip mill yet. If they only knew.

"Why not the old gasbag with the bell?" Charlie asked. After the groans died out, he added, "The only time I slept in was the morning of the murder, and that's because I was sleeping off a great time." He grinned. "I've been trying for a repeat performance ever since."

Four ales later, Amanda Mayfield took the stool next to mine and asked me to buy her a drink. I raised my hand and let her give her own order to the bartender, and while we waited, I reconsidered her purple hair and thought maybe it gave her a trendy look. And it wasn't as if it were permanent.

"You've been through the ringer." She gently touched my cheek, and I took it without wincing. "It's kind of sexy."

I removed her hand from my face and set it on the bar. "If you like your men roughed up, then I'm not the guy for you."

Her laugh was throaty, as if she weren't afraid to let it out. "You're a card."

"A shallow smart card."

She crossed her legs, and I noticed the gentle swell of her calf where it met her plain black skirt that, thank the heavens, was *not* crocheted. "I wanted to know if you're for hire. I don't know you well enough to ask you for a favor."

"I already have a job, thank you."

"I just need you for a few hours this evening."

I raised one brow. "I think I'm offended."

She laughed again and this time I joined her.

"You've been helping the police, so you'll know what I mean when I say they have to follow certain rules. Following the rules won't get us out of here any time soon."

She had my interest. "What rules were you thinking about breaking?" I noticed Charlie had been unusually silent, so I paid for the drinks, took her arm, and escorted her out the door for privacy.

"Why don't you tell me about it while I walk you back to your room?"

The color combinations she used with her yarn should have tipped me off to Amanda's vivid imagination. She had come up with a plan to call the chief suspects, disguise her voice, and tell them she'd seen them entering the Reverend Markham's room. She chose him because Luigi's murder had been talked out, but the alibis for Maggie's death weren't a known factor. She felt that gave her leeway.

I tried not to look at Maggie's nook when we passed it, and just before we reached Amanda's room, I thought I had better raise my objections. "What if the person you call says they had an appointment for a blessing?"

"I figured that in. I told them I would be happy to confirm their appointment with Mr. Markham."

I took her elbow and turned her to face me. "Told them is past tense, as in something that has already happened."

Amanda's brain cells had considered her idea and taken a vote. It was unanimous in favor of the plan. She had already made the calls.

I put my fists on my hips and frowned down at her. "What did you need me for?"

"I told them to meet me in the Atrium tonight at ten o'clock. It would be better to have a good fighter there in case the killer is someone large and things turn ugly. I've seen Jake's face."

"Okay. You've done something really stupid. Maggie and

Felicity baited the killer, and things didn't turn out so well for them. Of course, you may not be in danger if you were lucky and didn't get the right person on the phone. If that's the case, you'll just look stupid. I'll give you some advice and it won't cost you a nickel. Tell your plan to Timms—"

Amanda looked over my shoulder and gasped, and I turned my head and wished I hadn't.

"You'd better leave," I instructed. Amanda agreed and fled into her room.

Edward is larger than I am. He also outweighs me and it's all muscle, which I forget when he's playing Mister Manners. There wasn't anything civil looking about the Edward charging toward me. In fact, he looked dangerously angry, but I decided not to take the coward's way out.

"I was just coming to see you," I said.

That was all I got out before Edward grabbed my arm and wrenched it behind my back. "We're going to have a little chat."

"I can talk just fine without you—Ow!"

When he moved me toward our room, I had no choice but to double-time it to keep up with him. He only paused to offer a polite nod to Zali.

"Did you catch him cheating?" she called after us.

Our door stood open. He shoved me through and slammed it closed. I caught my footing before I reached the loveseat where Claudia Inglenook sat with her hands clasped and her elbows on her knees. She jumped to her feet on my entrance.

"What's going on?" I said.

Edward grabbed my collar and shook me so hard my teeth rattled, which my sore jaw wasn't in favor of. "What have you done, Nicholas?"

I got my hands between us and shoved, but it was like pushing a brick wall. I didn't know what he was talking

197

about, but a brother should know better than to ask a question only Mom has a right to ask. "Since I don't need your permission," I said, straining the words out as I pushed harder, "it's none of your business."

Using my feet for leverage and leaning into him with my shoulder, I pressed Edward back two steps. He made a quick move sideways, and when my momentum took me past, he shoved me into the wall. I got my head sideways in time to spare my nose.

"Who else have you called?" he demanded.

In my confusion, I relaxed my muscles. "Called?"

He shoved me again, so I slipped my left leg in between his feet and brought it forward around his right ankle, hard and fast. His foot went out from under him and he fell back on his rear, which gave me time to face him before he made it to his feet. He lowered his head and looked about to charge when I caught sight of Claudia Inglenook at the edge of my vision. I don't imagine she and Robert got into many physical fights when they were growing up, and the sight of my brother and I going at it had her clasping her hands together and biting her lower lip.

"Where are your manners, Edward?" I said between clenched teeth, jerking my head in her direction. "There's a lady present."

That had an effect. He straightened up and tried to look dignified, though the muscle near his right eye twitched. "A lady you harassed. How many others did you call? Did anyone take you up on your offer?"

"What offer?" The word call and offer suddenly connected with my conversation with Amanda. "Did you get a phone call that said someone saw you go into Markham's room?"

Edward snorted. "As if you didn't know."

"Was it my voice you heard on the phone?" I demanded of Claudia Inglenook.

"It sounded more like Amanda Mayfield."

Edward twisted my shoulder so I faced him and then shook his finger in my face. "How irresponsible can you be? You've put yourself *and* that silly girl in danger. You baited the killer. You made him think you saw something. Maggie and Felicity had a similar idea. Look at what happened to them."

I was tired of being knocked around. I stepped close enough to my brother that I could feel his furious breath on my face. Our chests were about two inches apart, and we both had our heads thrown back so that we were nose-to-eye. I kept my voice much steadier than I felt and said with precise annunciation, "I wasn't involved."

Edward's eyelids flickered with a glimmer of doubt. "You weren't?"

"Why would you think I'd have anything to do with such a hare-brained scheme?"

"I saw the two of you talking in the hallway."

"That's it? You see me talking to someone and suddenly I'm guilty?" I rubbed my elbow and rolled my shoulder a couple of times. "You don't even ask me about it?"

"He has a point, Edward," Claudia said.

"Thanks, but I don't need any help from you." I turned my back on her and directed my wrath at Edward. "This weekend has been an eye-opener. I knew you were a fake. You think you're Mr. Manners, but I could train a monkey to do what you do because that's all it really is. You going through the motions. Really, you're just a snob. All those fancy airs and graces were a put-on for your job, but I think you've played the part for so long that you actually forgot who you are. Let me remind you. Edward Mortimer Harlow."

"Mortimer?" Claudia said in surprise.

"Son of Alice and Jonathan Harlow. Born on the South Side of Chicago. Parents divorced. Moved to San Diego at age twelve. Oh, yeah. And my brother."

I rubbed the back of my neck. "Not only do I find you don't trust your own brother, but you think I'm a moron." I threw my hands in the air and backed away. "I've had enough."

I turned and headed for the door.

"Nicholas, wait," Claudia said.

I yanked the door open and paused for a last look. Edward's arms were crossed and his jaw set. She twisted her fingers together, and I'll admit she looked upset.

"Edward, say something. This isn't right."

He unclenched his jaw. "I never said you were a moron. Let's discuss this like two reasonable men."

"Discuss it with yourself. I quit."

And just to show him I meant it, I closed the door as gently as my mood would allow.

CHAPTER 24

The Atrium didn't provide much cover. A room lined with windows, a bright moon reflecting off the snow...we might as well have turned on the lights. What can I say? Edward said black, so I said white, and here I was.

Amanda sat on the floor and leaned back against the wall behind the plants. I preferred to keep my legs ready to move if anyone showed up, so I waited across the room by the entrance. Whoever walked in wouldn't see me until they were well inside.

"I think I mentioned this was a stupid idea," I said.

"Three times."

"Let's make it an even number. This was a stupid idea."

"I just thought we might get the killer to make a move so we could get this nightmare over with. I can't believe nobody saw anything."

"Maybe they did, but they never made the connection."

"Didn't Maggie tell you anything? It seemed you two were close."

I had liked Maggie, but I hadn't thought it had been obvious. "Okay. You were in the hallway making your breakfast delivery to Griselda. You're sure *you* didn't see anything that morning?"

"Not a thing."

I had an idea that walking her through the morning, as I did with Maggie, might jog her memory. "Maggie looked out of her nook and saw something that flustered her, and it was important enough to get her killed. It would have been around the same time you brought the tray in to your boss."

Her brows went up. "You sound as if you were there."

I nodded. "When I got upstairs, she had already knocked on Luigi's door in vain and delivered the breakfast tray to Griselda's door. I went back to her nook with her for some extra towels. I wasn't paying close attention, you understand, but I know that a door slammed, and Maggie leaned out and looked. She acted a little odd when she returned. It must have had something to do with whoever was in the hallway."

I went through the scenario again under my breath. "She knocked on Luigi's door. Heard the shower but got no reply. Dropped off the tray. Knocked on Griselda's door. Received some sort of reply. Went down the hall. Returned to the nook with me. Then ten minutes later heard the door slam. And you say you didn't see *anything*?"

She apologized and said she hadn't. "But I must have just missed the killer." She scrambled to her feet. "It could have been me instead of Maggie that got killed." From then on, she sat on the floor next to me.

By half-past eleven, I covered a yawn. "No one's coming." I reached down and helped her to her feet. "You were lucky."

"I suppose so," she said. "I guess I didn't think it through. I'm actually glad no one took me up on my offer."

She folded her hands in front of her and kept her gaze down. I felt sorry for her.

"If you come up with another bright idea, come to me for a second opinion *before* you act on it."

She grinned. "Promise."

My hands were in my trouser pockets, and I crooked my elbow out. "Walk you to your room?"

She slipped her hand through and rested it lightly on my arm. "Deal."

When we got to the second floor, I slowed down. I had a new problem. I wasn't about to crawl back into a room paid for by Edward just so I could have a comfortable snooze. Amanda must have sensed my reluctance because she invited me in for a drink.

"Won't your employer disapprove?"

Amanda barked out a laugh. "She's off in slumberland by now. Nothing could wake her."

She unlocked the door, and I stepped inside. Her room had a loveseat against the wall, just as we did, but a framed mirror lined the length of the wall above it. I leaned in and looked at my face. The jaw wasn't too bad, or maybe I had gotten used to it.

Amanda sat down, folded her legs under her and patted a cushion. I took her up on the offer.

"It's kind of creepy knowing a man died just down the hall from here. Makes me nervous."

I hadn't pegged her for the sensitive type, but maybe Edward was right and my instincts about people stunk. "I'd like to say don't worry about it, but I won't."

"You knew Maggie well?" She looked up at me through her lashes.

"She was a nice girl."

It then occurred to me that every woman I'd gotten close to at Inglenook had met a terrible end. "I should let you get to sleep." I made a move to leave and had already turned the knob on the door when she stopped me.

"Wait a minute. What about that drink?" She took my hand and walked me back to the loveseat. "Come on. I hate to drink alone."

"That's a sound rule."

She left me on the loveseat and went to a cabinet across from her bed. From the bottom shelf, she pulled out a bottle and held it up. "Bourbon is all I have. I keep it on hand for Grizzy."

I told her that was fine by me, and she took the bottle into the bathroom where the water glasses were. There was only one double bed in the room, so I squashed the idea of spending the night in Amanda's room. Then again, that wasn't an option from the start. Even if she invited me to sleep on the loveseat—or the floor if I wanted to stretch out —it's not in me to play with a woman's reputation.

She came back into the room, handed me my drink, and reclaimed her place next to me. I took a gulp and made a face. Bourbon's not a favorite of mine, so I threw it back, just to get it down.

I yawned and winced at the effect that had on my jaw. "Pardon me. It's been a long day."

She reached up to touch my face but pulled her hand back. "Did you get into trouble with your brother over my phone calls?"

I told her to forget it. "I'm always in trouble with Edward." I wound up giving her an outline of the conversation I'd had with him minus the acrobatics but including my desire to leave his employment.

"He's the most arrogant ass I've ever met. I bet you anything that right now he still believes that he's one hundred percent in the right. But here's the thing. I'm not apologizing. I don't care if I have to eat grass and sleep on a park bench; I'm through being his errand boy."

The more I talked about it, the more I wondered how I

had put up with him for so long. "Have you got room for an assistant at the Nappy Barn?" I asked, joking.

"Someday soon, I hope."

I blinked a few times and felt the exhaustion from the day wash over me so strongly it felt as if I couldn't have made it to Edward's room if I tried. Then I realized it wasn't just a feeling. The glass slipped from my hand, but Amanda caught it in time, almost as if she had been waiting for it.

"Srry." My tongue wasn't working and I slurred the word. I tried to stand up but slid off the couch. My legs were like noodles and they folded under me, and when I pushed off the couch with my arm, I couldn't get my muscles to cooperate. This was more than exhaustion. As my head hit the floor, it finally dawned on me what I'd missed the morning of the murder. What I hadn't heard. *You damn fool!*

The last thing I saw before I blacked out was Amanda Mayfield looking down on me, her cute features marred by a grim frown.

CHAPTER 25

The room came slowly into focus. Though it was dark, light shone through the connecting door between the rooms, and I could make out a table and chairs and the faint outline of red velvet roses on the wall. Snores loud enough to wake the dead came from somewhere far away. I was in Griselda Waterford's suite.

I widened my eyes to keep them open, but I didn't like it. The room jerked up and down. I blinked a few times, and it settled into place as I struggled to remember what I'd been talking about before my body had taken an unscheduled nap.

A vague memory came. I had fought with Edward. I might have quit my job. After that, things were a blank, but I knew in my gut that remaining on this floor wouldn't be good for my health. In my mind, I sat up like a shot, but my arms and legs and especially my head wouldn't cooperate.

I rolled over with effort and pulled myself along the rug until I felt a smooth surface and knew I'd come to the wall. Struggling to a sitting position took all the energy I had, so I leaned back with my legs stretched out in front of me while I worked myself up for my next move.

A shadow exited Griselda's bedroom and came to a stop where I'd been lying a few minutes ago. The light from the connecting door illuminated Amanda Mayfield's expression, and I readjusted my assessment. I saw nothing attractive about her, especially since she clutched one of Griselda Waterford's canes in her hand.

"There you are." She came closer. "It'll be harder with you awake. Sorry." Then she clutched the cane in both hands and raised her arms over her head.

What a stupid way to die, and apparently, I wasn't going to get a peaceful out. Even now, I heard Edward's voice shouting at me.

"Nicholas!"

Just as the cane came crashing down, a large mass moved in front of me. I heard a sobering thud but didn't feel anything, and then someone let loose a string of oaths that made my ears burn. Edward stepped over my legs, wrenched the cane out of Amanda's hand, and broke it in half over his knee.

"I heard someone moving in Mrs. Waterford's room," she said. "Nicholas, is that you?" She made a show of squinting and peering, followed by a gasp. "I'm so sorry. If I had known..." Then she looked over her shoulder toward the bedroom where Griselda Waterford slumbered. "We'd better go back to my room. Don't want to wake old Grizzy."

I clutched at Edward's pant leg. "How—"

"Amanda's front door was open," Edward said. I must not have closed it when she led me back into the room. "Fortunately," Edward continued, "so was the connecting door. The one that's always kept locked." He glared at Amanda. "Perhaps you needed to move something large but didn't want to drag it through the hallway?"

Amanda put a finger to her lips and glanced back at the bedroom.

I couldn't get my thoughts straight, but an image kept forcing its way to the front of the line. "The bell," I said, trying to make Edward understand. He half-dragged-half-carried me into Amanda's room where he dumped me onto the couch. He leaned over and peered into each eye, and then he gave each cheek an unnecessarily hard smack. I thought I heard him mutter *idiot* under his breath.

"He must have hit his head on something," Amanda offered. Good of her.

"I'm sorry he's caused you so much trouble," Edward said, still bending over me. I could see over his shoulder, and I watched, unable to move, as Amanda picked up a crystal vase and raised it high. I must have gurgled something because Edward raised his eyes to the mirror over the loveseat. My eyes popped open as she swung down hard.

Edward's hand shot out and caught her by the wrist, and then he turned toward her and twisted her arm until she dropped the vase on the ground where it bounced off the carpet.

"I think you've caused enough damage, young lady."

She threw back her head and screamed rape. Boy, did she have a set of lungs on her. To be fair, Edward gave her a choice. He ordered her to shut up, and when she took in a breath to scream again, Edward pulled a fist and popped her one, right in the eye. For Edward, it was a light tap, but she crumpled, and he hoisted her over his shoulder. Then he searched the room and, finding what he was after, he gave me an arm to help me stand.

"Can you walk?" he asked. I didn't trust myself to speak, so I bobbed my head and, using his shirt to pull myself up, got to standing.

He handed me a rolled-up paper to hold, and with one arm around my back to hold me up as I stumbled along, and

Amanda Mayfield over his shoulder, he carried us out the door. And that's exactly how he walked into the Gold Room, looking like a successful big-game hunter.

CHAPTER 26

When we made our grand entrance, Claudia Inglenook was tugging on Timms' arm with both hands while he sat behind his desk and tried to reason with her.

"You have to believe me. They could be in danger." Then she dug her heels in, leaned back, and pulled so hard that she jerked him out of his chair. "Get off your lazy butt!"

"Now, now," he soothed. "Tell me one more time who—" And that's when he saw us.

Sergeant Michelson's eyes almost popped out of his head, and his mouth hung open. It was worth everything I'd been through just to see a qualified expression force its way onto his face. Edward dumped Amanda Mayfield on the table like a sack of laundry.

"Book her!" he said.

"What's going on?" Robert Inglenook called through the open door. "Claudia? I've been looking for you. I want to take my dinner break."

"There's your murderer," Edward said, pointing his finger of shame at Amanda.

"What's the matter with Nicky?" Timms asked.

"Bad judgment," Edward snapped, though I could tell by the lowered volume that he wasn't that angry. My protest came out as a groan, and he deposited me in a chair.

"What in the hell is going on?" Timms said, throwing on his suit jacket as if that might suddenly give him control of the situation.

"That woman just tried to murder my brother, and for once it's not his fault," Edward said. "I caught her just as she was about to beat his head in." He rubbed his shoulder.

"With what?" Timms asked.

"There's nobody at the front desk!" Griselda Waterford waddled into the room in a humongous green bathrobe. "I want to file a complaint," she said. She looked back and forth at Claudia and Timms, not sure who to complain to first. She started with Claudia. "An awful racket awakened me. Aren't there rules about the noise level at night?" Then she heaved her bulk at Timms and held up a shattered piece of wood. "And someone has destroyed one of my canes. Malicious mischief."

Edward calmed her down and offered her a chair along with clucks of sympathy. "I have a question for you."

"For me?"

While he talked, I dropped my head into my hands, rubbed my eyes with my fingertips, and then sat up and blinked hard a few times. The ceiling lights were bright enough to make me wish I were back on Griselda's floor, minus Amanda and her staff of death.

"When Annabelle Inglenook married Henry McShane—the real one—did her father know about it?

"Let's keep calling him Luigi," Timms said. "It's less confusing."

Griselda snorted. "The couple returned to the house after the ceremony and informed us. I think Annabelle had the ridiculous notion her father would have to accept Luigi once the marriage was a reality. When they arrived, I told them about Doreen. Annabelle had packed for her honeymoon, and that's all she took with her when they left in a hurry."

"What about the rest of her things?"

"Her father had them packed and sent to her."

"What about the emeralds?"

I wished I had a pin so I could drop it to see if the axiom was true.

"Annabelle felt they belonged to her, since the family usually passed them down to the eldest daughter upon her marriage. I knew her father wouldn't see it that way, so I took the precaution of hiding them. Everyone assumed she had taken them with her."

"She never made a claim on them?"

"She wrote to me with her address so I could forward them."

"I assume with Annabelle gone you lost your job. That must have made you bitter."

"It's amazing how people rarely consider how their actions will affect others. I decided it was only fair that she should have to work for her prize."

"So, instead of sending the jewels, you sent the newlyweds a puzzle in the form of a drawing."

The air crackled with anticipation while Griselda decided whether to answer. She broke the mood with a toothy smile.

"I always was good at art," she said. "That's the one Girl Guide badge I earned myself."

Amanda groaned, and Griselda leaned forward and squinted. "What's the matter with her?"

"You knew the real Henry McShane would be here this weekend," Edward continued. "He wouldn't be able to resist the grand opening. It would be his first opportunity to come back to Inglenook and figure out the puzzle. Did you come here to stop him?"

"I came here to gloat. He never would have figured it out."

"I imagine, as angry as you were about the situation, that you couldn't help talking about the Inglenooks in front of your companion."

"I didn't give her details," Griselda said. "Nothing she could figure out."

Amanda Mayfield's eyes opened. "You think you're so clever. All that yakking and you finally said something worth listening to."

"And you, young woman, saw your chance to make the Nappy Barn a reality," Edward said. "So, you planned to steal the drawing and find the Inglenook emeralds."

She tried to sit up, put a hand to her cheek, and decided she preferred to remain prone. "That man hit me!"

Claudia gasped. "Edward?"

My brother flushed. "I promise you it was necessary."

"You can press charges as soon as we're done here," Timms said with little sympathy.

Edward clasped his hands behind his back. "This is conjecture, but I believe I can tell you what happened this weekend. It all started with the blue towels."

"The blue towels?" Timms looked to his sergeant for explanation. Michelson flipped through the pages all the way back to the beginning of his notebook and then shook his head.

"Miss Mayfield wasn't at the table that first night when Luigi Ferrara explained that he used the same towel all week. She had to use *his* towels to clean up the blood—a head wound bleeds a lot—so to replace them, she went to Maggie's cart and pulled out fresh towels to add to the rack. That's what Miss Zali meant when she said she saw a strange maid fooling around with the cart.

"When we went into Luigi's bathroom, Maggie noticed there were blue towels on the rack." He gave Amanda's shoulder a poke. "Why take mine? Did you plan to frame Nicholas or me? Why not take the white ones?"

Amanda lifted her head. "What do you mean, *your towels?*"

"My theme is Blue Bell. Luigi's is Birds of Paradise."

Amanda gaped. "The rooms have themes?"

"That you were looking for replacement towels before Maggie went upstairs meant Luigi Ferrara was already dead by then. However, I believe he was dead as early as six o'clock. Nicholas heard water running about that time."

"That could have come from any guest room." Timms shot an apologetic look in Claudia's direction. "This place is pretty old, including the pipes. I've heard the racket they make in the morning."

Claudia pressed her lips into a thin line. "Modern plumbing wasn't in the budget."

"You went into Luigi Ferrara's room that early in the morning because you thought he was in his fiancée's room. I assume you heard him go in there the night before, but that was actually her alleged cousin, Jake."

"That's just sick," Amanda said. "Wait. You said alleged."

"They're married," I mumbled. "You need to get around more."

She drew in a breath.

"You borrowed a maid's uniform," Edward continued. "If you were seen, no one would question a maid entering a guest's room. But he was there, and since he was fully dressed, I assume he was awake."

She turned her head sideways and looked at me with no sign that she had just tried to kill me. "Who gets up that early on vacation?"

I gave a feeble shrug in response. Not me.

"Are you claiming self-defense?" Timms asked.

She didn't answer. Her attorney would thank her.

"Assuming he caught you, the two of you struggled, you hit him with something that had a flat edge, and when it was over, he was dead."

"We didn't find the weapon in the room," Timms said.

"Since she wore a maid's uniform, she probably went in there with a tray. A good crack on the head with the edge of a wooden tray would probably match the wound left behind."

"I'll check the cellar," Michelson said. "She probably stashed it along with the towels."

Edward stepped up to the table and looked down on Amanda. "So, it's early morning, you have a dead body on your hands, and you have no idea if Felicity Hartwell will stop by. You had the bright idea to make it look like an accident, but it would take time to get the scene arranged. The sound of the shower running was to keep people out and to make them think Luigi Ferrara was still alive."

"When Maggie knocked on the door just after seven, the water was still running," I said, feeling good that I had made it through a complex sentence.

"You ran the hot water for over an hour?" Claudia cried. "No wonder there were complaints." She seemed relieved to cross the expense of a new boiler off her list.

"When Maggie knocked on the door, that must have given you a scare," Timms said.

Amanda just lay there like a slug.

"I don't think so," Edward said. "I think she wanted to establish that Luigi Ferrara was still alive to give herself an alibi."

"So she made the phone call to the front desk!" Claudia blew her bangs out of her eyes.

"The bell," I said. "Maggie didn't hear it."

All eyes were on Griselda. "I don't remember if I rang it or not. I had things on my mind."

"You were up early, rooting among the plants," Edward said. "Maggie thought you were going through your morning ablutions, but you were washing up after another round of digging. She knocked. You acknowledged, and then you went back to cleaning up."

"Amanda must have seen the tray in the hallway and thought she missed the bell," I said. "And Maggie noticed the tray had been picked up even though she hadn't heard the bell."

"Did Maggie try to blackmail you?" Edward asked.

Amanda pressed her lips together and folded her arms over her chest. I wished she would sit up. She looked stupid just lying there, and it was making me sleepy.

"And I assume the information that Nicholas shared with Felicity Hartwell gave her enough of a hint that she figured it out. Blackmailing was her specialty, and since she wouldn't back off, you killed her, too."

Claudia raised her hand. "Back up. Why has Mrs. Waterford been digging through my plants?"

"She was looking for the jewels," Edward answered. He unrolled the paper he had taken from Amanda's room. It was Luigi's drawing.

"I don't get it," Claudia said, leaning in for a closer look. "The man on horseback is looking at the woman in the window."

Edward jabbed at the drawing. "Look at the dog. What do hunters do? They point."

The dog was pointing away, tail stiff, left paw lifted.

"He's pointing at...the plant by the entrance."

Claudia gasped and laughed. "I moved that old thing years ago. It wasn't doing so well, so I dumped the soil and gave it a new home by the office."

Griselda teetered sideways in her chair. "You dumped the soil?"

"I would have seen if there had been anything in it." Claudia looked a little green. Pea-green, not emerald-green. "At least I think so."

We all marched down to the office, Michelson gripping Amanda's arm and Edward's arm around my back to help me along. When we got there, we stared at the large shrub in a plain pot positioned in the front desk office. Edward propped me up against the wall and tugged on the plant.

"Gently," Claudia instructed as Edward shook it loose and lifted it from the container. Robert dug through the soil.

"Nothing."

Edward turned the plant over. Tangled in its roots was a canvas package. It was Griselda's turn to moan. He gently loosened it and took it to the desk where he unrolled it.

The Inglenook emeralds—a little crusty with dirt and water spots, but otherwise unharmed.

Griselda Waterford summed it up nicely. "Unbelievable."

CHAPTER 27

The rest of the evening was a blur, but when I woke the next morning, I was back in our room. I'd had the strangest dream about Mother tucking me in. My blanket was snugly fitted around me up to the neck, and I hoped that Claudia Inglenook was responsible. If Edward had tucked me in, I'd never live it down. I sat up too quickly. My head felt as if elephants had trampled it. It wasn't as if I hadn't felt this way before. I'd just had more fun getting there.

I took advantage of Edward's absence and had a long bath —with hot water. I skipped shaving because my jaw hurt where the dark purple bruise had made an appearance. Then I dressed and shoved my clothes into my suitcase.

I was checking the room to make sure I hadn't missed anything like a pair of boxers or my comb when I noticed that Edward's computer was up. I took a closer look. He had altered his final response to Virgin Girl.

Dear Virgin Girl, (still, I hope)

I know at your age you think you've found The One, *but you haven't had a chance to experience life, meet different people, and discover who you are and what you want.*

Your question revolves around sex because that is what you think love is. You must ask yourself the following questions: If sex were impossible from this day forward, would you still want to be with your boyfriend? If romantic nights meant sharing a meal for two and watching a movie, would that be enough? Could you find something to talk about day after day? Find something to laugh about? If he lost his job and couldn't afford presents, would you still hang around?

These are questions you should ask yourself, and you should ask your boyfriend to answer them as well. If you can't both say yes, then do yourself a favor and save that precious part of you for the man who would gladly talk to you about nothing for the rest of his life.

Sincerely,

Aunt Civility

There wasn't a chance in heck his letter would do anything but offer the couple something to giggle over in their post-coital glow. Not that Edward wasn't right. It's just that in the battle of sex versus truth, I've found truth whacks people upside the head only after they've indulged in the sex.

Since I had quit and was no longer responsible for Edward's packing, I headed out to see if I could hold down some breakfast. Maggie's replacement had already started on the reverend's room at the end of the hall.

Charlie stepped into the hallway and closed his door. He hailed me with the hand that wasn't carrying brown leather luggage.

"Heard you had a rough time last night. Feeling better?"

I gave him a weak smile. "Much, thanks."

He handed me a business card and told me to keep in touch. It read *Titanic, Inc.*

"Boats?" I asked, pleased that I'd been right about his profession. If you worked with boats, you still qualified as a dockworker, sort of.

He barked out a laugh as he walked away. "Software engineers."

My arrival in the lobby coincided with the exit of Lipstick Teeth and her friend. After they asked after my health, Lipstick Teeth said, "You need to meet a nice young woman. One who doesn't get herself killed or murder other people. My daughter—"

"Eunice, don't be silly," the friend said. "Kit is going on fifty and she lives in New York. Mr. Harlow's a *young* man, and he lives in San Diego and works as his brother's secretary." She nodded at me. "That's what the article in *Senior Living* magazine said."

I smiled. "They would know."

I sent them on their way, wishing Alice the best of luck at finding her dream man, and strolled up to Edward who was pacing the lobby as he waited for his turn at the front desk. I had some gloating to do.

"If you need a referral for your second career, I'll be happy to hook you up with a venture capitalist in about four years. He's busy 'til then."

Edward stopped pacing, but he barely looked my way before fastening his gaze back on the front desk. "You're awake. Are you still in my employ? Because I haven't started packing."

"You might no longer be an employer. Hard to keep up the charade after you've thrown the rules under the bus, unless delivering a knock-out punch to a woman is new to the list."

Edward snorted. "You're talking nonsense."

"Oh, come on! You could hardly call your behavior last night civil." I added some frost to my voice because I rarely get the chance to lecture *him*.

"I came to the aid of someone helpless." He sneered. "Someone out of his depth, over his head, and acting like an idiot."

This was too much. I ticked off his offenses on my fingers. "You stormed into a woman's room uninvited on two separate occasions, dropped one like a sack of flour—"

"I should have let her bash some sense into you."

"Admit it," I said. "Civil behavior isn't always the answer. In fact, maybe we should reissue your book and call it *Civility Doesn't Rule.*"

"If a theater were on fire, would you chastise me for raising my voice and interrupting the actors to shout the alarm? If a woman were seconds away from drowning, would you reprimand me for grabbing a man's cane without his permission to give the poor lady a lifeline?"

It was my turn to snort. "No one carries a cane these days except Griselda Waterford. The woman would drown."

"Civil behavior does not preclude common sense. There are such things as emergencies. Saving your brother from certain death sounds like an emergency to me."

I could tell he liked the sound of that last sentence, but the discussion ended there. The final guest had walked off, and Robert Inglenook stood alone. Edward charged forward and blurted out his request.

"I'd like permission to court your sister."

Robert Inglenook had to smile at the look of terror on Edward's face. I know I did.

He said, "You have a shady record." He studied his computer screen with rigid concentration. "Fighting like a hooligan in front of my sister, mixed up in a murder, fright-

221

ening guests while playing I Spy with your little sidekicks. Oh, yes. I know all about it from the children." He looked up. "Though they do recommend you." He finally had mercy. "Come with me."

We found Claudia Inglenook in the office filing credit card receipts in the cabinet behind the desk. Robert cleared his throat, and she glanced over her shoulder.

"After discussing the pros and cons, I've given Edward Harlow permission to court you."

"What's that?" She stopped filing and turned around.

"In the absence of a father," Edward explained, "I approached your nearest male relative."

"You're both idiots," she said, and she returned to the receipts. Her breath quickened, and her sorting methods deteriorated until she finally slammed the file drawer and turned on us.

"I can forgive you, Robert, because I know you're just being a silly ass, but you!" She stepped up to Edward. "In my love life, I make up my own mind. Since you've been talking to Robert, maybe you'd like to date *him*."

Then she walked out of the room. A great exit.

Robert laughed. "I think she likes you. Maybe you'd better go after her." He winked. "If I were you, I'd just kiss her and talk things out later."

When Edward ran after her, Robert grinned at me. "He's off to ravage my sister."

"About time."

We moved out of the office and leaned over the front counter to watch. Edward caught up to Claudia, took hold of her arm, and spun her around. Her hands waved in the air as she made a heated point, and he stood there and took it, but he didn't like it. He folded his arms across his chest and huffed several times. When he caught sight of us standing there and grinning, Edward impulsively pulled her to him and planted a thorough kiss on her mouth. She stepped back, said something, and then they walked away hand-in-hand.

"I suppose I should change our airline reservations. Can we keep our room for a few extra days?"

Robert checked his watch. "It's almost noon. The bar's not open yet, but I own the place. Join me?"

As he came around the counter, I said, "I wonder what ever happened to Edward's VPS gang?"

"I didn't want to disappoint your brother, but his group made it into Chicago by the skin of their teeth and went ahead with their meeting at the airport hotel. Of course, you guys are always welcome to come back here for the next conference."

"Poor Edward," I said. "He never got to give his speech."

A maid I didn't recognize walked by with a clipboard clutched to her chest. I watched as she headed up the stairs.

"That's Deloris," Robert said.

"Deloris. A beautiful name for a beautiful girl."

Robert stopped walking. "Don't hit on my staff."

"Don't begrudge me," I said. "We'll find you someone. Too bad I don't have a sister."

"I'd feel safer with Zali."

"She's staying on then?" I took a quick look over my shoulder without thinking.

"You could say that." Robert grinned. "Aunt Zali lives with us."

I thought of Edward's face as I broke the news and realized today was going to be a great day.

The End

(Until you read the next Harlow Brothers adventure. Tap here to download BAD BEHAVIOR)

~

Continue Reading for a preview of BAD BEHAVIOR, Book Club Discussion Questions, and more.

AND DON'T FORGET to download your free story!

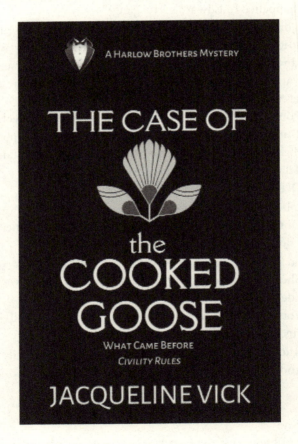

A HARLOW BROTHERS MYSTERY

THE CASE OF

the
COOKED
GOOSE

WHAT CAME BEFORE
CIVILITY RULES

JACQUELINE VICK

THE CASE OF THE COOKED GOOSE
A Harlow Brothers mystery prequel

When Nicholas Harlow accompanies his brother, Edward, to a conference at the Deer Stalker Hotel, he discovers his childhood idol, Sammy Spade, starring in the hotel's production of *Jekyl and Hyde*. During the evening performance, Sammy keels over onstage, poisoned. Unfortunately, Nicholas was the last one to see him alive, and the detective in charge is ready for an arrest.

Tap Here to Get the Free Story for My VIP Readers, the Mystery Buffs! Or go to www.jacquelinevick.com/subscribehb

A ONE CHAPTER PREVIEW OF
BAD BEHAVIOR

A Harlow Brothers Mystery Book 2

CHAPTER ONE

"Nicholas? What is this? A bad joke?"

My brother, Edward Harlow, author of the Aunt Civility etiquette books and columns, did a slow turn so he could take in the entire community room of the Babbitt & Brown Bookstore located on a downtown street corner of Citrus Grove, California, about twenty-five miles northeast of San Diego.

Admittedly, the room lacked character, being large and plain with cheap, beige carpet and off-white walls that looked a little dirty. The organizers had set up two long folding tables in front of a swinging door that led to the kitchen facilities and covered them with white paper tablecloths, the kind you'd find at a dollar store. Table number one held snacks provided by the Sweet and Sour Book Club, a group of enthusiasts who liked to read about food. Me, I prefer to eat it.

The second table held an assortment of desserts brought by Edward that related to his talk. Until my brother invited the crowd to partake, Mrs. Regina Robbins, a stout woman with short, gray hair who had the shoulders of a butcher, would guard the eats. Why make the audience members wait? Because Edward thought it was disgusting to watch people dribble crumbs down their shirtfronts and listen to lip-smacking noises while he lectured them. For around twenty-five minutes, they would be his captive audience, and by gum they could just suffer in polite silence.

Already attendees were slipping resentful glances at the woman who stood between them and free food since that was probably the only reason they showed up tonight.

I was more interested in the table directly across from the display of desserts. Stacks of Edward's latest masterpiece covered this table—*Conquering Shellfish and Other Messy Meals with Confidence* written under the pseudonym of Aunt Civility. My brother's sales were fine but, as one who depends on those sales for my paycheck, I wanted to keep a close eye on the book table. I hoped it would be empty by the end of the evening.

Bodies packed rows of folding chairs that filled the center of the room. It was an evening in early March, so most people had on sweaters and light jackets along with jeans and slacks, but a few stubborn sun-lovers, convinced that California's reputation for fair weather depended on them, wore shorts and sandals. Those people, especially the middle-aged man wearing the backward baseball cap, were the cause of my brother's irritation.

As Edward's secretary, my responsibilities include the usual chores of a personal assistant as well as duties not included in the job description: bucking the author up when he's feeling a typical writer's insecurities, calming him down when he has fits over silly details, and ignoring him when he doesn't like something that's for his own damn good.

I had arranged the event, and to say he wasn't pleased with the turnout would have been an understatement. A normal author would fret over a low head count, but Edward's complaint revolved around the large number of people. At least, the wrong sort of people.

My brother thinks his advice books on manners, etiquette, and general civil behavior are for those who share his opinion that barbarians have taken over the world. He only likes to give lectures to pre-qualified groups made up of members who would rather shoot themselves than interrupt or chew gum.

I deal in reality. Why would someone already on their best behavior bother with one of his books? So, I'd lied. I told him he would give his presentation on dining to the Citrus Grove Culinary Arts Council.

It wasn't a bald-faced lie. They were here. All seven of them. I mentioned in passing that the council members would invite a few guests and, when that didn't incite a tantrum, I had given them the go-ahead to open the event to the public.

I shrugged. "What can I say? They must have seen the event posted on your Facebook page."

He narrowed his eyes at me. "I don't have a Facebook page."

My grin held a hint of malice. "Yes, you do. I put it up myself last month."

His lips pressed together under his trim Van Dyke beard, and he took a deep breath through his nose, which made his nostrils flare like a bull getting ready to charge. Fortunately, Jeffrey Babbitt, a white-haired gnome and the owner of the Babbitt & Brown Bookstore, chose that moment to thank

Edward for coming. He gazed around the room, taking in the crowd with a reaction very different from Edward's. Jeffrey's eyes shone with delight, and he hooked his thumbs under the armpits of his green sweater vest.

"I haven't had such a popular signing since we had Whitney Sparks."

If Jeffrey was trying to get on Edward's good side, he blew it. Whitney Sparks was the antithesis of good manners. After the release of her book, *Whatever*, which was based on a blog of the same name, her popularity had soared among grungy twenty-somethings who felt that good manners were overrated. Mere mention of her name was enough to give Edward heartburn.

"I'm sure her crowd wasn't this big," I said with an encouraging glance at Edward.

"Actually," Jeffrey gushed, "it was enormous. Around the block, I believe."

"Vulgarians," Edward hissed.

Jeffrey beamed at him. "Vulgarians with money. I made an enormous profit that day." Profit reminded him of practical matters. "The books are on the table so you can stop by and greet Aunt Civility's fans after you're done. Customers seem to purchase more when there is an opportunity to shake hands with the rich and famous, even if it isn't the actual author. But you are related, and that's a plus."

When people thought of Aunt Civility, they got an image of a seventy-year-old grandmother type. Edward, at six-feet-two, with the physique of a football player, a head of black hair that kept trying to curl, and a trim beard, looked more like her arrogant, fat-headed nephew. The publicity department at Classical Reads had spread the word that poor Auntie suffered from agoraphobia, and her alleged favorite relative, Edward, traveled to events as her official representative.

My brother looked over Jeffrey's shoulder toward the table and his eyebrows joined in a frown. "What the devil is that?"

Jeffrey, surprised by my brother's tone, turned his head to look. "What is what?"

Edward would never point in public, but I knew exactly what was offending his finer sensibilities. Next to the book table stood a cardboard cutout of him smiling, and the cartoon bubble coming out of his mouth said, "Win your free copy here!" In front of Cardboard Edward stood a kind of ballot box on stilts.

"He means the raffle." I knew all about the raffle. I'm the one who emailed Jeffrey the photo of Edward smiling, and I thought he did a good job of blowing it up. Edward's likeness stood about six inches shorter than the real man.

The bookstore owner spun back around with his hands clasped at his chest. "Isn't it marvelous? I'm sure half the people here showed up because they heard about the raffle. People love free stuff."

Edward cocked his head and frowned. "I look ridiculous."

I leaned close to him and lowered my voice. "Not half as ridiculous as you would have looked if I had sent the photo of you in your bathing trunks. Now behave."

Jeffrey patted Edward's arm and said, "Nonsense, dear boy. You're lucky. Very photogenic. One authoress had a huge mole on her chin. When we enlarged her image, it looked like she was being attacked by a giant tick."

He gave a small shudder.

Across the room, an elderly woman with a walker struggled to stuff her raffle ticket into the slot on top of the box. Jeffrey excused himself and trotted off to assist her.

"A man who understands business," I said with approval. Edward grumbled something unprintable in response.

Call me an optimist, but I had extra books in the trunk of

our car in case the bookstore ran out. Since nobody but me and Edward's publisher knew he authored them, the books came already signed by Aunt Civility. He wouldn't have to sign them, but he would have to make nice with the public.

I scanned the potential buyers and wondered if this was the kind of crowd that would purchase Edward's books, or if most of them had showed up to kill an evening and get free food. The majority were over forty. In my experience, people between forty and, say, sixty usually had disposable income and weren't yet panicked about saving every penny for retirement. Unfortunately, it also meant they had enough life experience to be choosy about where they spent their dollar bills, and a book on fine dining might not make the cut.

There were a few younger people. Ms. Hattie Channing, spokesperson for the Culinary Arts Council, was probably in her early thirties. It was hard to tell. She dressed and carried herself as if inhabited by the spirit of her great-grandmother. Her high-necked blouse ruffled around her neck, and her polyester suit in yogurt pink matched the horn-rimmed spectacles that perched on the end of her nose. Black ortho-pedic shoes and a string of pearls added the final touch.

The rest of the council consisted of a grumpy old man named Ned, spinster sisters Dora and Flora, a former mili-tary man they referred to as The General, a short, balding banker, and a woman with a stylish, snow-white bob dressed in designer jeans and a peacock-blue sweater who carried a bag that said *Don't anger a knitter. We carry sharp objects.*

A man in his late thirties or early forties wearing a rumpled blue shirt and khakis, an impressive-looking camera hanging from a strap around his neck, approached Edward with his hand held out. My brother hesitated before proffering his own hand, taking a moment to eyeball the stubble on the man's face with disdain. When it comes to facial hair, Edward believes a man should be decisive.

"You must be the author's representative. I'm Charlie Grant, the reporter for the *Citrus Grove Courier.*"

Edward shook with him and murmured a lie about it being a pleasure.

Standing behind Charlie, so close he was practically clinging to his leg, was a boy around five. Charlie saw me noticing and grinned.

"This is my son, Zachary. I couldn't find a sitter. Say hello, Zack."

The kid held his hand up but didn't wave. Edward, who thought he knew something about children since meeting Claudia's niece and nephew at Inglenook, bent his head down and smiled.

"Are you helping your father?"

Zachary nodded. "I'm going to take pictures when I grow up."

"I'm sure you shall."

The photographer settled his son on a chair next to the dessert tables and handed him a peanut butter kiss from the Sweet and Sour Book Club stash.

"You stay here and be good."

When Charlie returned, he suggested Edward pose holding up Aunt Civility's latest book. This type of request always causes a dilemma. If Aunt Civility existed, would she appreciate her nephew holding up a copy of her book in a proprietary manner? Edward didn't think she would, but he agreed to stand next to the table with a book perched on a display stand to show the cover. Charlie agreed, and he took a few shots of Edward alone and some with him standing next to Jeffry Babbitt, who showed more enthusiasm for the publicity. When the reporter suggested Edward throw a friendly arm around Cardboard Edward, my brother declined.

"I'd like to interview you for the paper after your lecture," Charlie said.

My brother gave a brief nod. "Certainly."

Edward enjoyed hearing himself talk, so that was all right. I had hopes that his mood would take a turn for the better, but then his body went rigid. I followed his line of sight to a man wearing an orange t-shirt, sky-blue linen suit, and white tennis shoes who was sauntering in our direction. He was *Miami Vice* a few decades late and without the good looks of the lead actors. His skin had that weathered, dry texture that comes from too much sun exposure, his gray hair needed combing, and the beady, pale-blue eyes behind his glasses went fine with his smirk. To be fair, his bone structure hinted that he might have been handsome once, but age had finally had its way with him.

I didn't like him on sight. First, he had an arrogant saunter. Guys who saunter think they're doing you a favor by being in the same room. Second, he carried a metallic-blue aluminum water bottle in his hand as if it was a fashion statement. As he got closer, I could see it was personalized with an etching of a book and the initials JT, which gave me a third reason not to like him. Finally, his lips smirked. I dislike smirking lips.

When he made it to us, he clapped my brother on the shoulder. "Edward Harlow."

His voice surprised me. It boomed.

Edward strained his lips into a smile. "Professor Taylor."

Our parents separated when I was a kid, causing my mother to move with her boys from Chicago to San Diego. Even with child support, which my father faithfully paid, by the time Edward and I were ready for college, we were short of the kind of cash it takes to continue an education. Fortunately, a private school, G.W. Marston College, had a Division II football team and offered partial scholarships that allowed both Edward and I to get our bachelor's degrees. It was a small campus, and I had a vague recollection of a dreaded teacher named Taylor.

"I see my guidance has paid off." Professor Taylor nodded toward the table stacked with Edward's books. "I'd say you're doing well."

"You give us both too much credit," Edward murmured. "I'm merely the official representative."

Taylor scooted close to Edward and clutched his arm with long, bony fingers, and I moved in to make sure that my brother didn't lose his temper. Another of my duties. He doesn't like to be handled, and his reflexes can respond before his thought process kicks in. It was an asset on the football field and made him a formidable player. Here and now? Not so much.

"I recognized your writing style," Taylor said. "Pompous and verbose." He grinned, something he shouldn't do often as it showed a missing tooth next to his left canine. "You can't kid a kidder."

"I wouldn't dream of it," Edward replied between clenched teeth.

On Professor Taylor's approach, Charlie had melted back into the crowd to show his son how to photograph easier subjects than Edward, so I didn't have to worry about a head-line in tomorrow morning's paper calling Edward out as the author of the Aunt Civility books.

"How much is your secret worth to you?" Taylor winked. Maybe he shouldn't have because that started him blinking. He took off his glasses and cleaned them with his jacket, but when he put them back on his face, he frowned as if the exercise had been a waste of his time.

Although I thought readers would love to hear the male perspective on polite behavior, and I regularly told Edward he should go public as Aunt Civility, it was his decision. And

I dislike people who share other people's secrets on principle. I reached for his arm to escort him to the door, but the professor held up his hands in mock self-defense.

"Kidding. Only kidding."

He stuffed his hands into his trouser pockets to affect a casual pose, but to do it, he had to hold the water bottle under one armpit and wound up looking silly.

"You've got quite a turnout," he said, scanning the room. His gaze rested on someone by the snack tables behind us. "I think I'll mingle. It wouldn't hurt to promote my own book."

"You're an author now?" Edward stressed the now. "I seem to remember you were a stellar example of those who can't, teach."

"Edward," I said in warning. It wouldn't do for Aunt Civility's official representative to get into a public shouting match. Fortunately, the professor took it as a joke, and he threw back his head and laughed. I got another look at the gap in his teeth.

Just then, Miss Channing approached the microphone and tapped on it with one long fingernail as if she thought it might explode. The microphone, not her finger.

"Ladies and gentlemen. If I could have your attention."

Miss Channing's breathy, high voice didn't carry well, and she had to repeat the request several times before the remaining standees took their seats. Taylor jabbed a thumb in Edward's side and grinned.

"Talk to you after the show."

My brother watched him go with a contemptuous sneer, took a last look around the room, made a face, and, forced to admit defeat, settled onto his reserved chair in the front row. To leave now would be unspeakably rude.

After taking a seat in the chair next to him, I leaned my head in and whispered. "You don't think he'd spill the beans, do you?"

He didn't answer me, unless you count a low growl at the back of his throat as a response.

"We are so pleased to have a guest speaker tonight at the monthly meeting of the Citrus Grove Culinary Arts Council," Miss Channing began. "We are an interesting group and we're always looking for new members who share our passion for all things related to cooking, so please feel free to sign up at the table in the back. We'd love to have you."

A few people craned their necks to look at the table, but I would bet money none of them took her up on the offer. She then launched into the history of the council, and Edward leaned into me and growled, "We will talk about this later."

I held up a finger. "Shh. I think she's getting to your introduction."

She wasn't. She was talking about the suburbanization of Citrus Grove, which led to the annihilation of farmlands and a general decline in the tone of the place. Now that fast-food chains had taken over the outskirts of town leading to the freeway, a citizen's only defense was to bring fine dining into their homes. Mr. Edward Harlow, the official representative of that famous author, Aunt Civility, would help them reclaim that lost tradition, the family meal, and by gosh, armed with the correct etiquette, they wouldn't have to settle for hamburgers and meatloaf. Or if they did, they could do it with style.

I knew his talking points—the importance of the dining room in family meals, how to train your teenagers to be the perfect servers, how to eat finger foods without making a mess, and, for an exciting finale, the importance of adding color to your meals by serving brightly decorated confections for dessert. He thought it would thrill the crowd to mention some deadly ingredients that Victorians had used to brighten things up, including arsenic, iron, and lead.

I wondered how Edward would respond to people who

weren't blessed with separate dining rooms. What about those who lived in tiny apartments, or lofts that were one big room? I glanced around nervously, searching the faces of the friendly townsfolk for any signs of disgruntled activists. I wouldn't have missed it if a person had dragged in a sign declaring white males with dining rooms as the pinnacle of privilege.

When the people applauded, I realized that Ms. Channing had introduced Edward. He approached the podium and glared at the crowd. I coughed several times, and when he looked my way, I plastered on a big, fake grin as a hint. He adjusted his features into a friendlier expression and launched into his lecture.

Edward is rarely boring, at least not to first-time listeners, but I had gone over his talk with him at least ten times, so I settled back, closed my eyes, and let my thoughts wander. There had to be two hundred people here tonight, and I fully expected four, possibly five, to spend money on the book. Maybe, with Edward's added surprise of special desserts, he might lull three more people with sweet tooths to buy. Or would that be sweet teeth? That would make...

Before I knew it, they were applauding again. I had dozed off for the entire talk. Jerking straight, I craned my neck toward the back of the room. The volunteers had put out the final additions on the dessert table, and they had followed my instructions without a reminder from me. I thanked my stars for the efficiency of women over fifty and turned back to see how Edward had taken his audience.

My brother looked gratified by their enthusiastic response. The left corner of his mouth curled up, and his eyebrows were relaxed instead of pulled into a frown. He held up his hand to quiet them so he could deliver his grand finale.

"To celebrate Citrus Grove's fine history, I've brought

with me several citrus-based desserts. You can find recipe cards on the book table, courtesy of my beloved aunt. I've brought a Victorian treat called Kisses as well as lemon squares and sugared citrus peels. Lemon-barley water is available for anyone who's thirsty." He raised a finger. "And I promise you, any color in the desserts results from safe, modern color additives or nature."

They giggled and gasped, and the big showoff couldn't resist doling out additional tidbits about poison.

"If you think current makeup fashions are a pain, ladies used to use a couple of drops of arsenic to make their skin pale." The women shrieked, and the men guffawed. He nodded. "Gentlemen. Don't be so quick to laugh at the ladies. Victorian men regularly plastered bright green wallpaper in the family home—perhaps in the dining room—which also contained arsenic."

The women got a laugh out of that, and then Edward, finally out of steam, nodded again and thanked them. The applause this time was scattered, since most of the crowd was already on their way to the dessert tables. Edward stepped away from the podium and I stood and joined him.

"All caught up on your sleep?" he asked.

"Did I snore?"

He handed me his speech, and I packed it into his brief-case. The chairs were empty except for a few couples. His gaze moved toward the exit.

I shook my head. "Nuh-uh. You are required to mingle for ten minutes minimum."

Just then, the council members rushed up with hearty congratulations. The retired banker's name turned out to be Morton. Mort for short.

"I can't thank you enough for making the drive," Mort said with a smile that encouraged his fellow council members to agree. They did, which was funny since it only took us forty-eight minutes in rush-hour traffic to get here.

Grumpy Ned said, "I gotta get to the membership table," and he left us to join the Knitting Woman who was seated there and clicking away at a bulky project.

"You're right about teenagers," The General said. "They need a firm hand and something to keep them busy. If they pay attention to your instructions, they may be able to find employment at a restaurant."

Dora and Flora twittered at my brother and grabbed the opportunity to regale him with stories of what it was like to grow up in Citrus Grove before the town had condescended to allow people without livestock or crops to move there. They were both in their seventies with white fluffy hair and floral print dresses. The sisters weren't twins but they were interchangeable except for the mole on Dora's left cheek.

The story ended with the delights of drinking warm milk straight from the cow's udder, and then they joined the rest of their group in a procession to the snack tables.

My brother shot me a glare, but when he saw the line at the book table, his features softened into his typical expression of mild irritation.

"They seem to be enjoying themselves."

"You're a hit. There's a cake club in San Diego—"

"Don't even think about it."

"Edward, you've got to branch out. You refuse to use social media—" I held up a hand to stop the coming diatribe. "I started your social media sites in self-defense."

"Sites?"

We hadn't yet discussed Twitter.

"It's for your own good. People want to connect with the author, and you're her gateway. In fact, I had a thought about starting an account for Auntie. She'd be a hit."

"She's supposed to be mentally ill."

"She has agoraphobia. She can write from home unless you want to give her another social disorder that prohibits her from going online, but I don't recommend it. If Auntie has too many problems, people might get disgusted." I snapped my fingers. "Unless you had her share her difficulties in a book. People love reading details about the horrors encountered by celebrities, and she might actually help people who share her diseases."

"Mental disorders are not diseases," my brother snapped. "I don't understand your obsession with the Internet. What's social about typing a message on someone's paper?"

"Page. It's called their page."

"Sharing intimate details with strangers to whom you haven't been properly introduced... It's madness!"

I rolled my eyes and turned toward the book table. The line had grown, and it pleased me to have proof that Edward was wrong. Public appearances were good for his sales.

To reward myself, I cut our conversation short and joined the others at the table with the snacks. Not the desserts we brought, since I could enjoy our housekeeper's baking any time, but the ones supplied by the Sweet and Sour Book Club. I took a few meringue kisses and popped one in my mouth. When I reached for a napkin, the tables jerked. A startled cry was followed by the sound of breaking glass. I held my hands in the air.

"Wasn't me."

A glass pitcher, former home to the lemon-barley water, was scattered in pieces on the floor. Someone coughed, trying to smother a laugh, I assumed. Regina Robbins stooped over to pick up the pieces. Once she had gathered them up, she disappeared behind the swinging door that led to the kitchen.

"What did you do now?"

I tightened my muscles to keep from jumping. Edward had come up on me without making a sound.

"Nothing. Someone jarred the table, and the pitcher fell." I looked at the wet spot on the rug. "At least lemon-barley water won't stain. It could have been red wine. And why aren't you busy greeting book buyers?"

I glanced over my shoulder at the table. Jeffrey Babbitt sat alone; his grin gone. The crowd had transferred their interest from Edward's books to the free food. To make matters worse, Professor Taylor stumbled up to us. He put a hand on my shoulder for support, and when I firmly removed it, he leaned against the table to get his balance. I wondered if his water bottle held something stronger then H2O.

"Did you enjoy the talk?" I asked him. Not that I was eager to engage him in conversation, but I wanted to set a good example for Edward, who was clenching his jaw muscles.

"Gave me a headache," Taylor muttered. He squinted and blinked at me. He looked confused, and I was about to give him some sympathy, but then he coughed in my face. He removed his glasses and rubbed his eyes. Whatever was wrong with him, I hoped he wasn't contagious.

Regina Robbins returned with a full pitcher and filled a few plastic cups. I gave a small shudder. To me, lemon-barley water looked like a cloudy, dirty puddle, and I couldn't think of anyone more deserving of a serving of it than the man who was still coughing in my direction.

I picked up a cup. "Here. This might help."

He nodded, took the glass, emptied it in a few gulps, and then handed it back to me. I took it to be polite, but since I wasn't his waiter, I turned my back on him.

As I set his cup down next to the other empties, I noted that most of the lemon squares were gone. A glance in the wastebasket at the end of the table showed me what had happened to the citrus peels.

"I think people sucked the sugar off and tossed them," I said to Edward, shaking my head. "Told you they were too sour."

"What a waste," Edward lamented. He looked around at the attendees, now stuffing their faces, hooked his arm through mine, and pulled me out of earshot. "And speaking of waste, let's not waste any time getting on the road."

He led the way back to our chairs to collect his briefcase. No way could I talk him out of leaving this time. He had made it seven minutes longer than I expected.

"Where you come up with these foolish ideas..."

I scanned the room and considered the crowd, which had dwindled to half its original size. Still, it wasn't a bad turnout.

"Crazy!"

I held up a hand. "Fine. I got it. Foolish and crazy. I won't try to help you again."

He handed me his briefcase. "I didn't say anything."

"Crazy son-of-a—"

We turned toward the voice. Professor Taylor dropped his water bottle and folded his arm over his stomach as he doubled over. The other hand stretched out to point a bony finger at Edward. He gasped.

"You!"

And then he fell flat on his face.

"Someone call an ambulance," I yelled out as I crossed to him and knelt at his side. After rolling him over, I pulled at his shirt-collar to help him breathe and motioned the crowd back. His pale skin was clammy with sweat, and I thought *Great. Just great. I can't afford to get sick.* I forced a smile and told him to relax.

"Could everyone step back and give him room? Thank you."

A few people responded but most ignored me.

"Just relax," I repeated. "The paramedics will be here soon. You'll be fine."

His pale-blue eyes were fixed on something over my shoulder. I turned my head to look, but he clutched my jacket collar in a tight fist and jerked me to within a few inches of his face. I noticed an earthy smell that I assumed was barley and tried to turn my face away.

"Mwif." That's what came out. Then Taylor made a noise like "ack" and relaxed his grip.

I tried to find his pulse, but when you're panicked, it's not as easy as it looks on television. Resting one hand on his chest to feel the rise and fall of his breathing didn't get results, nor did putting my hand under his nose to feel an inhale or exhale. Nothing.

I searched the faces of the crowd for one of the volunteers. When I saw Miss Channing standing near the door with her hands clasped in front of her bosom, I said, "Did someone call 911?"

She nodded.

The professor's mouth went slack, with drool coming from one corner. "Get me a napkin." Someone shoved a handful at me. I swiped at the drool, placed one napkin over his mouth and started CPR on a dead man.

Jeffrey Babbitt crouched next to me; his impish expression gone. "Let me help."

While I handled the breaths, he pushed Taylor's shirt up so he could find the right spot and took over compressing the professor's chest. An hour later, or maybe five minutes, the medical professionals arrived and took over. Jeffrey and I moved out of the way and watched as they tried to revive him. Finally, they attached Taylor to a machine and took a reading. The female of the pair phoned the hospital, and a doctor pronounced the time of death.

I looked in the direction that Taylor had been staring when he made his last sounds. The council members stood in a huddle in front of the snacks, while Mrs. Robbins and her volunteers watched from behind the table. Maybe Taylor's last act was an attempt to complain about the food.

As the emergency personnel packed up their things, Jeffrey panicked. "You can't just leave him there!"

The female exchanged a look with her partner, who then concentrated on avoiding eye contact with anyone in the room. She looked up at me. "The medical examiner will be here shortly. And law enforcement. We'll wait until they get here."

Since I couldn't do anything for Professor Taylor, I returned to Edward's side. He demanded to know what was happening.

"I don't know how well you liked Professor Taylor—"

"I don't." He cocked his head. "Did you say liked?"

I nodded. "Dead as a doornail."

"Ye gads."

"You can say that again."

Edward searched the front of the room. "Where's my briefcase? Perhaps we should remove ourselves."

"Forget it. We're stuck."

As if to confirm my opinion, several San Diego County deputies walked through the door. The one in the lead, a tall blond man with a small belly, looked down on the late Professor Taylor and put his hands on his hips. "What happened?"

Miss Channing inched up to him and said, "I think he ate something that didn't agree with him."

Continue Reading!

THANKS FOR READING CIVILITY RULES

If you enjoyed this book, please consider leaving a review. Reviews help readers discover new books, and the author, who socializes mostly with dogs, appreciates the human feedback.

Thank you!
Jacqueline

Leave a Review

ACKNOWLEDGMENTS

Many thanks to my support group of brave souls willing to read proof copies and give me feedback and advice, especially Mary Grant, Andrea Voirin, and Gayle Bartos-Pool.

Finally, thanks to the Mystery Buffs, a community of readers who love mysteries as much as I do.

BOOK CLUB QUESTIONS

CIVILITY RULES

The story is told from the point-of-view of Nicholas. Does he make an engaging narrator?

Nicholas is very appreciative of the ladies. Does this make him "all man" or a chauvinist?

Edward has gradually taken on the personality of Aunt Civility's official representative. Do you think he is a faker? Or is he sincere in his efforts to be a gentleman?

According to Edward, the world is filled with cretins. People on cell phones in public and men who wear backwards baseball caps are particularly annoying. Is he being judgmental? Or is he right?

Luigi Ferrari was lured into a relationship with a beautiful, young con artist. Was this his own fault, or was he the victim?

Maggie turns to blackmail in order to further her dream of owning her own bed-and-breakfast. Nicholas seems to admire her. Was she being admirably assertive? Or is she in the wrong?

Zali never comes out and says she is related to the Inglenooks. Why do you think this?

Claudia Inglenook doesn't appreciate her brother's offer to help her at the computer terminal. She also takes offense when Edward asks her brother's permission to court her. Is she touchy? Or does she have a point?

Barbara Maggiano believes that Felicity is a scheming tart. If her father hadn't had money to leave in his will, do you think she would have cared?

The Aunt Civility etiquette books are the perfect reference for social situations. Do you think anyone cares about behaving correctly, and should they care?

ABOUT THE AUTHOR

Jacqueline Vick writes the Frankie Chandler Pet Psychic mystery series about a woman who, after faking her psychic abilities for years, discovers animals *can* communicate with her. Her second series, the Harlow Brothers mysteries, features a former college linebacker turned etiquette author and his secretary brother. Her books are known for satirical humor and engaging characters who are reluctant to accept their greatest (and often embarrassing) gifts.

Visit her website at www.jacquelinevick.com.

Made in the USA
Las Vegas, NV
14 August 2025

26312735R00152